SHARDS&ASHES

ALSO EDITED BY

MELISSA MARR AND KELLEY ARMSTRONG

Enthralled: Paranormal Diversions

SHARDS&ASHES

Edited by

MELISSA MARR AND
KELLEY ARMSTRONG

WITHDRAWN

HARPER

An Imprint of HarperCollinsPublishers

Shards and Ashes
Copyright © 2013 by Melissa Marr and Kelley Armstrong

"Hearken" copyright © 2013 by Veronica Roth
"Branded" copyright © 2013 by Kelley Armstrong
"Necklace of Raindrops" copyright © 2013 by Margaret Stohl
"Dogsbody" copyright © 2013 by Rachel Longstreet Conrad
"Pale Rider" copyright © 2013 by Nancy Holder
"Corpse Eaters" copyright © 2013 by Melissa Marr
"Burn 3" copyright © 2013 by Kami Garcia
"Love Is a Choice" copyright © 2013 by Beth Revis
"Miasma" copyright © 2013 by Carrie Ryan

All rights reserved. Printed in the United States of America.
No part of this book may be used or reproduced in any manner whatsoever
without written permission except in the case of brief quotations embodied
in critical articles and reviews. For information address HarperCollins
Children's Books, a division of HarperCollins Publishers, 10 East 53rd Street,
New York, NY 10022.
www.epicreads.com

Library of Congress Cataloging-in-Publication Data is available.
ISBN 978-0-06-209846-7 (trade bdg.) — ISBN 978-0-06-209845-0 (pbk.)

Typography by Carla Weise
13 14 15 16   LP/RRDH   10 9 8 7 6 5 4 3 2 1
❖
First Edition

CONTENTS

INTRODUCTION

Melissa Marr and Kelley Armstrong

In recent years, there have been a plethora of disasters and political upheavals. The news makes a person pause and ponder. Yet . . . we could've said the same thing in past years—and undoubtedly we will be able to say it in the future. Somehow, to us, the news has seemed more poignant of late. We see threats looming, ways things could go horribly awry, and wonder at the uncertainty of the world. Maybe it's as simple as being mothers to teenagers who are leaving the nest. In discussing this one sunny afternoon, we thought it would be interesting to ask various writers/friends to envision a dangerous future. Oddly (or not), they thought this sounded like a grand idea.

A couple of the contributors already write of dark futures in their novels. One of them, Beth Revis, returned to us with a story set in space, in the world of her Across the Universe series, while Veronica Roth created a new future where one can hear songs of life and songs of death. Carrie Ryan decided to unsettle us with a world facing a plague that gave at least one of the editors a case of the shivers. Other authors who are not writing near-future novels created worlds very different from their novels. Rachel Caine delivered a chilling story of advanced technology and age-old class divisions; likewise, Kami Garcia tackled questions of class in a society where the sun is deadly. And then Margaret Stohl and Nancy Holder came in and offered up stories of hope, glimmers of light among these shards and ashes.

In this anthology, you will meet a mythological corpse eater and the Erl King, as well as reluctant heroes and those who are neither hero nor villain. You'll walk in the swamp, desert, forest, and city. You'll visit a ship hurtling through space, and a cavernous underground world. Without any planning beyond selecting the authors themselves, we've collected vastly different visions of dark futures. The one constant, in our editorial opinion, is that these are stories we feel fortunate to have read and to share with you.

—Melissa & Kelley

HEARKEN

Veronica Roth

"BLACK OR RED?"

The woman in the lab coat held up two small containers: one with a red substance caked inside it and one with black. It sounded like she was asking Darya a question of taste, rather than the question that defined her future. The only question, Darya believed, that would ever matter this much.

The question was not "Black or red?" It was "Life or death?" And Darya would not have been able to answer before that moment.

She had been seven years old when her father first realized what she could become. Her older sister, Khali, had been playing piano in the living room, an old piece by Schubert. Darya sat on the couch, humming along, a book in her lap.

Her mother dozed in the recliner, her mouth lolling open. Darya thought about drawing a mustache on her face. She wouldn't notice it when she awoke. She would be too dazed by the alcohol. Even at seven, Darya knew. But it was not uncommon, with the world as it was. Half her friends' parents had the same problem.

Darya's father stood in the doorway, listening, a dish towel in his hands. He turned it over a plate to the rhythm of the notes, which came in stilted intervals as Khali tried to read the music. Darya stopped humming, irritated. The music was meant to be smooth, and it sounded like Khali was chopping it up into bits.

Khali turned the page and adjusted her hands on the piano. Darya perked up, letting the book drop into her lap. Her mother snored. Her sister began playing, and Darya stood, walked over to the piano, and stared at her sister's hands. To her the notes sounded *wrong* . . . the intervals were too large, or too small; they did not mesh together in the right way.

"That's wrong," she said, wincing.

"No it's not," said Khali. "How would *you* know?"

"Because I can hear it," she said. "It's supposed to be like *this*."

She reached out and shifted her sister's index finger one note over. Then she moved Khali's pinkie finger, and her middle finger.

"There," said Darya. "Now do it."

Khali rolled her eyes and began the piece. Darya smiled as

the notes came together, ringing when they touched each other.

"Oh," said Khali. Her skin was too dark to reveal a blush, but her sheepish expression betrayed her. "You're right. I read it wrong. It's supposed to be in B minor."

Darya smiled a little, walked back to the couch, and picked up her book again. Her father moved the towel in circles even when it started to squeak against the dry dish.

A few weeks later, Darya's father started her in music classes. There they discovered that Darya had perfect pitch—one of the prerequisites for becoming a Hearkener.

Khali quit piano after Darya surpassed her in skill, which took only a year. It was useless to try to play piano when you were in the same family as a Hearkener.

"Come on. Today's the day!"

Darya yawned over her cereal. It was too early to be hungry, but her father had warned her that she would need to eat a good breakfast because today would be a long one. She was going to be tested by the Minnesota School for Hearkeners later that morning to see if she was qualified to enroll, and the test could last several hours. That was a long time for an eight-year-old.

Her mother shuffled into the kitchen in her old robe, which was threadbare at the cuffs where she pulled it over her hands. She held a mug of coffee, which Darya eyed suspiciously. Her mother had carried it into the bedroom several minutes ago.

A few weeks before, Darya had found a brown bottle under the sink in her parents' bathroom. She had sniffed it, and its contents burned her nose, and the smell seemed to linger there for several minutes. The bottle and the coffee and her mother's running-together words were part of a familiar pattern that she had always recognized, even before she had the words to describe it.

Her mother's eyes wandered across Darya's face.

"Where're you going?" she asked.

"I'm taking Darya to get tested," Darya's father said, too brightly.

"Tested for what?"

"Dar has perfect pitch." Her father set his hand on Darya's head and tousled her hair. "She could be a Hearkener some-day."

A Hearkener, to Darya's mother, meant two things: being employed by the government—a stable job; and carrying an expensive piece of equipment, the implant, in your head—which meant immediate evacuation if the country was quarantined. She snorted a little.

"D'you really think you should be putting that idea into her head?" Her mother's eyes were cold and critical. Darya couldn't look at them. "Almost nobody becomes an Ark . . . 'Arkener."

Darya stared at her bowl. The little bubble of excitement that had risen inside her as soon as she woke up was gone, like it had floated away.

Her father rose and took her mother's arm. "Maybe you should get back to bed, Reggie. You don't look well."

"I just meant," her mother said angrily, "that I don't want her to be *disappointed*—"

"I know," he said.

He ushered her from the room. Darya heard the bedroom door close and muffled voices getting louder every second until something banged shut. No longer hungry, she dumped her cereal bowl into the sink without finishing.

"Your mom's not feeling so good, Dar," her father said as they walked down the sidewalk in front of the apartment building. "She didn't mean it."

Darya nodded without thinking.

They would have lived in the suburbs if they could have— it was safer there, since the attacks came less frequently—but her father's job only paid well enough for a small apartment downtown.

The attacks had always been a part of Darya's life. They could come from anyone, and they were waged against everyone with a pulse. That was why Darya and her sister had to wear face masks on the way to school.

Her father had taught them both to know bio-bombs when they saw them, but their minds had a tendency to wander when they were together, and he didn't trust them to look for bombs yet. Kids at school teased them for the masks, but they couldn't persuade their father to let them go without. "Prove to me that you can pay attention," he always said.

Death was too real a possibility. Most people didn't make it past fifty nowadays, even if they lived in the suburbs.

Her father pulled her tight to his side as they walked, scattering old cans and bits of paper with the toes of their shoes. She craned her neck to see the tops of the buildings—they seemed so far away, though her father said they were shorter than the buildings in most cities. Most of the windows in the building next to her were blown out completely from the days when destructive bombs had been in fashion. But it was the loss of people, not buildings, that made a war destructive, and the fanatics had figured that out.

They stopped walking and stood next to a blue sign marked with graffiti. Darya itched her leg with her free hand and gazed up at her father. He was not a tall man, nor was he short. His skin was dark brown, like Darya's, and his hair was black and smooth, shiny like her hair, too. He had moved to the States from India before the quarantine. India had been one of the first countries targeted when the attacks began because of its condensed population. Now the infection was so rampant that the borders had to be closed to prevent a worldwide epidemic. Her father's parents had gotten infected, so they hadn't been able to leave with him. She had never met her grandparents. She assumed they were dead by now.

"Will the test be hard, Daddy?"

He smiled. "Most of it will be things you already know how to do. And the rest you will be able to figure out. Don't worry, Dar. You'll do great."

A bus trundled around the corner as he finished speaking, and creaked to a stop right in front of them. The doors opened, and Darya's father paid the fare. They sat down in the middle, next to an old lady who was shifting her dentures around in her mouth, and across from a middle-aged man with a mask covering his mouth and nose.

Her father leaned in close and whispered, "Okay, so what do we do when we get on a train or a bus?"

"Look for masks," she whispered back. They would have been wearing masks too, if they had not had to leave the two they owned for Darya's mother, who had to walk Khali to school later, and Khali. Masks were expensive. But she was safe with her father, who could spot a bio-bomb anywhere.

"Why do we do that?"

"Because only people with masks will set off bio-bombs." Her voice dipped even lower at the word *bio-bombs*, as if saying it any louder would provoke an attack.

"Right," he said, "and after we look for masks, what do we do?"

"We watch."

The enemy could be anyone, anywhere. All that bound them together was a commitment to bringing about the apocalypse. They believed the world ought to be destroyed. They did not believe in ending their own lives. Darya didn't understand it and didn't want to try.

He nodded. And they watched, both of them, as the bus bumped and thudded around corners and down streets. Darya had not seen much of the city because she spent all her travel time eyeing the people around her. She was usually in a bus, rather than a train, because buses were easier to escape from.

"You know, when I was young, people didn't like Hearkeners much," her father said.

Darya watched the man across from her. His eyes remained steady on the floor. She could hear his breaths through the slats in the mask—not loud, but louder than unfiltered breaths.

"Why not?" she asked.

"Because they were seen as an unnecessary expenditure," he said. "Not worth the cost, I mean. But the people over at the Bureau for the Promotion of Arts were very insistent that music would help a troubled world. And then when people started dying . . ." He shrugged. "Everyone started to understand why Hearkeners were so important."

"Why are they so important?"

"Because what they hear . . . it's like hearing something beyond us. Something bigger than us." He smiled down at her. "It reminds us that there's more going on in this world than we can see with our eyes and touch with our hands."

Darya didn't quite understand what her father meant, but she knew there was something beautiful in it all the same.

Then she heard something—quickening breaths from the man across from them. She saw a bead of sweat roll down the side of his forehead. He looked so harmless—he was short, with salt-and-pepper hair and a white, collared shirt.

His slacks were pressed, creased. He was not a killer. But the peculiar blend of fear and determination in his eyes was enough to make Darya's breaths stop completely.

As the man in the mask moved to get off the bus, he took a canister from his bag and dropped it on the ground. It was an object she had only seen in pictures—dull metal, about six inches long, as thick as her wrist, with an opening at one end to let out the gas.

Someone screamed. Darya's father clapped his hand over her mouth and nose, and lifted her up from the abdomen. He ran toward the front of the bus, shoving people out of his way with his elbows. Darya fought for air, but the hand prevented her from taking a breath.

Her father shouldered his way out the bus door. Against her will, Darya's body began to struggle against her father's grasp, fighting for air. Her father sprinted down the street and into an alley just as she began to see spots.

He took his hand from her mouth, and she gasped.

He had not had time to cover his own mouth. What if he inhaled some of the gas? What if he was infected? She choked on a sob. What if he died?

"It's okay, Dar." He gathered her close to his chest. "I held my breath. We're all right. We're just fine."

Technically, the only distinguishing feature of a Hearkener was the implant. It was placed in the temporal lobe of the brain. It didn't protrude from the skin, but it contained a dye that created a weblike pattern on the right temple. Hearkeners were required to pull their hair away from their faces to reveal the pattern. Its purpose was to make them easily identifiable.

The implant made them what they were. They heard music everywhere—as long as there were people, there was music.

The first time she saw a licensed Hearkener was outside the Minnesota School for Hearkeners, on the fifth step from the bottom of thirty long, low steps. They had not made it to the testing center the day of the bio-bomb, but they went three days later, this time walking the whole way instead of taking the bus.

Her father stood beside her, clutching her hand. They both paused to watch the Hearkener woman walk past.

She was tall and slender, with hair the color of earth and the same pale skin Darya's mother had. She walked without a bounce in her step, but at the same time, her feet were light on the cement. She wore a knee-length coat that snapped when the wind caught it. The pattern on her temple was iodine black, but it was the last thing Darya noticed.

All Darya could think was that this Hearkener of Death was the most beautiful woman she had ever seen, and she wanted to be just like her.

As the Hearkener passed Darya and her father, she tilted her head, the way a person does when he is trying to hear something. Her footsteps slowed for just a moment, and she closed her eyes.

After the moment passed, she looked Darya's father in the

eye and smiled. Despite the curl of her lips, a troubled look remained in her eyes. She kept walking.

Three weeks later, Darya's father died of the infection, and that Hearkener was the only person who ever heard his death song.

Darya passed the test, and her mother enrolled her in the Minnesota School for Hearkeners that fall. Though Darya's mind was still muddled with grief, it was what her father had wanted for her, so she went.

Her first impression of the place was that it was too large for her. Even the front steps were vast, made of wide slabs of a dark, matte stone. The building itself was tall, made of black glass with girders that formed a huge X across the front. A giant clock, fixed to the front of the building, told her she had five minutes to get to her first class.

She looked at the piece of paper the school had sent her, along with half a dozen packets and information sheets, to tell her where to go on her first day. All the new students took classes together until they tested into particular levels of musical study or until they chose their instrument specialties.

The schedule said: *Hour 1, Introduction to Hearkener History, Room A104.*

Darya looked up when she passed through the doors. She couldn't see much past the security barrier. A stern-looking man in a black uniform told her to put her bag on a black conveyor belt that would take it through a scanner. She then had to stand in what looked like a globe with a tunnel cut through it so that it could scan her body. She had gone through both when she took her tests here, but her father had been with her then. This time she was afraid. What if they didn't let her through?

But another man, on the other side, handed her the bag and let her pass him. The hallway here was completely different from the dingy, green-tiled hall that had been in her old school. Here, the floors were white marble—or at least something that looked like marble—and the walls were navy blue. Even the lockers were elegant—made of dark wood, they lined the walls as far as she could see.

She looked at the first room she passed—room A101. She was close. She walked past another section of lockers and glanced at the rooms to her left and right. A104 was on the left. Taking a deep breath, she walked in.

The room was oddly silent. Ten other children, her age, sat at long wooden tables inside. She found an empty seat near the back, next to a densely freckled boy tapping out a rhythm on the table with his pencil.

The bell rang. An older woman with gray, curly hair and a chunk missing from her eyebrow strode in. She wore the Hearkener uniform: a black trench coat, buttoned up to her throat, and gray pants. Darya leaned to the side to see what color the woman's implant was. Red. That meant she heard life songs rather than death songs.

The woman cleared her throat, though there was no reason to—no one was talking.

"Hello," she said. "Let's not bother with introductions. Oh, except me. We go by surnames here, and mine is Hornby. I'll be giving you the rundown of Hearkener history."

Darya knew the basics—that the Hearkener implant had something to do with string theory, and what it did was channel the vibrations of the human body somehow and make them into music. But she felt strangely exposed, without knowing more.

"String theory became widely accepted in the early part of the century," Hornby said. "Can anyone tell me what string theory is, basically? Yes—how about you—what's your name?"

The boy next to Darya had raised his hand. "Christopher Marshall, ma'am."

"'Hornby' will do, Marshall. Go ahead."

"String theory is the theory that subatomic particles like electrons and quarks are one-dimensional strings instead of three-dimensional, and that the one-dimensional strings form the fabric of the universe."

"Good," said Hornby. "Also, the strings are constantly vibrating. That's important to remember because when Dr. Rogers created the first implant, all it did was channel the vibrations and their various frequencies and translate them into music. It was her successor, Dr. Johnson, who refined the implant to filter out all frequencies but those of human cells, so it was only people who made music. Anyone want to tell me why he would do a thing like that? You, there—your name . . . ?"

"Samanth—uh, I mean Brock," a girl in the front row said. "He said he just wanted to see if it was possible."

"In fact, that is what he said, but we have since determined it was so he could hear the music his dying wife made." Hornby added, "He had a friend try out the implant so that she could transpose the music. She was the first Hearkener. But the implants didn't stop there."

Here she paused and tapped the red dye on her temple with her index finger.

"The last developer of the implant discovered that he could filter out either the vibrations of decaying cells or the vibrations of regenerating cells. In other words, he could make the implant play the sound of a person's life or the sound of their death. For a long time, hardly any Hearkeners chose death. Now that death is so common, those Hearkeners are in high demand."

Darya remembered the look the Hearkener who had heard her father's death song had given him. She had seemed almost bewitched by it. Darya didn't think that woman had chosen the death songs because they were in higher demand.

Hornby clapped her hands. "Now that that's out of the way, I would like to call each of you up so that I can listen to your life song and tell you what instruments it seems to include. Not, by the way, that a life song actually incorporates instruments. It's just that certain sounds remind us of them. Anyway—this is important because you will be selecting two of the three instruments you are required to master in your first year here. Much of your time will be spent trying out each of them to see which ones you gravitate toward. Hopefully my evaluation will steer you in the right direction."

It had been a very brief history lesson. Darya sat in her seat with her hands clutched around the edge of the chair as each of the eleven children in the class walked up to the front of the room so Hornby could listen to them. She didn't want to go. She didn't want to let that woman analyze her. She didn't know why, but it felt far too personal, far too intimate for a setting like this.

It wasn't long before Hornby pointed to her and bent her finger, beckoning Darya forward. Darya got up—too fast; she knocked the chair over and had to set it right again—and walked to the front of the room, her hands fidgeting at her sides. When she stood right in front of Hornby, the woman asked her, "Your name?"

"Darya Singh," she said.

"Singh." Hornby laughed a little. "Well, that's convenient. Let me listen to you for a bit."

Hornby focused her attention on Darya's face, though she wasn't exactly looking into Darya's eyes. She stared for a few seconds, and then a few more seconds . . . and then Darya became aware that Hornby had been staring at her for much longer than she had stared at anyone else . . . and then Hornby rocked onto her heels, as if something had blown her backward.

"My goodness," she said quietly. Then she seemed to come to her senses and said, more briskly, "I hear . . . violin, cello, piano, some voice, trombone, trumpet, drum . . . there are more, but those are the dominant instruments."

She leaned a little closer to Darya's face, so that Darya could see a dart of blue in her otherwise green eyes.

"I've never heard so much dissonance in a life song before," she said quietly, so that only Darya could hear.

And that was the beginning of Darya's education as a Hearkener.

"When do you get the implant?"

Darya stabbed a piece of lettuce with her fork. After seven years at Hearkener school, she had passed the final test, an achievement half of her class hadn't managed. And all Khali wanted to know was when she would get to work. But that was Khali—all work and no play.

"A week from tomorrow," she said.

"Oh."

"It's soon, I know."

Khali frowned. "What?"

"A week. It's hardly enough time to determine my entire future."

Khali's expression was still blank. Darya felt like she had started speaking another language without meaning to. She raised her eyebrows at her older sister.

It was midday, but the windows were boarded up, so it felt like night in the kitchen. Wood wouldn't keep the infection at bay if someone set off a bio-bomb nearby, but it was better than nothing. The battery-operated lantern on the table glowed orange, with fake flickers so that it imitated fire.

Khali lived with their mother now, in their childhood home. Darya had stopped coming back during the holidays three years before, and now only saw Khali when they went out to eat, or when she was sure her mother would be asleep.

"I don't understand," Khali said. "What decision needs to be made?"

"*The* decision." Darya scowled. "You know—life songs or death songs? It's a huge choice. It changes everything."

"But you're going to choose death songs," Khali replied tersely. "Right? Because you want to record Mom's song before it's too late. Right?"

Darya pushed the piece of lettuce around her plate.

"She's only got a few weeks left if she doesn't get the transplant. At most, Darya."

Darya did know.

"She won't get another Hearkener! We don't have enough money as it is!" Khali was shaking her head. "I can't believe you wouldn't do this for her. I can't believe you."

Darya looked up, her lips pursed.

"I can't believe *you*," she said. "She's already controlled my life enough; I'm not going to let her control the rest of it too!"

"What do you mean? She hasn't controlled you."

"What little childhood we had she took from us," said Darya. "Kids aren't supposed to think, 'Oh, Mommy's drunk again, so I'd better stay away from her.' Kids aren't supposed to take care of their parents. We've done enough for her. I'm not doing *this* for her."

Khali's mouth was open, but she wasn't saying anything. She just looked stunned.

Then she said, "You've only met the real her a few times, Darya. The woman you know is just the alcohol, stifling her."

"The implant isn't something you can undo, Khali. You choose death, you choose it forever. You can't tell me it's my duty to choose something just because our shitty mom is finally getting what was always coming to her."

Darya clutched the edge of the table, waiting for Khali to scream at her, or call her names, or something. But Khali's eyes just filled with tears, and her lower lip started to wobble.

"Then . . ." She gulped. "Don't do it for her. Do it for me, so I can hear. . . . She's the only parent I . . . Please, Darya."

Darya carried her plate to the sink and scraped the remnants of her salad into the garbage disposal. She took a long time to clean her plate, scraping slowly, rinsing slowly. She didn't want Khali to see the tears in her own eyes.

"I don't know if I can," she finally said.

"Black or red?" the nurse asked again.

All her life Darya had been developing a resistance to obligation of any kind. No one had taught her to; maybe the world had taught her to. People who set off bio-bombs did so out of a religious obligation to hasten the apocalypse. The pictures she had seen of them did not reveal any delight in the prospect of the world ending—they tried to stay alive in the aftermath of their attacks only so that they could attack again.

Obligation was dangerous because it muddled the mind. Did she want to choose red to defy her mother or because she really wanted it? Did she want to choose black for her sister's sake? How could she know what she really wanted with so many competing obligations—to herself, to her mother, to her sister, to her late father?

Darya remembered the Hearkener's face as she listened to Darya's father's death song, distress and warmth competing for dominance, like she protected a secret, and Darya longed to understand it. It was that whisper of longing that made the decision for her.

"Black," she said.

The nurse put the red cylinder aside and set the black cylinder on a tray next to the hospital bed. She wrapped rubber tubing around Darya's arm to make the veins stand out. Darya felt her pulse in each one of her fingertips, and a harsh sting as the needle went in. The nurse removed the rubber tubing and, with a small smile, flipped the switch that would start the IV drip.

Darya was supposed to be awake for the procedure, so the doctors would know they hadn't damaged her brain while inserting the implant. But she wouldn't remember any of it, thanks to whatever was in the IV bag, and she was grateful. She didn't want to remember them peeling back her scalp and drilling into her skull and inserting things into her temporal lobe, the part of the brain that processed sound.

A haze of passing images was all she retained to remind her that time had passed. Gradually she became aware of someone sitting in front of her, but it looked like she was hidden behind a white film. Then a face surfaced, and it was Khali's. Her mouth was moving, but Darya couldn't hear her. There was something over her ears.

Khali covered her eyes momentarily, as if chastising herself, and then took out a pad of paper and a pen. On it, she wrote, *They don't want you to hear anyone yet. Said it would be too overwhelming. Keep the ear covers on. How do you feel?*

Darya's head throbbed, especially over the right side, where the implant was. Other than that, she just felt heavy, like she could drop right through the mattress.

She didn't want to try to explain all that to Khali, so she just put her thumb up and tried to smile, though she was sure it looked more like a grimace. Even her cheeks were heavy.

Khali's eyes were wet. She scribbled another note on the pad:

Thank you.

Darya knew what Khali was thanking her for. If she hadn't been so tired, she might have tried to say that she had not made her choice for Khali, had not made it for their mother—that she wasn't even sure she wanted to hear her mother's song, despite what she had chosen. But soon the weight collected behind her eyes, dragging her back to sleep.

She woke up later to dark skies showing between the blinds and a nurse peering at the incision in her scalp. They had buzzed some of her hair—eight square inches of it, in fact. She had demanded to know the exact amount. Another thing her mother had told her: a woman's hair is the most beautiful part of her.

Darya's mother had had beautiful hair when she was younger, a reddish brown that shone like a penny in sunlight. It had come down to the middle of her back, incorrigibly wavy—no matter how hard she tried to straighten it, it refused to stay that way. Darya had often thought that it was a shame that neither she nor Khali had inherited her mother's hair.

It was a strange thing, but in the moments right before she fully woke, a memory of her mother had come to mind. It had been during one of her mother's sober streaks. Darya had come home from school for spring break, and her mother had been restored—one month sober, rosy-cheeked, smart, pleasant. She and Khali had been making cake batter in the kitchen as Darya's neighbor nailed boards on all the windows, and her mother had been singing in a thin soprano.

"Sing with me!" her mother had said. "You have a beautiful voice, Darya."

She had started on a song that Darya knew, and though Darya had felt that this woman was a stranger, she could not help but join in. She had made up a harmony on the spot, slipping her lower voice beneath her mother's, and tears—happy ones—had come into her mother's eyes.

"Beautiful," she had said.

That was the week Darya chose violin as her third instrument—every Hearkener needed to be proficient in three—even though her fingertips were too soft for the strings, and she had trouble holding her fingers in tension for so long. She chose it not because she liked it, but because it was challenging, because she knew bearing through the pain would result in greater joy.

The nurse checking the incision site noticed that Darya was awake, and she smiled. She said something Darya couldn't hear, thanks to the glorified earmuffs she still wore. The nurse removed her rubber gloves and tossed them into a nearby trash can. Darya was finally awake enough to look around—she was in a large room full of beds, with curtains separating each one. She could only see the toes of the man next to her.

A stack of books stood on the bedside table—some of Khali's favorites and some of her own. Darya slid one of Khali's from the stack and started to read, propping herself up on the pillows.

About an hour later, Khali walked into the room, dabbing at one of her eyes with a handkerchief. Her face was discolored—she had obviously been crying. *My face looks like raw hamburger when I cry,* Khali used to say. *It's so embarrassing. I can never hide it.*

Khali clutched a phone in her right hand, the one without

the handkerchief. Her grip was so tight it looked like she was about to crack the battery in half with her fingernails.

"What?" Darya said. She could feel the word vibrating in her throat, but she had no idea how loudly she had spoken. Khali didn't shush her, so she assumed it hadn't been that loud.

Khali picked up the notebook and pencil resting next to the stack of books, and started to write.

Mom's request for a liver transplant was denied.

Darya nodded. Obviously. They didn't give new livers to alcoholics.

So I had her transferred here, so she'll be close to us. She's in room 3128.

Darya wanted her mother to be as far away as possible.

She looks awful.

Khali stared at her, wide-eyed, waiting. *Waiting for what?* Darya wondered, but it was a silly question. She knew what Khali was waiting for: an offer, *I'll go record her death song for you.*

But Darya didn't offer. She took the pad of paper from her sister's hands and scribbled, *Okay. Thanks for telling me.*

It was midnight. Khali had left hours ago, right after Darya wrote back to her, but not in a huff—that was not Khali's way. She always made sure to smile when she said good-bye.

Darya put her feet over one side of the bed and let them dangle for a moment before touching them to the tile. It was cold, or her feet were warm from being buried under blankets for so long. She stretched her arms over her head and felt her back crack and pop, though she didn't hear it. The noise blockers were still over her ears.

She walked into the bathroom and looked at her reflection. What she saw shocked her. She had not expected the implant to transform her the way it had. The black veins sprawled across her temple, arching over her eyebrow and down to her cheekbone. She turned her head to see how far back the dye had traveled—it stretched over her scalp as far as the bandage that covered the incision site. Soon her hair would grow over it.

She touched the layer of fuzz that was already growing in. It would grow back faster than normal hair, she knew— the nurse had told her, with a wink, that she had put some hair-regrowing salve on it, the kind they used for vain men and cancer patients. Looking at her reflection, Darya didn't think she would have minded keeping the shaved portion for a while. It made her look tough, just like the implant dye.

She made sure the back of her gown was tied tightly, slipped her shoes on, and walked down the hallway. At the end of it was a large waiting room that looked out over the city. The hospital was one of the taller buildings in this part of Minneapolis, so she would be able to see more than usual.

She shuffled down the hallway, her head aching, but not enough to stop her. In one corner of the waiting room, by the television screen, were what looked like a brother and sister.

The sister was rocking back and forth, her hands pressed between her knees. Both stared at the television but were not really watching it.

Standing near the window on the other end of the room was a young man with the same ear covers she wore, but his whole head was buzzed instead of just eight inches of it. When he looked to the side, she recognized him as Christopher Marshall.

He smiled at her and beckoned for her to come closer. She did, scanning the tables for something she could write on. But then she saw that he was already holding a notebook, balancing it against the railing near the windows, and there was a pen behind his ear.

She stood next to him and touched her fingertips to his chin to turn his head. She wanted to see which implant he had chosen. The red dye on his temple disappointed her. She had hoped that their paths would intersect in the future, but if he had chosen life songs, he would be in different classes for the next two years and work in different places thereafter.

He wrote something on the pad of paper:

What made you choose it?

She sighed and took the pen from him. She paused with the tip of the pen over the paper for a few seconds before she began to write, then scribbled out what she had written and began again. It took her several tries to find a response she liked: *Life's something we already understand. Death is a mystery.*

He nodded, looking impressed, and wrote, *I've heard dying people are ornery toward Hearkeners. Hornby got that scar above her eyebrow because one of her clients chucked an alarm clock at her head.*

Darya laughed and reached across him to write back. *So is that why you picked life? You can just wear a helmet, you know.*

He shook his head. *No. I guess I just wanted to . . . People don't celebrate life as much as they used to. I think they should.*

She nodded and leaned her elbows on the railing. He did the same thing next to her. Their arms, side by side, were as different as the paths they had chosen—his were pale, dotted with freckles, and long; hers were brown and short.

The city lights were beautiful at night, glowing from distant offices and blinking atop buildings, like the Christmas lights her father had put up because he liked the way they looked, though he only turned them on for an hour a day to save on the electric bill. But there was no limit on these lights—they would be on all night, as long as it was dark enough to see them.

Christopher was writing in the notebook again.

Have you listened to anyone yet?

She shook her head.

He bit his lip and wrote, *Do you mind if I listen to you?*

Darya hesitated. Hearkeners had listened to her life song before, but this was different. This was his first one, and he wanted it to be her? She doubted he was thinking of it that way, but it seemed that way to her.

You can say no. I just want it to be someone I know, not whoever runs into me first when I walk out of the hospital, he wrote.

He made a good point. She would be the first, but she would also be the first of many. She took the pen from him and wrote, *Go ahead*.

He took off his ear covers, slowly, so they didn't slip and hit the incision site. She turned to face him, though she knew it wouldn't be any easier for him to hear her song if he was looking at her. He stood with the headphones clutched in front of him for a few seconds, frowning and squinting as he made sense of the new sounds in his mind.

Then, after a few seconds, he stopped squinting or frowning. His face relaxed, and his mouth drifted open, forming a loose O. Darya shifted, holding the railing with one hand, uncomfortable as he stared at her. And he *stared*. His eyes, normally so courteous, were wide and *on* her, pressing against her until she was forced to look back at him.

When she did, she saw a tear in his eyelashes. He wiped it with the back of his hand and shoved the ear covers back on.

Did he not want to hear her anymore? Had it hurt him?

Far from staring now, he was looking at his shoes, at the railing, at anything but her. After she had let him listen to her, after she had exposed that part of herself to him, he had nothing to say, not even a glance to give?

She handed him the notebook and the pen, and walked away without another written word.

Darya walked the hallways of the hospital for a long time after that, not sure where she was half the time. She walked through a cafeteria, and an atrium full of plants in large clay pots, and a hectic corridor with gurneys lining the walls. At 2:00 a.m., she realized that she was in a hallway in which all the rooms started with a 31. Sighing, she walked until she found room 3128 and peered through the window next to the door.

Her mother, with her now-scraggly red hair and yellow-tinged skin, lay in the bed, hooked up to an IV and a few monitors. Khali sat beside her mother with her head on the edge of the mattress, fast asleep. Resting against the wall was a violin case. For if Darya changed her mind, probably.

Not for the first time, Darya wondered what it was that made Khali so attached to their mother. Their father had told her once that their mother hadn't started drinking until two years after Darya was born, when Khali was seven. There wasn't an inciting incident as far as Khali knew—no great losses, or deaths, or arguments—but the strain of the world had weighed on their mother always, more than it weighed on other people. And she had cracked under that weight.

A sad story, maybe, but Darya did not feel particularly sympathetic. The world was terrible for everyone these days, and they still got up, got dressed, went to work, kept their families together.

It didn't really matter, though, did it? It didn't matter whether she felt sympathy or not. Khali had asked her for something. Khali had always been there for her. And Darya would give it to her.

She opened the door. The sound roused Khali from sleep, but not their mother. Khali stared at her sister like she was an apparition, and Darya supposed she did look like one, in a pale hospital gown, her hair half shaved, wandering in uncertainly. The door closed behind her.

She walked to the violin case and crouched over it to open it. Khali had probably brought the violin because it was so portable; she could not have known how perfect it was for this occasion. Darya had chosen it as her third instrument because it was so difficult for her. It seemed only fitting that she should play it on an occasion that would also be difficult for her.

Usually Hearkeners listened to death songs with a computer in hand instead of an instrument, to transpose the music so that it could be preserved and played later. Khali didn't have a computer to bring, and neither did Darya, so the instrument would have to do.

She sat down in a chair opposite Khali, with their mother between them. Khali opened her mouth to speak, her eyes full of tears, and Darya pressed her finger to her lips. She didn't want to hear Khali's gratitude—it might make her too stubborn, might make her want to take back what she had already done.

Darya reached up and removed her ear covers. She put them on the floor and set the violin in her lap. She understood, then, why Christopher's face had screwed up when he took his ear covers off. At first all she heard were sounds—clapping and clamping and stomping and banging, like a crazy person in a kitchen full of pots. She scowled for a few seconds as the sounds transformed into notes . . . into instruments.

And then the song of her mother's dying came to life in her mind.

The notes were low and consistent, at first, like a cello solo—but not like a solo, more like a bass line. And then, arching above it was something high and sweet—painfully sweet—faster than the cellos—but not too fast, not frantic. Then the low notes and the high notes melded together into one melody, twisting around each other, straightening out in harmonies. She thought of the song she and her mother had sung in the kitchen. Her mother had had cake batter on her fingers.

Darya stared at her mother the way Christopher had stared at her, *staring*, trying to extract from her mother's face the genius of this song. It took a few seconds before she realized her mother was awake—awake and staring back.

The melody changed, turning darker. If it had had a flavor, it would have been unsweetened chocolate, bitter, smooth. Her mother's eyes were on hers, clearer than they had been for the years that Darya lived with her, but bloodshot, ugly. She remembered the night she had awoken to her mother breaking plates in the kitchen, raging at their father for one reason or another. She felt a surge of anger.

But still the music went on, lifting again, swelling, louder.

It was so loud Darya moved to plug her ears, but she couldn't plug her ears against this song, she couldn't block out the sound of her mother's death. The sound of her ending.

Loud and pounding, a heartbeat contained in a song, low and high, vibrating in Darya's head. Even if there had been a thousand symphonies playing alongside it, Darya still would have picked it out from the rest—it was insistent—she had to hear it—she picked up the violin and wedged it between her chin and her shoulder.

Darya didn't know what to play first. There were too many competing melodies at work in this complex death song, hard to pick just one. Finally she isolated what seemed to be the dominant notes and began to play them. She had not been in school long enough to be good at this, but she remembered what she had learned: Listen first, and trust your fingers to play what you've just heard. Don't listen to yourself; listen to the song.

Darya trusted her fingers. She played furiously, her eyes squeezed shut and her jaw clenched, as the song swelled again, the notes turning over and over each other. Her arms ached and her head throbbed but still she played, not for her mother and not for herself and not for Khali anymore, but because the song required her to play, to find its strongest moments and bring them to the surface so that someone else could hear them.

Her fingers slowed, then, finding the melody she had heard first, the low, persistent notes. They moved into the high, sweet notes, the notes that hit each other so hard she thought they might crack each other in half. They were weak like her mother was weak, sprawled on the couch in her night-gown—but beautiful like her mother, too. They were the smiles that surfaced in the afternoon, when her mother was more lucid, and the happy tears she cried over her daughter's voice, and the light fingers that went through Darya's hair as she brushed it on her better mornings.

And then the notes were low again, low and slow and barely changing, barely moving, a vague utterance in near solitude. They were the weight, the weight her mother bore, the world that crippled her.

The song, moving in Darya's brain—melodic—dissonant—fast—slow—low—beautiful.

Then she felt tears on her face, and she threw the violin onto the bed and ran.

She ran back to her room. As she ran, she heard pieces of songs all around her and clapped her hands over her ears, but it did her no good. The world was *loud*, too loud to bear. Still, no matter how far she ran, she could hear her mother's death song in her memory, the most powerful of all the music she encountered in her sprint back to the room.

The nurse saw her on her way back in and grabbed her by the arm. "Where are your ear covers? Where have you been?"

Darya just shook her head. The nurse ran down the hall and returned a few seconds later, new ear covers in her hands.

She shoved them over Darya's ears, and all the music stopped. Relief flooded Darya's body like cold water. The nurse steered her to her bed.

Darya crawled under the sheets, gathered her knees to her chest, and stared at the opposite wall.

She slept past noon. Khali came in to speak to her, even touched her hand lightly, but she pretended that she couldn't feel it. She had done what her sister wanted, but she had not done it with a good heart; she had done it out of obligation, something she had always avoided. And she felt angry—angry with herself, for doing it, and angry with Khali, for making her feel like she had to, and angry at the death song itself, for refusing to leave her alone from the second she awoke.

Darya sat in bed for the rest of the day, eating small spoonfuls of flavored gelatin and watching the news report on an attack that had happened in Kansas City earlier that morning. She stared at the death tolls, numb. Sometimes it was weeks before a person showed signs of infection, and sometimes it was minutes—it depended on the potency of the bio-bomb. How long would it be before the world ran out of people?

Darya winced as part of her mother's death song played in her mind again. It ached inside her, feeble but intricate, and every few seconds she felt tears pinching behind her eyes like tweezers. She tried to suppress them, but they came anyway, blurring the news. She didn't know what to do, so she just sat there.

That evening she left her food uneaten on her tray and walked down the hallway again to the waiting room. There were more people in it now, most of them reading magazines or staring at the clock. And Christopher was there, too, sitting in one of the chairs with a stack of paper in his lap. His eyes moved straight to her when she walked in.

He beckoned to her again. His ear covers were off now, and he looked slightly agitated, twitching at sounds she couldn't hear. But the songs didn't seem to pain him. Maybe he had learned to tune them out.

She sat down next to him and removed her own ear covers. This time she didn't hear a series of random sounds when they were off—she heard music right away, everywhere, but not as loud here as it had been in the rest of the hospital. These people weren't sick.

Everyone had a death song, no matter how young or healthy they were, and everyone had a life song, even when they were dying. Everyone was both dying and living at the same time, but the death song grew louder as death approached, just as the life song was loudest at a person's birth. She could hear Christopher's death song, so faint it was barely over a whisper, but she thought she could hear an organ in it, and a clear voice.

"I stayed here all day, hoping you would come back," he said. "I wanted to tell you I was sorry for last night, how I acted."

"You could have asked them for my room number," she said.

He frowned, like this hadn't occurred to him.

"Well," he said, "it felt more like paying penance, this way."

Darya couldn't help it—she smiled a little. Then she remembered how hastily he had shoved the ear covers back on, and her smile faded.

"It was overwhelming," he said. "Your song. I couldn't get it out of my mind. Even while I was listening, it was too much . . . it was too much to bear, so I had to stop." He showed her the first sheet on the stack of paper he was holding. Written at the top was *Daria*. She ignored the misspelling and stared at what was beneath it—crudely rendered musical notes, line after line of them.

"I wrote some of it down," he said. "Do you want to hear it?"

Did she want to hear her life song? Of course she did.

Slowly, Darya nodded.

"Come on, then," he said. He reached for her hand, and led her out of the waiting room. Darya stared at their joined hands as they walked through the hospital corridors. Then she stared at the side of his face, which was also covered in freckles, but these weren't as dark as the ones on his arms, except on his long, narrow nose.

He led her to a set of double doors. The one on the left was marked "Chapel." Christopher pushed it open, and they walked down the aisle between the pews. No one was inside, which was good, because he was heading straight for the piano.

He sat down on the bench and put the first few sheets of music on the stand. He looked at her furtively from beneath his eyebrows, set his hands on the keys, and began to play.

At first the song was unfamiliar—a few chords, some isolated notes, slow and methodical. After a few seconds she felt like she recognized it from somewhere, though she could not have said where. Was it simply that a person always recognized their own life song, whether they had heard it or not? Because it belonged to them, maybe?

His fingers moved faster, pressing harder into the keys. The notes swelled, became *loud*, fierce, as if giving a voice to her own anger. And then, when they began to clash, she knew where she recognized them from.

She put her hands on the piano, an octave above Christopher's, and played, as best she could, the section of her mother's death song that had been going through her mind since the night before. It fit in perfectly with a section of her life song. It was not quite harmony but not quite repetition—sections of notes matched up perfectly, and other sections layered above her life song, bringing out by contrast its richness, and still other sections were similar but came just a second too late, like her mother's song was chasing her own across the piano.

And she realized that her mother was like her—angry, weak, complex, sensitive—everything, good and bad, moving together in this song that made Darya's song more beautiful. Darya had never seen the similarities before, but they were there—buried, but emerging in her mother's occasional lucidity, emerging in Khali's memories of a woman Darya had barely known, and now, emerging in Darya herself.

She felt herself smile, and then laugh, and then cry, and then all at once.

"It's not exactly beautiful," Christopher said, as he played the last note on the last page. He glanced at her. "I don't mean that as an insult. I'm very attached to it. It keeps following me around."

When she didn't respond, he looked slightly alarmed. "I'm sorry, was that rude?"

Darya shook her head and set her left hand on top of his right, guiding it to the right keys. His fingers warmed hers. He glanced at her, smiling a little.

"Play that again," she said quietly, pointing at the place in the music where the section began. She took her hands from the piano, and listened as Christopher played the section again. She closed her eyes and swayed without knowing it to the rhythm of the notes.

She had been wrong to say that death was the mystery, not life.

Her mother's death song had revealed a secret beauty inside of her, something Khali had known, but Darya's anger had prevented her from seeing.

The anger had not left her, might never leave her, but it now had to share the space with something else, and that was the certain knowledge of her mother's worth.

BRANDED

Kelley Armstrong

THERE'S NOTHING AS boring as civics class, and in the fortress, that's really saying something. Still, monotony can be good, if the alternative is fighting for survival every second of every day until you die a horrible, violent death, your bones gnawed and sucked clean by scavengers, not all of them animal. That's the message of civics class, and students get it every six months to remind us how good we have it in the fortress. After seventeen years, I could recite it in my sleep.

As the minister droned on, Priscilla elbowed my ribs. "Braeden keeps looking at you, Rayne."

I glanced over. Braeden smiled. He mouthed something, but I didn't catch it—I was too busy looking at that sad twist of a smile. Maybe there was still time. Maybe I could—

But I couldn't. It was done.

The minister had now begun the history lesson, just in case we'd somehow forgotten how we all got here.

"The end began when the world discovered the existence of supernatural beings. Witches, sorcerers, vampires, werewolves, and others, all living among us. When they were revealed, the natural order was destroyed forever, and the very earth revolted. Famines, earthquakes, tsunamis . . .

"Then those supernatural beings decided that infiltrating our world was not enough. They needed to infiltrate our very selves. They convinced scientists to modify ordinary humans with supernatural DNA, promising superior soldiers for our wars against those who sought to take our food supplies and our habitable land.

"And so we took refuge in our fortresses, where we continued to live as civilized beings, protected from the Outside. Yet even here, we are constantly under siege from another threat, equally dangerous. Overpopulation. That is why—"

The classroom door flew open. Two regulators burst in, one armed with a cudgel; the other, a syringe.

"Braeden Smith," barked the cudgel-wielding one.

Every kid surrounding Braeden stumbled over himself getting away—chairs toppling, desks scraping the wooden floor—until Braeden was alone. He rose slowly, hands instinctively going to the pockets of his grease-and-soot-streaked trousers, then thinking better of it and lifting them.

"Is this about the Fourth's horse?" he asked. "He says my father didn't shoe it properly but—"

"Braeden Smith." The regulator with the cudgel walked toward Braeden. "You are hereby charged with breaking the First Law of the fortress." The whispers and gasps of the students almost drowned out his next words. "You have been accused of having supernatural blood. Werewolf blood. You will be taken to the stocks and watched for signs—"

"What? No! I'm not a—"

The regulator grabbed Braeden by the arm and twisted it, but Braeden broke free. He looked around, as if lost, then his gaze fell on me. He let out a snarl and flew at me. I stood my ground as Priscilla and the other girls ran, shrieking.

"You did this!" Braeden said as he charged. "You treacherous bitch!"

I made a move to dive for safety, but he grabbed me in a headlock, still ranting as I struggled. The regulator with the syringe crept up behind Braeden. As he injected him, Braeden stiffened. His hand dropped to mine. A quick squeeze. Then he hit the floor, unconscious.

A day later, they had their proof. Braeden had transformed into a wolf. We'd known he would. Braeden had grown up on the Outside and knew the gene ran in his family. As with most supernatural powers, it left whole generations untouched. We had hoped it would pass Braeden. It didn't.

On the day of his branding, nearly everyone in the fortress crowded into the square. I read once about hangings in the Old World, how people would watch with great delight and baskets of food. There was no joy here, certainly no feasting. We came because if we did not, then someone—a regulator, a minister, a prefect—might notice our absence and decide we were not as committed to the laws as we should be. Or, worse, that we had cause to fear the same fate for ourselves.

They'd given me a place of honor, on the raised platform with the First's and Second's families. As Priscilla clutched my hand, I noticed her mother frown, but Priscilla's chin shot up in a rare show of defiance, and she held my hand tighter. Her father noticed and nodded, first at me, then at her. She glowed at his approval.

Priscilla and I had always been schoolmates, but now that she believed I'd informed on a werewolf, I had risen to the status of friend. Friends with the Second's daughter. How my mother would laugh if she were here to see it. No, she wouldn't laugh. She'd rub her hands and plot how to use it to her advantage. That's what it was all about in the fortress—getting ahead, surviving and thriving.

For my mother, surviving had meant accepting life as a whore. It's a real job in the fortress, just like a blacksmith or a doctor or a farmer, and it's considered just as necessary for the stability of the community. She accepted it. I wouldn't. There were other ways to survive, if you were willing to take chances, including the chance that you wouldn't survive.

They led Braeden out. He'd been stripped to the waist, his feet bare, his trousers even filthier than they had been when the regulators had taken him in. His face was unshaven, dark shadow on his cheeks; his hair unwashed, falling over his face. Making him look like an animal. *See? This is what we saved you from.*

I looked at his chest—the lean muscles, the old scars, the healed burns—and remembered all the nights lying in our cubbyhole, touching him, whispering with him. There were new marks now, lash welts crisscrossing every inch of bare skin.

"They'll beat me, Rayne," he'd warned. "You need to be ready for that."

"I know."

I tried not to see the welts, but of course I did, and the rage built inside me until Priscilla's hand twisted in mine. I realized I was clutching too tight and loosened my grip.

Taking deep breaths, I forced myself to look at the figure on the stage and see another Braeden. To see the boy who'd been bought from the Outsiders to replace the blacksmith's dead son.

In the fortress, couples are allowed only one child. If that child dies, they can have another baby, but that isn't a solution for someone like the blacksmith, who needed a replacement for the strong, healthy ten-year-old son who'd been his apprentice.

The day that Braeden was brought in, everyone had again found an excuse to be in the square. They'd ogled the boy, who'd looked much as he did now—barefoot and filthy. They'd whispered about his eyes, how savage he looked, how angry, how dangerous. But I hadn't seen anger—I'd seen terror.

I remembered him again, at twelve. A prefect's son and his friend had cornered me behind the schoolhouse and decided that since I was going to be a whore someday, I should be willing to take off my shirt for a credit, and if I wasn't, then they'd take it off without paying the credit. Braeden came around the corner and sent them scattering with an ease that made my weak kicks and punches look like the struggles of an infant. I'd asked him for lessons in fighting and said I'd pay. He'd said he didn't need that kind of pay, and I'd lost my temper, snarling that I wasn't a whore and when I said pay, I meant credits. He'd been amused, I think. But he agreed. Only he wouldn't trade for credits—he wanted me to teach him something: how to read and write.

When they lifted the brand, I was thinking of Braeden again, at fourteen, the first time he kissed me. I tried to focus on the memory, but I could smell the fire and see the glowing metal.

"The brand is nothing," he'd said. "I've had worse burns. You know that."

I'd seen those burns. Some accidental. Some not. Mr. Smith might call Braeden his son, but he slept in the barn and worked from sunrise to sunset, and if he didn't do a good enough job, he'd be beaten, sometimes burned.

Yet this was different. I saw that glowing metal coming toward Braeden's back, and I had to drop Priscilla's hand before I squeezed hard enough to break bones. I gripped my legs instead, my fingers digging in.

The brand sizzled as the metal touched his back. His body convulsed. I swore I smelled the stink of burning flesh. He didn't cry out, though. They always cried out, even the grown men, sometimes dropping to their knees, howling and weeping. But after that first flinch, Braeden stood firm, gaze straight ahead, biting his lip until blood trickled down his chin.

Next the regulator pressed soot into the wound. That's when Braeden almost lost it. His eyes bulged with agony, and tears streamed down his cheeks. His gaze rolled my way. His eyes met mine and he mouthed, "Just a burn," before looking away again.

"He saw you," Priscilla whispered. "He said something."

"Cursing me to a thousand hells, I'm sure," I said, my voice thick.

She put a thin arm around my shoulders. "You did the right thing. Can you imagine if no one had discovered him? A werewolf?" She shuddered. "The last werewolf in the fortress ate three children before he was caught."

I doubted it. I'd been with Braeden when he changed to a wolf, and he'd never even nipped at me. Priscilla's story was an old one, passed down as an example of how horrible supernaturals could be and why they must be rooted out at all costs. There probably had been a werewolf. And children might have died in the years leading up to his discovery, but that was hardly unheard of in the fortress. Disease and death stalked the young and old here. It grew worse with every passing year, as supplies and food sources dwindled.

There were no words after the branding. The charges and the sentence had been read beforehand. Now all that remained was the final part of that sentence. The casting out.

A horse-drawn cart waited beside the stage. The regulators prodded Braeden toward it. When he gazed about, as if blinded and befuddled by pain, they gave him a tremendous shove off the stage, and he hit the cart with a thud, crumpling at the bottom. A regulator jumped in after him and forced him to stand. It took a moment for Braeden to get himself steady—there was a post in the cart, where they often had to tie the convicted to keep him upright—but Braeden managed it and stood there as he had on the stage, gaze forward, expression blank.

The crowd followed in a procession behind the cart. Now there was a little spring in their steps. This was the part they looked forward to, as they jostled and jockeyed for a spot near the front. Not to watch a convict cast out. Again, that struck a little too close to everyone's gravest fear. But they were about to see a sight they'd talk about for days. The Outside.

The cart rolled along the dusty streets, past the wooden buildings. Children too young to watch the branding leaned out the open windows. Mothers tugged at the children, but only halfheartedly. It wasn't a sight for a child, but fortress life would be better and easier if they understood the alternative.

The cart stopped at the gates, and the regulator took longer than necessary fussing with the locks, making people stamp and twitch and whisper with excitement. I pulled my gaze from Braeden's whip-striped back and looked up at the structure that kept us safe.

The walls of the fortress stretched twenty feet in the air. Our buildings might rot and list, but no expense would be spared for this wall. Voyager parties traveled for days and lost members to the hybrids and the tribes, all to bring back wood to repair the wall. Sixteen feet up there was a platform that stretched around the perimeter. Guards patrolled it at all times. One was permanently stationed at the gates, bearing one of the few guns we still had from the Old World.

As the gates began to open, Priscilla gripped my arm, her hands trembling.

"Don't be afraid," she whispered. "We're safe here."

That was the point. That was what this drama was all about. As those gates swung open, there was a collective gasp. A few women who'd fought to the front now shrieked and pressed back into the crowd. Men snorted at their cowardice, but even they shrank as the gates swung open to reveal . . .

Nothing.

That's what you saw at first. That's what was so terrifying. The gates opened, and you looked out to see miles of barren, rock-strewn dirt, stretching in every direction.

The sun beat down, baking and cracking the earth. It was so bright that it took a moment for your eyes to adjust. Then you noticed the plain was not empty. Far to the left, there was a mountain, dark with trees and capped with snow. To the right rose a thin ribbon of smoke. You didn't need to wonder what was at the base. Not a bonfire—no Outsider would be so foolish as to announce his presence with that much smoke. It was a camp, now burning. Torched.

Braeden told me once about coming across a burned camp, back when he was with the tribe. They'd seen the smoke and gone to it, holding back and sending scouts until they were sure the raiding party had left. Then they'd swooped in for the scraps the raiders hadn't wanted, bits of fur or wood left unscorched. They'd ransacked the bodies, too, taking whatever they could from the corpses of those too proud or too foolish to flee when the raiders sounded their horn.

"We didn't take the bodies," Braeden had said. "Sometimes the elders argued about that. Other tribes took them. For meat."

I remembered how disgusted I'd been. I remembered how angry Braeden got.

"You don't understand what it's like out there, Rayne. You do what you have to. I really don't want to eat another person, but if it was that or starve . . ."

He was right, of course. Later I found out that, sometimes, in the long winter, when someone died in the fortress, their body wasn't taken out to be burned. People did what they had to, and it was no different in here than it was out there.

There were piles of bones on the landscape, too. We sent out voyagers to scavenge those when one of the craftsmen needed material, but we didn't bother storing any. The piles weren't going anywhere, and space inside was already at a premium.

Off to the far left there was a body not yet reduced to bones. Carrion eaters attempted to remedy that, silently ripping flesh from the corpse. From the looks of the body, it had been a hybrid, I could no longer tell what kind. Maybe part bull or part bear or part cat. Those were common ones.

The hybrids were the end result of the overreaching ambition that began with the supernaturals. The minister taught us that supernaturals had convinced us to use their DNA, but Braeden's family told him it had been the humans' idea. They'd rounded up the supernaturals and taken that DNA. The scientists had started with careful, controlled studies, but then the wars for food and land broke out, and there wasn't time for caution.

Eventually they decided there was no need to limit themselves to creating ultrapowerful werewolf soldiers or spellcasting assassins. If they could use the DNA of supernaturals, could they use animals, too? That was near the end of the Old World, when the situation was so dire that no one cared about limits. So they created hybrids. Then the Great Storms came and the Final War came, and when it ended, the hybrids and modified supernaturals broke out of captivity and fought back. It took only a few years for the first fortress to rise, shielding a small group of uninfected humans against that endless wasteland overrun with hybrids and roving bands of survivalists.

That's where Braeden was born. Out there. When he was five, his parents had been killed by hybrids. He'd survived and been found by a tribe of wanderers. They'd taken him in—as a slave whose job was to roam from camp and attract any nearby hybrids so that his tribe could kill them for meat.

So Braeden knew the hybrids better than any fortress dweller. We were told they were just animals with humanoid features, but he said they could be as cunning as humans, setting traps and raiding camps. Some even had language. The point of the lie was to convince us they weren't human so that we wouldn't feel guilty when we slaughtered and ate them.

The hybrid rotting outside our gates hadn't accidentally perished there. I'd heard the shot two days ago. It had ventured too close to the fortress, and a guard had killed it. The carcass would warn others away. To me, that proved the hybrids had some human intelligence.

When the gates opened, the regulators drove the cart through, then stopped just past the walls. By now, Braeden had recovered enough to walk on his own. Once he was out of the cart, the driver led the horses to the side, and two regulators flanked Braeden as the First stepped from the edge of the crowd and solemnly walked toward him. A young prefect followed.

The elderly First stopped in front of Braeden.

"Braeden Smith," he said in his reedy voice. "You have been found to possess werewolf blood, which has been proven to manifest itself in the form of a physical transformation. For this, you must be cast from the fortress. However, in recognition of the fact that you have been an otherwise loyal and productive member of the community—and that this curse comes through no fault of your own—this is not a sentence of execution. We hope that you will find your place in the Outside. To that end, we will provide you with the tools necessary to do so."

He motioned to the young prefect, who stepped forward and handed him a dagger, the metal flashing in the sunlight.

"A weapon for defense."

He dropped it at Braeden's feet. A small bow followed.

"A weapon for hunting."

A filled skin and a bound package.

"Water and food."

Another parcel.

"Clothing and shoes."

Finally, a bag.

"And a pack with which to carry it. You are young and strong, Braeden Smith, and I trust that you will not perish in this harsh land. Go forth with our gifts. And do not return."

Everyone waited for the inevitable final outcry from the convicted. Some attacked the First, and their exile turned into a speedy execution. Some raged and had to be forcibly dragged into the Outside. Most dropped to the First's feet, wailing and begging, promising anything, should they be permitted to stay.

Braeden bent and picked up the shoes first. He put them

on. Then he stuffed the food, the waterskin, and the rest of the clothing into the pack. He slung the bow over his shoulder. When he reached for the knife, the First tensed, but he could not recoil, could not show fear. Braeden picked up the knife, thrust it into the discarded sheath, fastened it to his belt, and hefted the pack. Then, without a glance at the First or the fortress, he began to walk into the Outside, bloody soot falling from his branded back in a trail behind him.

The gates closed as soon as the cart was brought back in. I left then, mumbling apologies to Priscilla as she told me again how brave, how terribly brave, I'd been. Before I could escape, her father clamped a hand on my shoulder and said I must come to dinner, soon, that the fortress needed more young women like me.

If only he knew.

I got away, then raced to the smithy. Braeden's "father" wasn't there. He hadn't gone to the ceremony, more out of shame than because he couldn't bear to watch his boy branded and cast out. I made my way through the stables, past the horses that were the fortress's most valuable commodity. That's what Mr. Smith had used to buy Braeden—a horse. The tribe wanted it because horses were the only way to cross the barren lands one step ahead of the predators, human and otherwise. As Braeden said, though, he doubted their foresight had lasted past the first harsh winter, when they'd have looked at five hundred pounds of meat and decided having a horse really wasn't that important after all.

When I ducked out the stable's back door, the smell hit me, like it always did. The dung heap. Almost as valuable as the horses themselves—or it would be, once it rotted into fertilizer for the fortress garden's near-barren soil. Given the stench, this was one treasure everyone steered clear of. It was Braeden's domain, one he never argued about, because that dung heap kept everyone from discovering his cubby.

The "wall" was actually two layers with empty space between. In other parts, the space was used for storage. Here, because of the dung heap, it was left empty. Years ago Braeden had cut through a board behind the heap and made a narrow door. I had to twist out a nail to get the board free. Then I swung it aside and squeezed in.

There used to be straw here, covering the ground and masking some of the smell, but a drought two years ago meant Braeden couldn't afford to steal enough from the barn to replace it, so I'd brought rags instead. As for the smell, you got used to it.

On the other wall Braeden had carved out a peephole. He'd covered it with a nailed piece of old leather, in case light from inside the fortress revealed the hole at night. I pulled the leather off and peered through. Braeden was a distant dot on the horizon now. It was still daylight, and the hybrids rarely came out then, but I knew they were there, hiding in the outcroppings of rock or the rare stand of scrubby bush. Braeden knew too, and steered clear of all obstacles.

"I know how to survive out there, Rayne," he said when he came up with the plan.

"You were ten."

"But I survived. And I've been out with the voyagers. I'll be fine." He'd paused then, peering at me through the dim light in the cubby. "It's you I'm worried about."

"You've taught me well."

"I hope so," he'd whispered, and kissed me, a long, hungry kiss as we stretched out on the rags and told ourselves everything would be all right.

I stared out at his distant figure.

"Everything will be all right," I whispered. But I didn't quite believe it. I don't think either of us did.

I fell asleep in the cubby that night. I knew I shouldn't—it was risky. But I had to trust that everyone in the whores' dormitory would think I was just too upset to come back. Why did I stay? I don't know. I guess it made me feel like, if things went wrong, and Braeden came back, I'd know and I could save him from the guard's bullets. I couldn't, of course. If he returned, even pursued by a pack of hybrids, he'd be shot.

When I woke to the sound of voices, I bolted up so fast I hit the wall and froze. Then I heard another whisper—a male voice, from outside—and I scrambled over to the peephole. I couldn't see anything. It was night and pitch-black. Then, slowly, I made out figures moving along the wall. More than one. Not Braeden. I started to exhale, then stopped.

There were figures. Outside the wall. That was not a cause for relief.

I crept toward the door, to race out and warn the guards

that we were under attack. Then I heard a child's voice.

"Are we going to live in there, Momma?"

"Shh!"

"But—"

A man's voice. "We will . . . if you can be quiet, child. Just for a while longer." A pause as they continued creeping along the wall, then he said, "Do you remember what we told you, child? What you need to say? It is very important."

"Yes," the girl lisped. "I am to say that I am hungry and cold, that I do not eat very much, but I am a good worker, like my mother and my father. Then I am to cry. If I do not, you will pinch me."

"Only to make you cry, child. It is very important that you cry. They will not listen otherwise."

I cursed under my breath. Outsiders, coming to try to persuade the Six to let them into the fortress. It happened nearly every moon cycle. They came and they begged and they pleaded, and their cries fell on deaf ears.

It had been a generation since our fortress accepted refugees. Yet the desperate still came, only to be refused and sometimes . . .

I shook off the thought and reached for the cubby door. It was not my business. It could not be my business.

And yet . . .

Any other time, even the child's voice wouldn't have moved me. You learn not to be swayed by useless emotions like mercy and pity. But tonight, listening to the child, I thought of

Braeden, alone out there, and I thought of the branding, and I thought of what would happen if these Outsiders approached the gate and refused to leave.

I returned to the peephole and pulled back the leather.

"You there!" I whispered.

It took a moment for me to get their attention, but when I did, they came over and gaped around, as if the very wall had spoken.

"You need to leave," I whispered. "Now."

"What?" the girl said. "We have walked—"

The woman reached out, scowling, and pulled her daughter closer. "Ignore her, child. It is only a fortress girl, not wanting to dirty her pretty town with the likes of us."

The man stepped forward. "There is no need to fear us, girl. We are hard workers, and your town needs hard workers, so you do not need to dirty and callous your pretty hands."

I looked at my already dirty and calloused hands and bit back a bitter laugh. What did they imagine when they pictured life in the fortress?

"I don't fear you," I said. "I'm trying to warn you. Whoever told you this town takes refugees has lied. It hasn't taken one in my lifetime, and it does not take kindly to those who ask."

The girl whimpered. Her mother pulled her closer, scowl deepening.

"It is you who lies, girl. We know what you fear. That we will take some of your precious milk and your honey and your fresh water. You want it all for yourself."

Milk? They'd killed the cows decades ago, when they realized the milk was no longer worth the cost of supporting them. We had goats now, but their milk was reserved for children and, on special occasions, made into cheese. As for honey, the bees had started dying almost from the start, and the few that remained were coddled like princesses, because if they perished, the crops would no longer be pollinated. We would never risk disturbing them by removing honey from their hives.

Water was another matter. We did have it. Every fortress was built around a spring, encompassing just enough land to grow crops and keep livestock and support the community forever. A noble dream. After generations, though, the water didn't flow as freely as it once did. And the land? There must have been no farmers among those early settlers, or they would have warned that you could not keep using the same land year after year and expect bountiful crops.

"We have nothing to spare," I said. "We have too many to support as it is."

We're dying. Don't you get it? We're all dying. Out there. In here. It makes no difference.

I didn't say that—I didn't want to scare the little girl—but she started to cry anyway.

"They won't take us, Momma. You promised they would—"

"They will," the woman said. "Do not listen to that foolish

girl. She is greedy and wants it all to herself. Come. We will speak to the guard."

"If you try, then you are the fool," I whispered, my voice harsh, anger rising. "I only hope you are not fool enough to persist when the guard tells you to begone, or you will see your daughter's blood stain the—"

"Enough!" the man roared, and he leaped forward, challenging the very wall itself. Behind him, the little one began to sob. "You are a wicked girl, and you had best hope I do not find you when I am in there, or I shall teach you a lesson."

"Come," his wife whispered. "While the child cries. It will soften their hearts."

Nothing will soften their hearts, I wanted to rage. *You don't get it. You really don't get it. We have nothing to share. We are dying. Every third moon, the Six meet to assess the food supply and discuss new ways to decrease the population. They don't just cast out the supernaturals anymore. The smallest crime is weighed against your contribution to the community, and if the balance is not in your favor, you are exiled.*

Nothing I could say would stop them. They were determined to make a better life for their child, which only made me all the more angry, because it made me feel pity. That love of parent for child was nothing I'd ever known. My mother had cared for me, in her way, but thought more of what I could do for her, the credits I could bring if my looks blossomed while hers faded.

When she'd died three years ago, she'd been pregnant.

For that, she was executed. Those in the fortress were allowed only one child, and in trying to secretly have a second, she'd committed high treason. She'd begged for mercy, pleaded and wept that she had been blinded by maternal instinct, which would have been much more touching if I hadn't known the truth—she'd promised the child to the doctor for an outrageous sum. His wife was barren, and the new population rules did not allow adoption. They'd conspired to pretend the doctor's wife was pregnant, while hiding my mother's condition. It failed. She died. A community that would kill one of its own for the crime of attempting to bear a second child was not about to admit three strangers.

I stayed where I was and strained to listen. They hadn't even reached the gate before a patrolling guard tramped over, platform boards shuddering.

"Who goes there?" the guard called.

I could hear the parents prompting the child to speak, but she was too distraught, crying loudly now.

"I asked who goes there!"

"We . . . we are refugees," the woman said. "Our tribe was raided by the Branded. We are the only survivors. We throw ourselves on your mercy and—"

The child cut in, finding her voice. "I am hungry and cold, sir. I do not eat very much, but I am a good worker, like my mother and my father." She snuffled loudly.

"There is no room for refugees here," the guard said. "Begone."

"Where?" the woman said. "There is no place for us to go."

"Find a place. Now leave."

"We'll leave," the woman said. "Just take our child. She's strong and she's healthy and she'll be no bother at all. She'll prove her worth. Just take—"

"We have more than enough children of our own. We need no extra mouths to feed. Now, begone!"

He cocked his gun, the metal clank ringing out in the silence. The woman started to wail as her husband begged the guard to take their daughter. Another guard joined the first and ordered them to leave.

"Yes, all right," the man said. "We are going, but we will leave the child."

"You will not—"

"Stay there, child," he said. "Just stay there." To his wife: "Come. We will leave. They will take her."

"No, we will not," the guard said, his voice growing louder as the parents' footsteps trampled over the hard earth. "Come back and get the child or you are leaving her for the hybrids."

The girl wailed. I heard her try to run, but her father caught her and forced her back, whispering, loud enough for the guards to hear, "You will be fine. No one would be so cruel." His voice rose another octave. "No one would be so cruel."

His footsteps retreated.

"Come back for the girl!" the guard shouted.

"You would not—"

"If I open this gate to your child, my own life is forfeit. If you do not take her, there is only one way for me to show mercy: kill her before the hybrids do."

"You would not—"

"I would! Now get back here and take your child and begone before—"

"You will not. I know you will not."

"I must! Are you a fool? A monster who would sacrifice his own child?"

The guard continued to rant, his voice growing louder, his partner joining in, entreating the parents to come back, do not do this, come back. Inside the fortress, people began to stir, doors opening, then closing quickly as they realized what was happening. Stopping up their ears because they knew what was coming. What had to come.

A shot.

A single shot, barely audible over the guard's voice, choked with rage and grief as he cursed the parents to deaths in a thousand hells. The father shrieked and raged, and his wife wailed, and they raced back to their dead child, and the guards told them no, they must go, leave her, she was gone, and the scent of the blood . . .

The parents didn't listen. I could hear them still sobbing and cursing as they carried their child's body into the wasteland.

Then, reverberating through the night air, a growl. Joined by a second. I opened the peephole to see eyes reflecting in the darkness.

"Drop the child!" the one guard shouted, his voice raw. "Drop her and run!"

The guard continued to shout as his partner tried to quiet him, to tell him it did no good. The growls continued, seeming to come from every direction. And then, as if answering some unknown signal, feet and paws thundered across the baked earth, coming from the left, from the right, too many to count.

The woman screamed. She didn't scream for long.

Growls. Snarls. Roars. The wet sound of ripping flesh.

I stumbled from the peephole, fumbled open the door, and raced back to my quarters.

For two nights, I scarcely slept, racked by nightmares of the child at the gate, the creatures beyond, those eyes, those snarls, that horrible ripping sound. I thought of that, and I thought of Braeden. Out there. Alone.

"It's the smell of blood that draws them out, Rayne," he'd said.

"But the branding. There will be blood—"

"The soot does more than mark the brand. It covers the blood. As long as I take shelter at night, the only hybrids who will attack are the ones who are starving. Easily fended off with a blade."

He was right. The hybrids hadn't attacked until the child was killed. They must have heard and smelled the three refugees, but they were still human enough to have learned lessons about attacking healthy targets.

At least ones who were in groups.

Braeden was alone.

He'll be fine. He'll be fine. He'll be fine.

And if he wasn't? This fate had been chasing him from the day he began his first transformation. He couldn't have hidden that forever. Either way, he would have been cast out, and all we could do was take control of the situation. Make plans.

Plans.

The morning after Braeden was cast out, Priscilla had come to the livestock barns, where I was tending to the chickens. Except for civics class, most children stopped school as soon as they were old enough to work. My true "job" might be six months away, but that didn't mean I could laze around until then. I had chores that paid for my room and board, and I worked extra tasks for credits that could be bartered for everything from shoes to rations. These days, for most people, credits went to rations, which only drove the price higher, until it was a rare night you went to bed with a full stomach.

Priscilla had asked me to lunch in the dining hall of the Six, and I'd come away sated for the first time in memory. There'd been extra tasks I'd planned to do that afternoon, but she had wanted to spend the time with me, and I knew that was more valuable than any paper token in my pocket.

In another life, would Priscilla and I have become friends? Probably not. She was sweet and kind, but too timid by far. As hard as I struggled to remind myself that she had not chosen her place in the world, I couldn't help but feel guilty niggles of contempt when she twittered about the refugees at the gate, telling me they had escaped into the night, as her father told her. There was no reason to correct her. It would only turn her against me.

For the next three days, I accepted all her invitations, both to meals and quiet times together. Did she see me as a friend? Perhaps. But I think, in truth, I was more of a pet. An exotic pet in a world where children made cages for mice because anything larger was a source of food, not companionship.

On the third evening, when I was supposed to meet her in the square to watch a rare dramatic performance, I did not show up. She found me in tears behind my quarters. Hearing her, I leaped up and wiped my cheeks.

"Wh-who's there?" I squinted into the twilight. "Oh, Priscilla. What are you doing—?" My eyes widened, mouth dropping open. "Oh! I was supposed to—" I looked up at the stars. "The performance. I missed it." I hurried over to her, tripping as I did. "I'm so sorry."

"What's wrong?"

"Wrong?" Another wipe of my eyes as I cleared my throat. "Nothing. I was just"—I pointed up—"admiring the night sky."

"You've been crying."

I denied it. She pushed. I continued to deny. This went on

for a few minutes before I blurted, "I heard a rumor."

Thus far in our relationship, while Priscilla was the Second's daughter, she'd treated me as an equal, more recently as someone she looked up to. I was a year older. I was more mature. I was certainly more worldly. And then, of course, there was the matter of my recent estimable "bravery." When I said this, though, she pulled herself up tall and smiled, shaking her head as a mother might with her child.

"There are always rumors, Rayne. You can't pay them any mind."

"But this—this was about Braeden."

"Oh." She paused, as if uncertain how to react, then reached to grip my hands. "I know you must feel some guilt, but you shouldn't. You really and truly shouldn't. You did the right thing, and I'm sure he's fine. He grew up Outside, remember?"

"It—it's not that."

"I know it is." She enunciated each word carefully, as if I truly were a child. "You did the right thing."

"I didn't do any—" I sucked in breath. "It doesn't matter. What I heard was about the interrogation. When they forced him to transform." I paused. "Who witnesses that?"

She frowned. "Hmm?"

"When an alleged supernatural is forced to reveal his or her powers, who is there to witness it? Is one of the Six present?"

"Oh, no."

"So it's . . . just a prefect."

"And a regulator, of course," she said.

"But no one else?"

"No. Why?"

"I heard—" I stopped myself. "Nothing. I heard nothing. I'm sorry."

I broke from her grip and fled into my quarters.

I avoided Priscilla for the next two days. It wasn't easy, but I stuck with others or in places where I knew she wouldn't follow, like the whores' quarters. Then on the second evening, I was playing ball with a group of young people in the square. Priscilla was there, watching us. Partway through the game, I started hesitating, as if overcome by my thoughts. Finally, I made my excuses and fled. She followed.

I raced behind the dining hall to a stairway that led to the wall platform. This section was blocked off—it had been unstable for years, and we couldn't yet retrieve enough material to fix it. I climbed over the barrier and ran up the stairs. At the top, I grabbed the wall and stood there, leaning out.

"No!" Priscilla shrieked.

Her dainty boots tapped across the platform as she ran.

I turned and waved her back frantically. "It's not safe!"

She kept coming. "Whatever you're thinking of, Rayne, don't do it. Please don't do it."

"Don't . . . ?" I looked down and stepped back with a wry smile. "It's twenty feet, Priss. At most, I'd twist my ankle. I wasn't going to jump." I took another step from the wall to reassure her. "I was just . . ." I looked out at the setting sun. "Thinking, I guess. Of him. Of what I did."

I stared out until she got a little closer, then wheeled and blurted, "I didn't turn him in. Not on purpose." I took a deep breath. "Braeden and I. He was . . ."

"Your boyfriend."

I nodded. "One night, we were out together, and he told me that there were werewolves in his family. I—I went a little crazy. We'd been together for years and he'd never said a word, and now he tells me he could turn into a wolf? That we could be alone together, and he could suddenly transform? Kill me? Eat me? He insisted it was no big deal—it might never happen. Might? Might?"

I stopped and gulped breath.

Priscilla came over and patted my back. "That must have been terrible."

I nodded. "It was. We fought. Really fought. I yelled at him and I think—" Another gulp of air. "I think someone heard. Someone told the regulators."

"But not you."

I shook my head. "No. But when they came, I didn't . . . I didn't stand up for him. I didn't defend him. I knew it was right—that he needed to be taken. To be tested."

Lies. All of it. I'd known about the werewolf blood since Braeden and I became more than friends. I had been the one who'd informed on him—as part of the plan, our plan.

"I thought—I thought he'd be fine. I told myself that he needed to know for sure. Then . . . when they said it was true—he did transform—I knew there was nothing I could do, nothing I should do. He had to leave. For the sake of everyone, he had to leave."

"Of course. A werewolf cannot be allowed—"

"But he's not a—" I clamped my hand over my mouth, eyes going wide. "I-I'm sorry. I shouldn't say anything. Just . . . just leave me, Priss. I know you mean well, but I can't involve you in this."

"What did you hear?"

"Hear?" More feigned terror and horror. "I didn't hear anything."

Once again, I let her press, and I pretended to resist until I finally blurted, "They say he didn't transform. That the prefect lied. I overheard the regulator—the one who was with Braeden—and he said that after the last two accusations, when they didn't find anything, some of the Six were angry with the prefect. They thought he wasn't doing his job right. So he . . . he lied."

"But if Braeden didn't transform, he would have said something."

"Accuse a prefect of lying? What good would that do? Every accused denies they manifested powers. They're beaten for the lie, then cast out." I looked beyond the wall. "I need to get to him."

"What?"

I turned back to her. "I need to get Braeden and bring him back. I could tell what I heard, but they wouldn't believe me. I need proof. I need Braeden."

"You—you—" She sputtered for a minute, unable to find words, then took my arms again. "You'd never find him out there, Rayne."

"No, I can. I know where he'd go. We talked about that, in case something ever happened to either of us. Where we'd go. What we'd do. How we'd survive. We had a plan. It made us feel safer."

She looked confused.

"Everyone has a plan, Priss. Everyone who isn't the Second's daughter. What they'd do if they were accused of having supernatural blood. If they were accused of a crime. If they were cast out. How they'd kill themselves quickly or how they'd survive. Braeden used to live out there, and he traveled with the voyagers, so he had a good plan. He told me about a spring where I could camp and wait for a tribe to come by, then join them. That's where he'll be—until a tribe comes. Which is why I have to go now."

"Go?" Again she sputtered. "Go how? You can't go out there. You'd never survive."

"Not alone."

Her eyes shot wide. "You—you want me—"

"No, of course not. I'd never ask anyone to do that. I meant a horse. I could do it with a horse. I just need help—"

I stopped, and now it was my eyes widening in horror. "I

don't mean—I shouldn't ask—I'm sorry. I just . . ."

I turned back to the wall and looked out, pouring every ounce of despair into my expression, imagining Braeden out there, alone, waiting for me, and I never came. That must have done the trick because Priscilla reached for me. I sidestepped, then feigned a stumble and let myself collapse in a heap on the platform, tears starting to stream.

"I just—I love him so much. He's the only boy I've ever loved. The only one I will ever love."

I continued in that vein for a while. It was, in some ways, more of a struggle than the lies. It shouldn't be, because this part was true, but to pour my heart out in such melodrama felt like a mockery of the truth. I loved Braeden. I wanted to spend my life—any life—with him. But, to me, love isn't mooning and moaning—it's taking action to protect the one you love. Deed, not word. Priscilla needed words. She was still very much a child, a princess locked in a tower, dreaming of her prince. She actually did have one—she'd been betrothed to the Third's son for a decade. But he was still a gangly, pimple-faced youth of thirteen, and she was a pretty young woman noticing all the handsome young men around her, and knowing she couldn't so much as share a lingering glance with one.

She might never have read a romantic story, but she yearned for what I had. Or a prettied-up, fantasy version of what I had, in which the young couple wouldn't set off to a harsh life together in the bleak wasteland, but would ride home, victorious and vindicated, living happily ever after within the safe bosom of the fortress.

So she promised to do whatever was in her power to make this dream come true. I argued, of course, but the more I fought, the more resolved she became. She would aid in the cause of truth and true love, whatever the cost. She would be brave, too.

Finally I agreed, on one condition.

"You must tell them I tricked you," I said.

"Tricked me?"

I nodded. "I set you up. I used you. You considered me a friend, and I abused your trust and tricked you into helping me escape with a horse. Then they cannot punish you."

"But then I won't seem brave; I'll seem a fool."

I took her hands. "Don't think of that. Remember that this might not work. I might be killed. Braeden might have already been killed. Even if we return, they might not permit him to stay."

"They will. I know they will. I heard Father telling the First how sorry he was to lose Braeden. He was strong and healthy and already a skilled blacksmith, and now another will need to be trained, and the smith is an old man. That prefect is old, too, and it is not the first time he has given my father reason to doubt his loyalty. They will exile the prefect and welcome Braeden back, and hail you as a hero." Her eyes clouded. "But I will be seen as a fool."

I told her we'd work that out, that I'd be sure to give her credit when I returned—if I returned. She wasn't happy, but she saw my point, and turned instead to excitedly planning my trip, as if I were heading off on some grand adventure.

I was leaving that night. When I told Priscilla, I panicked her a little, and I began to think I'd miscalculated, but when I said I had my bag ready, she agreed tonight was best. And it was—not giving her time to rethink everything I'd said and realize that, as stories went, it was rather ludicrous: "I think my boyfriend was wrongly accused, so I'm going to ride to near-certain death to bring him back, and hope the Six will believe a blacksmith and a whore over a prefect and a regulator." But it was heroic and it was romantic, and that was all that mattered, so long as I didn't give her too much time to ponder it.

Getting the horses was easy. They weren't guarded—the penalty for disturbing one was exile, and you couldn't exactly ride through the fortress without anyone noticing. Or you couldn't unless you were the Second's daughter, in which case they'd notice but wouldn't dare stop you. The Six and their families were allowed to exercise the horses between their rare forays into the Outside. So too were the blacksmiths, which was how I'd learned to ride.

When Priscilla arrived at the stables, I was filling the saddlebags with goods Braeden and I had been saving for weeks. She'd brought more—as much as I had two times over, all gathered easily in the space of an hour or two.

We each selected a mount. If anyone challenged us, she

would say she was treating her friend to a midnight ride, as was her prerogative.

We headed along the lane of shuttered homes to the gates. The main gates were enclosed in a courtyard, for added security from the Outside. The gates into the courtyard were simply latched. Not much need for added security from our side—no one in their right mind would sneak through.

I unlatched the gate, and Priscilla rode through first. I followed and closed it behind us. The gate guard noticed, of course, and started down from his post. Priscilla swung off her mount and raced up the stairs to meet him, breathless, as if she'd run the whole way. I moved my horse into position alongside the main gate, where I could reach the locks.

"Father needs you," Priscilla panted. "He needs every regulator he can find. It's—it's—"

The guard made her slow down. As he focused on her, I began undoing the locks.

"It's the regulator who guarded Braeden Smith," Priscilla said. "The werewolf bit him and he didn't tell anyone and now he's transforming and Father needs help—"

The regulator started down the steps again, faster now, then stopped. "The gate—"

"Father is sending someone. He says not to wait."

As the regulator raced down, I stopped working on the locks and moved the horse in front of them. He cast a quick glance my way, but didn't pause when he saw me. Everyone in the fortress knew I was the new pet of the Second's daughter.

He didn't question Priscilla's words. Why would anyone lure him from him post? No one ever left the fortress. No one ever tried to sneak someone in—the fortress was not large enough to hide a stranger. So he saw me, gave a curt nod, and hurried off.

"Quickly!" Priscilla said as soon as he was gone. "The patrol will come soon."

I'd timed the patrols of the night guard and knew we had only a few moments before one reached the gate.

I was on the last lock when I heard the thump of boots.

"Hurry!" Priscilla breathed.

I resisted the urge to glower at her and tugged at the lock. It was sticking. It'd been the first I'd tried to undo, but when it didn't come easily, I'd moved on and now I was back to it, and it hadn't magically popped open in the interim.

I yanked at it as Priscilla urged me to hurry and the guard's boots came ever closer until—

It came free. By the time it did, my hands were shaking so badly, I could barely grab the rope to pull the door open. I fumbled, then caught it and yanked. It barely budged. Priscilla rode over and took the end from me, and I held the middle and we pulled.

The gate swung open.

"Go!" Priscilla whispered.

I wasted only a moment to whisper back a thank-you. Then I rode, heels knocking my horse's flanks to spur her ever faster. I listened for the shouts of the guard or a shot from the

gun, but none came. He'd still been too far away. I kept straining, but all I could hear was the thunder of hooves. Then, as I
passed the first outcropping of rock, a dark shape leaped out. I
passed it easily, but as I did, I heard a shriek from behind me,
and turned to see Priscilla on her horse, fifty feet back.

I spurred my horse around. Another dark shape raced on
all fours across the baked earth. I caught a glimpse of fur and
fangs as my horse passed it, and I circled back to Priscilla.

"Ride!" I shouted. "Just ride!"

The first hybrid snarled up at me, and I could see it now, a
hairless, naked bearlike thing with tiny eyes and claws as long
as my fingers.

I pulled something from my pocket. A hunk of dried meat,
put there for just such a purpose, as Braeden had advised. I
held it out. The hybrid lunged for it. I spurred my horse, meat
still held out, leading the beast away from Priscilla. Then I
threw the meat and jammed my heels into the horse's sides.
She didn't need the encouragement—the moment I gave her
rein, she was off, following Priscilla's horse across the wasteland.

I didn't stop riding until I reached the first waypoint. When
Braeden and I had planned our escape, he'd mapped out every
step of it for me. The first waypoint was a large outcropping of
rock five miles from the fortress.

"Don't stop until you reach it," he'd said. "If you do, the
hybrids will come out."

So I couldn't pause long enough to say anything to Priscilla, let alone try to send her back. We rode until I saw the outcropping, then veered toward it, my horse breathing hard now, sweat rippling down her neck.

"Leave the horse outside," Braeden had said. "She's been trained to defend herself. The hybrids will eventually work themselves up to attacking, but you'll both have time to rest."

I did as he'd instructed. Priscilla stayed mounted, waiting for me to speak. I ignored her, filled the horse's water bag, and headed into the cave-like outcropping. It was dark, but I could see a pile of brush at the mouth. Dried brush. Left for me. When I saw that, I let out a sigh of relief so hard it was more of a sob. I quickly lit the fire, then hurried into the cave. There, on the wall, he'd written with a flint rock: "Be safe." I smiled, struggling not to choke again, then quickly wiped the note off as Priscilla approached the fire at the cave's mouth.

"Rayne?" she said, her voice nearly a whisper.

"Get in here," I said. "Past the fire. Before you attract a hybrid."

"I—"

"Did you water your horse? Did you even bring water?"

"I—I did."

"Had it all planned then, did you?" I glowered at her as she carefully stepped around the tiny blaze. "Because, really, this wasn't going to be difficult enough for me. Now I have the Second's daughter to look after. What did you think you were doing?"

"Helping. You can't do this alone. Even you said—"

"If you're saying I asked—or even hinted—"

"No, you didn't, but it was the right thing to do." Her chin shot up. "I wasn't going to stay behind and pretend you tricked me. I'm tired of being treated like a fool. I can be brave, too. I just never get the chance. This is my chance."

I argued, but there was little to be done. She couldn't go back now.

"Have a drink," I said. "We can't stay here long. Now that I have the Second's daughter with me plus two horses, they'll have a search team out already."

"I . . . I didn't think about that."

I grumbled and scowled. Yes, they'd come looking, but the ground was baked hard, no tracks left behind, and it was hours until daylight. The fortress had no experience tracking people in the Outside. For a horse, they'd come. For two horses and the Second's daughter, they'd definitely come. But they'd be ill-equipped for the task. As long as we kept moving, we'd be fine. As for the part where Priscilla thought we were "rescuing" Braeden and bringing him home? That could be dealt with later.

We stopped at two more posts that night. As long as it was dark, we had to keep the horses moving fast, which meant they needed regular breaks with water. Braeden had planned for that. I found his messages at the next two posts, telling me he'd gotten at least that far. As for the rest . . . ?

At dawn I let the horses slow. Daylight would not keep all hybrids away, but now I could see them coming and kick the horses to a gallop.

Soon we came into a field of rock and upturned earth, the scars left by earthquakes a century ago. It went for miles in each direction, and we had to pick our way through it.

"This will be the most difficult part," Braeden had said. "You'll feel more secure, because you aren't on the plains, but if you feel sheltered, so does everything else. Get through it as fast as you can and back out to the plains where you can see again."

I looked around. Twisted earth and upheaved rocks turned the land here into something almost beautiful. Hills and fissures, overhanging rocks, even patches of green where the upheaval had brought underground springs closer to the surface. It smelled of water, too, a rich scent, like lush crops in the rare year when the baking sun didn't stunt their growth.

Behind me, Priscilla was lagging, and I had to keep waving for her to catch up. She was sulking because when she'd seen the greenery, with its promise of fresh water, she'd wanted to stop. I'd explained why we couldn't, but it didn't matter. She was tired and aching and wanted rest, and I wasn't giving it to her.

When I looked back again, I caught a flicker to the east, where the sun was, already so bright it hurt. I squinted and shielded my eyes. The landscape was empty. I'd seen something, though. A dark shape against the gray-and-beige rock.

As I motioned Priscilla forward, I caught another movement, almost directly to my left. A figure perched on a furrow of upturned earth. A human figure. When I turned, it dived for cover.

I frantically waved for Priscilla. She pretended not to notice me. Another figure climbed over a rock to my left. My horse whinnied and sidestepped. I jabbed my finger at the figures, but when Priscilla looked, they were gone, and she just kept trudging along.

I measured the distance between us. Too far for me to whisper a warning without the watching figures knowing they'd been spotted.

"Outsiders won't attack like hybrids," Braeden had said. "The horse is too valuable to risk killing. They'll follow you and wait until you dismount, but if they know they've been seen, they'll swoop in."

I'd stopped looking around now, but could catch glimpses of movement in every direction as our pursuers crossed the rough landscape, drawing closer. I tried to turn my horse around and go back to Priscilla, but we'd been traveling down a narrow path between a fissure and a line of rock, and while there was room to turn, my horse disagreed, whinnying and balking, hooves stamping the hard earth.

I waved for Priscilla. She pulled her horse up short and sat there, scowling.

"I can't go any faster," she called, ignoring my frantic gestures for silence. "My horse is tired and the rocks hurt his hooves and I don't understand why we can't just—"

A stone hit the ground, right at her mount's front hooves. He reared up.

"Priscilla!"

I yanked the reins, hard enough that my horse finally started to turn. Priscilla managed to stay on her mount, but one foot fell from the stirrups and she clung there, leaning over the beast, reins wrapped around her hands, eyes wide. Another rock struck near the horse's rear hooves. Then another hit his flank, so hard that I heard the impact. The horse bucked. Priscilla flew off. The Outsiders charged, seeming to rise from behind every outcropping of rock, swarming toward us.

My horse tried to twist and run. I held the reins tight and spurred her on. I reached Priscilla before the Outsiders did. I grabbed her outstretched arms and heaved her up, nearly unseating myself. I managed to haul her on just as an Outsider leaped. He caught her foot. The horse's back hoof kicked him in the stomach, and he sailed through the air, spitting blood.

I righted myself in the saddle. We were surrounded. Eight Outsiders. All men. They were filthier than the refugees who'd come to the fortress, some wearing ragged clothing, some wearing only a loincloth, one wearing nothing but a bluish paint streaked across his body. Their hair was as long and matted as their beards. Savages, ultimately not much more civilized than the hybrids. But they were human enough to keep their gazes half fixed on the riderless horse, now snorting and pawing the ground.

I looked for an escape route. There wasn't one, and even if they were watching the horse, making sure they didn't lose it, the other half of their attention was on us and the second horse. I pulled my dagger from my boot. One saw it and snarled. He charged, but I was already in motion, spurring my horse toward her stablemate.

"What are you—?" Priscilla began.

As we closed in on the horse, I raised my knife.

"No!" she shrieked, both hands clutching me, fingers digging into my sides.

I slashed the knife and caught the other horse in the flank. He let out a scream. Then he bolted. Seeing their prize escaping, six of the Outsiders tore after it. The oldest one shouted and snarled and waved, as if trying to call some back, but none listened.

I gave my horse full rein then, and she galloped back the way we'd come. An arrow whizzed past. A second caught the folds of my shirt. But they didn't dare risk hurting the horse—or wasting arrows—so after two shots, they settled for chasing us, howling and raging as they fell ever farther behind. Twice, the horse stumbled on the rocky ground. Once, I thought she was going down, but I managed to rein her in, slowing her enough to get her footing and keep it, and we continued on through the rocky divide.

When we reached the other side, I took us a little distance out onto the plain, then stopped my horse and slid off.

"You don't need to do that," Priscilla said. "We can both ride."

I certainly was not walking so that she could ride. I resisted the urge to snap that and said, "You need to get off, too, before the horse keels over from exhaustion."

"O-out here?" She looked around. "It's not safe."

"That looks like a sheltered spot over there," I said, pointing to a pile of stone, oddly out of place in the empty plain.

It was the next stop on the mental map Braeden had given me. He'd called it something I hadn't quite understood—an Outsider term. As I drew closer, I realized it was a pile of ruins. The remains of a building from the Old World. There weren't many of them left—they'd been scavenged decades ago. But this one was a twisted mass of man-made rock and metal rods that looked as if it had been fused together in a giant oven.

"Wh-what is it?" Priscilla asked as we drew closer.

"A building from the Old World," I said. "Destroyed by some kind of bomb, I think."

"Bomb?" She said the unfamiliar word like I must have repeated Braeden's Outsider term. If you hadn't read every book in the fortress's collection a few times, there were a lot of words you wouldn't know—ones that had dropped from our vocabulary because we had no use for them. Even I wasn't sure exactly what a bomb was or whether one had done this.

I crawled through what must have been a doorway. Inside, it was hushed and cool. I picked my way through the rubble until I saw Braeden's message: "Soon." I wiped it away quickly, but there was no rush—Priscilla was still outside.

"Get in here," I said. "We need to rest, and this is safer than any pile of rock. We can stay here for a while."

She finally came in. She didn't look around, just walked straight into the main room, stretched out gingerly on the ground, and laid her head on her arm. As she rested, I continued poking about.

When I first heard the growl, I was near the back wall, in a separate room. I wheeled, ready to race back to Priscilla, but the rational part of my brain said it was only the wind whistling past. A real growl meant hybrids, and if one got anywhere near the ruins, the horse would have let us know. But when the growl came again, closely followed by Priscilla's shriek, I stumbled back to her so fast I reached the main room only to trip on the rubble and fall face-first, barely catching myself as I hit the ground.

As I lifted my head, Priscilla raced over to help me.

"It's okay," she whispered. "I think it's Braeden."

I looked up to see a massive black wolf in the doorway. Saliva dripped from its open mouth. Blue eyes held mine. Human blue eyes, one of them filmed over, as if blind.

"It's a werewolf," I whispered. "But it isn't Braeden."

"How would you know?"

I didn't answer. I'd seen Braeden in wolf form. His dark eyes stayed the same and his fur matched his hair—medium brown. This wolf was almost black, with grizzled gray around his mouth. Older. Bigger, too. A lot bigger.

"Don't break eye contact," I whispered. "We're going to back up—"

"To where?" Panic edged into her voice.

I reached out and gripped her arm, my gaze still holding the wolf's. "We'll find another way out."

There wasn't one. Not that I had seen. But she nodded and rose to her feet.

"Don't break eye—" I started.

The wolf growled, the sound reverberating through the hushed room, and Priscilla leaped up to run. The wolf lunged. I dived out of the way. Priscilla flew into the wall, as if the wolf had hit her, but he was still running. I looked up to see a man in the doorway, his hands lifted, fingers sparking.

A woman appeared behind the man, pushing past as the wolf brought Priscilla down. I started to run to Priscilla, but the first man hit me with magic, knocking me off my feet. I saw Priscilla twisting under the wolf as she tried to fight it off. The woman said something—words I didn't understand—and Priscilla stopped. Just froze.

Something hit my side. I caught a flash of fur, felt claws scrape my leg. I tried to rise, tried to drag myself away, but a second wolf had me. Still I fought. Then fangs clamped down on the back of my neck, pinning me to the ground, and I stopped struggling.

"The Branded," Priscilla whispered. "We're dead now. Worse than dead."

She moaned and huddled on the dirt floor of the hut. Our

attackers had brought us there, thrown us in, and left us. It felt like half a day had passed, just sitting there in the dark, waiting, listening to Priscilla.

When the door flap opened, the sudden blast of sunlight was so strong it blinded me. I felt fingers grip my forearms. Someone yanked me to my feet. Priscilla screamed at them to leave us alone, that she was a Second's daughter, and her father would hunt them to the ends of the earth if she was harmed.

The man who held me only laughed and kicked at her when she tried to attack. Then he dragged me out, stumbling, into the bright midday sun. As he led me, I blinked hard and looked around. I'd been blindfolded when they brought us in. Now I saw that we were in a camp filled with leather tents. People milled about, mostly men, a few women, no children or elders. A raiding party. Some looked over at me as I passed. Most continued with their tasks—sharpening weapons, cooking food, tending to the small herd of horses tied nearby, my own mount now among them.

My captor said nothing, just led me along, one hand on my arm. When we reached another tent, he opened the flap and prodded me inside.

Again, I was blinded, this time by the sudden dark, and I stumbled. Fingers gripped my arms and steadied me. They pulled me inside, and the door flap closed. Then arms went around me, lips coming to mine in a deep kiss.

"You did it," Braeden whispered when he pulled back.

I blinked. There was a small lantern blazing, and after a moment, I could see him in the dim light. His cheek was cut, healing now, along with a blackened eye. I hugged him, tight and fierce, and when he stiffened a little, I remembered his back, whipped and branded. I tried to pull away, whispering an apology, but he hugged me again.

"You really did it," he whispered.

I looked up at him. "We did it."

A smile. A kiss. Then he led me to a blanket, where dried meat and water waited. I took the water first, gulping it.

"You weren't hurt?" he said.

I shook my head.

"You knew it was me, didn't you?" he said. "The wolf that took you down? I thought you would, but then I wasn't sure you did."

"I knew," I said. "I'm just a good performer." Another gulp of water. "So it worked? The Branded took you in?"

"I had to fight a few rounds to prove my worth, but they can always use werewolves, and young and healthy is even better. It doesn't hurt that they lost their blacksmith in a raid last year."

"Good. So now . . ."

I took a deep breath. My heart hammered so hard my hands shook. Braeden squeezed them.

"It'll work. The hard part is over. Now we just need to—"

The tent flap opened, and in walked a massive man with grizzled black hair and blue eyes, one cloudy and sightless.

"So, girl," the man said. "What are we going to do with you?"

The Branded. That's what those in the fortress called them, in hushed tones with averted gazes. They might fear the hybrids and the tribes, but it was the Branded they invoked to frighten children. The greatest danger in the Outside, one the fortresses themselves created by casting out those with supernatural powers and branding them. Did they not realize that those branded outcasts would find each other? That they'd create their own tribes, more organized, more powerful, and more dangerous than anything in this barren world?

This was why I had informed on Braeden, rather than just helped him sneak over the wall. He needed that brand. While not every branded Outcast was accepted—those rejected were killed on the spot—we knew he'd be a prize recruit. As long as he bore the mark.

A mark I did not bear.

"The boy tells me you have no powers," the grizzled man said. "You're certain of that?"

"As far as I know." If I had, this would have been much simpler. I didn't say that, of course, only dropping my gaze respectfully.

"That's a shame. You would have made a good addition to our tribe."

Beside me, Braeden stiffened. "She brought you—"

I quieted him with a hand on his arm. I tried to be discreet, but the man noticed and laughed.

"He said you were a smart one," he said. "I see he's right.

I'm well aware of what she brought, boy. Reminding me is not appreciated."

"I'm young and strong and healthy," I said. "I can read and write. I can cook. I can sew. I can farm. I can tend livestock. I can fight, too. With weapons or without. I can ride. I can hunt. I can slaughter and skin. I can do anything the tribe requires of me."

"*Almost* anything," Braeden said, his voice a growl as he gripped my hand.

"Put your back down, boy," the man said. "You've made the situation clear, and I don't need that reminder either."

The man circled me, his gaze critical, assessing my health, my strength.

"Anything I don't know, I can learn," I said.

"I'm sure of that. Braeden tells me this plot was your idea?"

Not entirely true, but it did me no good to be modest, so I nodded.

"I don't know what you're expecting, girl, but life here isn't going to be as easy as it was in the fortress."

"No life is easy," I said. "It's just a different kind of hard."

"True." He looked toward the door. "It's a good horse. We were hoping for two, but we can raid those that stole the other one. About the girl, though . . . You're sure her father wants her back? She's not a son."

"Yes," I said, "but without a son, she's the only way he can hold on to power and pass it along to his kin. The First is old. He will die before next winter ends. Everyone is certain of it. He has no living child. Both the Second and Third will want the position, and they know that an alliance is the best way to solve the problem. If Priscilla marries the Third's son, both can rest assured of their legacy. They will each move up one post with the promise that the son will become First after Priscilla's father."

The grizzled man shook his head. "It's all too complicated for me. But that's the fortress way, and if you're as smart as you seem, you'd know that your gift is useless if they don't want her back."

"They will."

"You took a big risk, expecting her to follow you. Would have been easier just to take her."

"I knew she'd come, and it worked better if she thought it was her idea. Also, this way, the fortress will never know I betrayed her, so they won't have the excuse to exile my friends."

The man smiled. "Good. Loyalty is important here. All right then. We accept your gifts. Welcome to the Branded, girl. There's just one more thing we need to do. . . ."

I stood by the fire. There was no crowd here. No onlookers at all. Only those who needed to attend. Everyone else continued with their work.

It was Braeden who held the brand in the fire. The camp had been using the stable master as a smith, and the grizzled man—the camp leader—offered to let him do it, but Braeden said no. The leader seemed surprised, but I understood.

Braeden didn't trust anyone else to do it right.

Braeden gave me a piece of leather to bite down on. I didn't refuse it. I couldn't start my life here screaming in agony.

"If you have to cry out, they'll understand," he whispered as he took out the brand.

"I won't." I smiled back at him. "It's only a burn."

"I wish I didn't have to—"

"I trust you."

"I mean I wish it wasn't necessary."

"It is."

He moved me into position, lying flat on my stomach, which he said would be easier. I lifted my head and looked at Priscilla's tent. If I strained, I could hear her crying. Did I feel guilty for what I'd done? Yes. Did I wish I hadn't? No. I knew what I had to do, and I did it. Sometimes, that's the only choice you have.

Braeden lowered himself to one knee beside me, and I could feel the heat of the brand over my shoulder.

"I'm sorry," he whispered.

"I'm not," I said, and closed my eyes as the metal seared into my flesh.

NECKLACE OF RAINDROPS

Margaret Stohl

1. RAMA

Everything is loud in the air.

Partly it is the wind. Partly it is the machine, the blades slicing the blue-black above him. *Zhishengji* are loud, even for sky choppers.

Partly it is his heart, pounding itself into a broken arrhythmia. Beating itself literally to death.

His breath in his ears.

The boy, Rama, sits on his scuffed boot heels, staring out into the dying day and the growing night. Beneath him, the faded sprinkling of lights that was the Southlands, that is what remains of the Southlands, spreads like the scattered beads of a snapped necklace.

Behind it, in the distant black, is the ocean. *Haiyang*, as they call it. There are no lights there at all. It looks like death.

Siwang. The great darkness.

How Rama imagines it.

Vivid. Lightless. Gone.

Rama steadies himself, catching his breath as the chopper twists and the metal floor panel slides backward, swinging his legs out from under him. They dangle through the open shaft, and he grips the open metal edge that much more tightly.

The lights below him blur. He rubs his eyes.

Don't be afraid.

It's too late to be afraid.

Everything seems important in the air.

No. It's not that.

It's me.

I am important in the air.

Being above something, becoming larger, makes everything smaller. But it's an illusion; Rama knows this. It's optics. Perspective.

I am as small as that, he thinks. *I am a scattered light on the ground. I am one of many.*

Why should this one drop mean more than any other? Why should one life be different?

Why should mine?

"Ready?"

The pilot shouts back to him. Rama only nods. He's ready to jump. He's been planning this jump for months. Nothing about this night is a surprise. But that's not the question.

Is he ready?

Is it worth it?

To live, and to die?

This jump is expensive. They don't call it getting high for no reason, and he's at least a thousand feet higher than he planned.

The chopper lunges in the opposite direction.

"*Goupi!*" the pilot curses. "No offense, kid. If you're gonna jump, you gotta go now."

Rama reaches into the pocket of his orange jumpsuit, pulling out an envelope. Paper, like in the old days. The time before now, when there were things like minutes and hours and days and weeks and years.

The luxurious, indifferent time of time. The era of eras. The epoch of epochs. When life was quantitative, not qualitative. Something to be measured, not judged.

Not dropped.

Not bartered.

Not sold.

Back then, Rama thinks, *I would still have my whole life ahead of me. How old would I be? Seventeen? Eighteen? In man years?*

Rama sighs and turns back to the pilot. "Can you give this to—my *xinfeng*—to whoever? Whoever comes for me?" Rama stumbles over the words, because he isn't sure.

Who will be left? Who will come?

Who will care enough to waste a precious tear, a millimeter of water in an economy of small waters, on him?

Probably Jai. Jai will come.

He hopes she will, for her as much as him.

The pilot nods, without even turning back to look. "Stick it in the box with the others."

Rama looks behind him, where a metal postbox sits welded to the chopper floor. He flips open the lid marked XINFENG to see a hundred letters, no different from his own.

Nothing is different for anyone, not anymore. Not now.

I am different, thinks Rama.

I am ready.

It is finished.

I was here, and I will be here no longer. But as I drop, I will have that. I will have the rush, and the pounding, and the burst of adrenaline in my blood. And I will know that before I died, I was really alive.

I lived.

Even I could afford that.

Then, as deliberate as a last gesture can be, he folds a photograph of a girl into the paper, and drops it into the box.

"You want a parachute? I know it's kind of pointless, but it makes some people feel better. On the way down."

The pilot turns to look at Rama, but he isn't there.

He's slipping through the darkness, searching for the end of his story, feetfirst and falling.

He's a hundred yards down before the pilot can even turn

the chopper around, back toward the base.

Wondering, as he does every night, how long it will be until he'll be making that last drop for himself.

The pilot shivers and heads for home. He has a wife and a child and a love for meat and beer.

It is nearly enough, while he has it.

To keep the drops and his thoughts away.

2. JAI

There it is.

I hold Rama's letter in my hand.

The cat looks up at me expectantly. Purring. Perhaps she has missed him, too.

Mao is a stupid cat.

I have been waiting, watching for it, ever since he left for the Mojave Desert last week. I could see it in his eyes. He hadn't told me his count, but I wasn't a fool. I knew how he'd been living. I'd added up the late nights, the motorcycle trips, the sudden interest in mountain climbing. The thick rolls of tobacco leaves, bound in rice paper. The cheap Mexicali beer.

Rama was burning through beads like nobody's business. Like he wanted it that way. Like he wanted to go.

It was my business, though. I have learned this through experience. It is always our business, the ones left behind. The business of the dead belongs to the living.

I slice open the folded paper, smiling to myself. Paper. Of course, paper. Old paper, from trees, not rice. Rama would have liked that. He would have combed the off-market shops and dealers until he found some.

Our mother was like that as well. Before she dropped. There was something about dropping that made everyone anachronistic. We looked for what was old about our lives, what came before. What things endured.

Because we could not.

Words, the few we could remember.

Bread, when we had it.

Babies, when they surprised us, finding their way to life in spite of every modern manner of escaping them.

The sun and the dirt and the sky, though the thick brown layer of toxins in the air made it difficult to see, sometimes. The *Yanwu* never clears over the Southlands, that's what they say. It only turns our brown skin browner, our lungs blacker.

The old things matter more, when you're dropping.

That's what I've been told. That's what it seems like, to me. I have no one to ask, now that Rama's gone.

He was the last of my family to go. His necklace used to be as long as mine, as full of teardrops. We wept for our parents together. There was him, before, and now there is only me.

I shiver, looking at the paper without seeing it. I knew what it was. Dropletters were a painful burden. Everyone wrote them, everyone left them. It was a commonly held custom to burn them. That I could do.

I don't know if that means I have to read it.

I don't know if I want to.

Instead, I push my way into the smallest of the quiet, empty rooms in my quiet, empty quarters.

"Come on," I say to myself, and the cat. "Let's get on with it."

Inside the tiny room, the room where my family's secrets had always been hidden, there is only one object. An enormous cabinet.

That's where I keep it.

That's where we'd always kept them.

Hidden inside the top drawer of the big blue cabinet, in a box lined with velvet, in a pouch lined with satin.

I ignore the empty pouches next to it, crumpled inside empty boxes. The ones left holding nothing but empty strings.

Not now, I think.

Never.

I turn my attention back to the only true thing left in the cabinet.

"It's beautiful," I breathe, opening the drawer and taking the pouch with both hands. I'm talking to myself, just as I always do. Every time I come to see my necklace.

I would never let anyone else see it.

My secret.

I smooth it in my lap, crouching in the heap of clothes piled on the bed. I immediately forget everything but the pouch, as soft as water in my hands. Perfect. Cool. I wish I was the pouch. Or the box. Or even the big blue drawer.

I wish I was the thing that held my necklace of raindrops safe, never spending it, never losing it. I wish I'd keep it inside me always, the way the pouch does, never threatened in any way at all.

Never threatening.

Never anything.

How do I feel? Scared. Small. Like there is nothing I can do that will ever be worthy of the treasure inside that satin purse.

I can't let myself think how much treasure is inside it.

And I can't let anyone else know.

I slide to my heels next to the dresser and close my eyes, crumpling the letter in my hand.

Damn him. Damn him for leaving. Damn him for wanting to leave.

It is left to me. Time to mourn, again. Like before. Like always.

As I did for my parents.

As I did for Hana and Issa.

And now Rama.

The tears slide down my cheeks, surprising me.

I did not know tears could be so cold. The coldness of my tears frightens me. I stop crying.

Instead, I open my letter and begin to read it to the cat. Just as I did the four that came before.

Rama is waiting for me.

3. RAMA

My sister.

I know. I understand.

You are angry. You think I am weak.

I am.

I am unmoored, as lost as the little boats in the harbor after the floods.

Ropeless. Rudderless. Anchorless.

I can't live my life like you, if you can call what you do living. I can't hide away in our chambers, wasting my days and nights.

I know life has a cost. I know adventures are expensive. You can get hurt, you can die, you can drop.

I know.

I know everything you want to scream at me right now. I don't care.

I had to see for myself.

I had to go.

In the last year, I saw every phase of the moon, from every continent on the planet. I shivered on the frozen ground in the middle of a wolf pack before the dawn, listening to them howl and scream at each other. I followed the curve of a river down falls and through gorges. I stood in the path of a mother bear. I painted chalk circles on a sacred elephant. I ran with the bulls down the streets of a crowded village. I watched the *sunrise with a beautiful woman.*

It was worth it.

All of it.

Once I determined to blow through my life, drop by drop, I knew I could not look back. I could not stop.

Every day of the last year was a transaction. I knew, every time I handed another precious drop into a Counter, that I was going to leave you, and soon.

The thing I realized was, it didn't matter when I left. Not to us, our story. The bond, my heart, yours— everything between us had already happened.

Has happened.

You're big sister; I'm little brother.

You will always be my sister. In death and in life. That was never going to change. It hasn't now. But the rest of my life needed to. It had to begin.

I know I was your younger brother. I know you were supposed to drop first. But Jai, you're not going to. You're too afraid.

Let me give you this one gift. Let me tell you what I have learned.

Don't be afraid to live.

Your life will be long, but it won't be life.

I have loved someone. I have been loved. I have been here, everywhere.

I haven't left a mark on the world, but is that so bad? Considering how deeply the world has marked me?

Know this.

When I drop tonight, I will be thinking of you.

I'm not scared.

I'm ready.

And I hope you will find your way to your own last drop, before your beads leave you to drop in your bed alone, a thousand years from now.

If nothing changes, and you keep going like this, you will. Live forever.

But eternity at what price, big sister?

I crumple the letter in my hand and hold it toward the candle.

The edge of the envelope catches on fire, and I drop it into the brass bowl in the center of the room.

The cat and I watch as my brother explodes into a final flame.

I try to think of something to say, something important, something befitting a life and a death like my baby brother's.

My mind is completely blank, and all I can do is cry. I can't bring myself to burn the rest of the paper, his paper, and I fold it into my pocket.

Good-bye, Rama.

Zaijian, little brother.

And peace.

---

4. JAI

I lock the door behind me, sliding my c-card through the slit above the handle one last time. I straighten my ancient army jacket, buttoning it over my clothes. It warms me, even if the edges are frayed. It used to belong to my father.

Then Rama.

Now everything belongs to me. I don't want it, any of it.

Everything is heavy, a lot to bear. Too much to carry, or even remember.

I look both ways before I cross the busy center street of *Pinminku*, my ghetto. Scooters and cars and cats scatter like noisy cockroaches as I step into the street. The Southlands, where I live, are full of ghettos like mine. And *Pinminku* is even more full of *zuifan*, neighborhood criminals who will steal your drops as easily as your coins. Not the greatest people to run into.

I reach with my hand into my left pocket, fingering the bare length of broken knife blade I hide in the cloth, sewn into my jacket.

I have to protect myself now.

I am all I have.

I stay in the shadows at the side of the long, straight roads of the city. Over in the fringe, the fruit and vegetable sellers shout as I pass.

I don't even look at them. I can't afford it.

There is a market for drops like mine. Long life for the wealthy and the ruthless.

I have to be careful.

I have a necklace. My *Xianglian*. That's not a secret.

We all have one, everyone does, in *Pinminku* and all the ghettos of the Southlands. A necklace of raindrops, that's how I think of them. Standard issue, my *Xianglian*, right at birth. They're not made of raindrops, not really, though I couldn't tell you what they are made of. Not even my father knew that, and I used to think he knew everything. But I have always thought of it as my necklace of raindrops, ever since my mother read me a bedtime story about an actual necklace of raindrops.

As I duck around the corner, I try to remember.

I can't recall the story, not exactly, but the way she told it went something like this: There was a girl who had a necklace of raindrops. Each drop was powerful. Each drop had a different power.

One by one, the girl used the drops, and the drops dissolved or disappeared. I can't recall.

When the story ended, the girl had what she wanted, but the necklace was gone. At least that's how I remember it.

This is like that. Only not quite so happy. More like the reverse:

When the necklace is gone, the story ends. At least, my story ends.

This is how my necklace story goes:

I have a necklace of raindrops, only it's not made of raindrops, and the raindrops don't have powers. All they have is time. And I can spend them as I choose, but when they're gone, my life is over, and I will die.

I find I am standing in front of the building where I work. It is still early, but I am even earlier. I have little else to do.

I swipe my card, this time my e-card, through the doorway. I wait as the door recites my numerical code, swinging open without another greeting.

One Nine Six Seven.

Rama used to tease the door, calling it different names every time we passed through.

I try not to think about Rama.

Rama is gone, I tell myself. *There are things I need to do now. Because Rama is gone.*

I slip into the elevator and stand staring at the back of the faceless man in front of me.

Here, on the South Coast, we have something called death. It means you have to leave when you run dropless. When your life thread—the thin, twisted chain that holds your drops together—is bare.

You do not want that to happen, not anytime soon.

But it does. It happens to all of us.

Not all drops are the same. That would be ridiculous. But everything has a price, and everyone is expected to pay it.

The elevator opens and I move toward my cubicle.

I don't nod at the people I pass.

I don't say hello.

I am thinking of Hana.

Hana is crazy, I mean, was crazy. She spent her drops like

nobody's business. My parents, of course, tried everything they could to get her to stop. They dropped her out of school, kept her in her room, told her to eat her vegetables. But nothing worked. Hana, she was what some people called a Lifer. A *Shenghuo* girl. They just go for it.

Not me.

I'm what you'd call a Keeper. A *Baocun* baby, a Saver. I'm the best at keeping my drops hidden away. You won't ever see me doing anything that costs more than a drop at the most.

I'll be around forever.

I'm the opposite of a Lifer.

Even if what I'm leading is the opposite of a life.

I slide into my cubicle at the Shenzen Life Insurance Company, a Fanzui Five Hundred Corporation. Regulated by the FEIC, the Federal Expiration Insurance Charter.

There are no photographs, no plants. Nothing that reveals anything about me, Expiration Claims Processor #25883704222. A medium-level employee. With a medium complexion, medium-length hair, a medium build. Only notable for not graduating fifth form, not sitting for my upper-level exams, and not taking a single vacation day.

Why should I? Where do I have to go? And who would notice if I was gone?

Who would care?

I wonder.

I flip on my vid screen.

As I wait, the screen is blank, black.

It's as if I do not exist at all.

It only looks that way.

That's my secret, the thing no one can know. People would kill for a full set of drops like the one I hold in my hand.

Killing for life. How ironic is that?

I thought I had this all worked out. I thought I had a plan for myself, a way of engineering things so they were never too dangerous, never too fast—never too unexpected or creative or different.

I was in control.

I understood my place in the game.

Then Z moved in, right across the hall, in another nameless cubicle of our government-subsidized office. Here at the job I only qualify for because of my grandfather and the role he played in the founding of the FEIC, and the mass production of *Xianglian* necklaces.

Pioneer of the FEIC Expiration Monitors.

The shackles we all wear around our necks, hide in our boxes.

My grandfather was a doctor.

All he meant to do was save lives. That's the punch line— or it would have been. If the *Xianglian* were jokes.

He sat at the head of the federal organ-donor lists. He watched while good hearts went to waste, time and again, when they were given to unfit recipients, simply because of their youth. He began to develop a database, youngest to oldest—until he computed their LC, life calculus. Junkies dropped lower, taking alcoholics and prescription-drug users with them. Convicts, prostitutes, high-risk behaviors dropped again. There were so many factors. So many reasons to be denied key organs, additional days and months and even years of human life.

Time, he realized, was a factor. Just not the determining factor.

The nature of the life, that was the true cost. That was the math that mattered.

The Feds noticed when his patients' surgical outcomes soared. My grandfather's agency grew.

I don't blame him, any of them. I understand why they did it. It's possible I would have done the same thing. My grandfather was a good man. He was only trying to help.

That's when he realized the database had other uses, so many other uses. To think that he could imagine a new world, and bring it to life, whether or not it was right or wrong. He was as a god among men.

When people wanted to end world hunger, they didn't consider how the ends could justify the means. When faced with overpopulation and the erosion of global resources, they didn't perform the cost-benefit analysis.

The FEIC database did it for them.

And so our grandfather became a god, before I was even born. You know how they say we have to make the world we want for our children, and our children's children?

I am that child.

I didn't tell Z that. I didn't tell him any of this.

I look up to see if he's there. He's not. He's late. Of course he is.

I am never late.

I don't know why Z works here. He's never told me how he got the job. Only his name, over lukewarm tea in the break room, since our break isn't long enough to steep it properly.

Laurence Horatio Hanzicker.

An old name, from an old time.

Z's what you'd call a Stringer, the kind my mother warned me about. Bare string, nearly the length of it. World traveler. Pilot. Rebel. Thrill seeker.

He makes Hana look like a medical librarian. Like a research botanist.

Like, well, like me.

I have 99 percent of my necklace, fully intact. My life, preserved in a box. In a drawer. In a pouch. In a room so locked up and lonely, it might as well be Fort Knox.

My grandfather's granddaughter.

I've memorized the database. I've eliminated my risk calculus, almost entirely. I'm a perfect candidate for anything.

Z is not.

He's on his last drop. That's what people say about him.

He's final.

Zuihou. That's what he says. Z for short.

I don't know when it will happen. Any day. Any hour. Any minute could be his last.

If what they say is true, Z's life is all used up, while I hold mine here in my hands, bagged and boxed up in satin and velvet and drawers.

I don't know why I'm crying.

For Rama or Z or me.

My family, everyone who has gone before.

Everyone who has dropped or will.

I don't know which one of us I'm crying for.

My screen lights up and I deaden my mind for another day at work. The interface logs me in. One Nine Six Seven. That's all I am.

I wipe my eyes and lift them for the scan.

This is my life.

Is it any wonder Rama jumped?

5. Z

She's there when I finally get to work.

Late as usual. The Shift Super glares at me as I walk by the front desk with my helmet stuck under one arm. She looks at me the way my old aunties did, after I came home from school. Like pit vipers.

Rough.

My hair stands straight up after I ride. I let it dry that way.

Also rough.

I see her there, across the room, in the little place where her cubicle stares at mine.

One Nine Six Seven.

She doesn't know why I'm always late. That I ride my motorcycle all the way down to *Pinminku*, waiting in the alley until she locks her little door and leaves her little cat inside.

I follow her, two blocks behind. I'm her guardian angel. That's what I told her little brother, before I set him up with the drop. I told him I'd do it. That's how he knew he could do it. Leave all this. Her.

She just doesn't know.

That, or how badly I wanted the job.

She's beautiful, the most beautiful thing I've ever seen. The only beautiful thing in the room. Everything else is made of smoke.

Smoke and steel and ash.

All around us, everyone is dying, and they feel it. It's no way to live.

She's not dying.

She may never die.

I watch her. Her head fixed, eyes staring straight ahead. Her mind is wild, though, a thousand mountains and moons away.

Even I know that. Even from here, my desk, all the way across the corridor.

She hasn't seen me come in. Not yet.

She's a flower, I think, the moment before it's cut. She's a puddle of rain in the street, before a tire has yet to run through it.

Jai.

Even her name is a petal and a puddle to me.

She stands. She hangs her jacket on the hook behind her. Pulls something from her pocket.

Paper.

Strange.

A letter? A paper letter. Her face looks tired, drawn. It isn't good, whatever it is.

I try to remember. Her family is gone. She has only Rama. He'll be gone soon, if he's not already. He's been preparing for months. That's why I came back.

I came because he asked me to help.

I stayed because he asked me to help her.

Her glossy black hair bobs as she reads, again and again.

Is she crying?

It's him.

It's her brother.

It's either her brother, or a lover I know nothing about.

I smile at the idea of Jai, my Jai, having a lover. Jai, who would not risk the rain without an umbrella. Jai, who keeps a spare train ticket in her pocket at all times, in case she has to flee.

Then I stop.

I want to tell her about tigers.

I want to throw her into a river, and see which one of us can swim the farthest.

I want to walk her out into the ocean, one step at a time. I don't care if we ever come back.

What does it matter to me?

What difference would it make now?

I flip on my computer.

It grunts into blank white light. Then, an animation pops up onscreen.

"Hello, Valued Employee of Cubicle Two Zero One One. We at Shenzen salute your contribution."

"Thank you." I look the animation in the eye. If I don't, my terminal won't finish loading.

I prefer the other kind of security, where they shoot the criminals in the face and don't make the rest of us endure this. That's how we do things in the North, where I'm from. Hinter. Here in the Southlands, where the Feds are crawling up your ass all day, that's not an option.

The face nods, accepting my retinal scan. I guess I'm not as bloodshot as I thought.

"Begin your day, Two Zero One One. We hope you find personal fulfillment as you are of use to the world around you."

"Super." I hit a key, and the face disappears, my database scrolling across the screen. Name after name, number after number, risk after risk.

It's not rocket science.

You do the math, you hit the key.

The plus sign to add a drop.

The minus to delete one.

You do the math.

You hit the key.

Sometimes it's just a tear that drops.

Sometimes it's a person.

That's how it works.

You hit the keys.

But I don't.

I never have.

I never will.

Instead, I reach around back and flip on my off-market modem.

My screen becomes another screen, and I see a face again. This face isn't an animation, though. In fact, it doesn't move at all.

"Jai," I whisper, leaning closer to the microphone at the base of my monitor.

"Are you there?"

She looks down at the camera, which I know is only a blinking green light at the corner of her monitor. I know this, but it feels like she is looking at me.

When she smiles, which isn't often, it feels like she's smiling at me.

"Z."

"In the flesh."

"You're late."

"I'm always late."

"You're going to get fired."

"So?"

"So."

She falters, biting her lip. She looks away, but she has nothing else to look at. Not even a mug, with a cat painted on it. Not even a pen. There is nothing but me, a small blinking light above a keyboard and below a stretch of reflective plasticine.

She looks back at me.

"So. That would not be a positive contribution to the world around you." She's mocking the Corporation's log-in screen, and I grin. That's Jai, that spark deep inside. It isn't easy to get to, and you have to work hard to find it, but I try.

I will never stop trying.

I crave it, more than anything else in my day.

"So?" I say it back to her, smiling. I straighten in my seat as the Super walks by, then slump back toward her. "What's it to you whether or not I contribute? Whether or not I get fired?"

"It would be . . ." She smiles at her fingers, playing against the keyboard. They type and retype the same letters, over and over again. "It would be sad if you weren't here."

"It would?" I grin again. *Say it, Jai.* Her lips are pursed with a smile that they struggle to keep to themselves, like a kiss, like a secret.

"I would."

"Meet me in the break room at the hour."

"No."

"Please."

"We can't be alone there." She says the words, not me. I wonder what is happening to her today. Maybe it is her brother. Maybe it's Rama.

Better and better, I think.

"Okay. Meet me outside, after work."

She pauses, and I sit back and wait, watching the screen.

After a century, after one million years, she nods, so slightly you would have missed it, if you were not me.

Then she hits a key in front of her, and all I can see is the database once again, scrolling down my screen.

6. JAI

"What are you doing?"

I say the words to a stranger passing by me, who looks startled, but they're meant for someone else.

For him.

The man pulling me by the arm the moment I step out onto the sidewalk, pulling me into people and traffic and pass-ersby, dragging me around the corner until we are pressed against the side of a building hung with shadow. It is after six, rush hour, and the crush of the commute is everywhere. Not for us. We are the only ones standing still.

I don't dare look at him.

I haven't seen him all day.

I drank my lukewarm tea alone at break, ate my Spam roll alone during lunch. I kept my book with me, a statistical primer of risk calculation. I didn't read it. I only pretended to read, so I didn't have to talk to anyone around me.

There was no reason to speak, because the only person I wanted to speak to wasn't there.

He disappeared right after we talked in the morning. His chair sat empty all day, his cubicle dark. Two Zero One One had been logged out, flagged a sick day, the seventh this month.

"Why did you go?"

"I was sick."

"You aren't sick." I glance at him, sideways, though I know even before I look at him that he's perfectly fine.

"Of course I am. I'm dying, One Nine Six Seven. We all are."

"Jai. Call me Jai." I say it quickly, and he smiles.

"I know your name, Jai." His lips curl as he says it, and I want to touch them. Instead, I wrap my hand around the blade in my pocket. I grip it so hard I am afraid I will cut myself.

"I know your name better than they do, Jai." He curls himself around my name again, looking up at the building behind us, and I realize it is the far corner of our own building. We haven't gotten very far.

I shiver.

"Very funny." I don't smile.

"Your grandfather didn't think it was. Your grandfather thought it was very smart, the database."

I feel myself growing colder.

"His database," Z says, again.

"Z." I stiffen and pull my army jacket more tightly around me. I don't want to talk about that. Not with him, not with anyone.

This was a bad idea.

All afternoon, I have imagined this meeting, this time we have. I have imagined it so many times. The two of us, together at an out-of-the-way teahouse or, even more daring, a bathhouse.

The two of us, riding on the back of his motorcycle, my hair streaming in the wind behind me.

Of course, that would be impossible.

I would have a helmet. We both would.

It's little improbabilities like that—impossibilities, really—that are why fantasies are so stupid, and why I don't have them anymore.

"I should go." I look toward the busy street. The night is thick and humid, graying in the fading light. It looks as sticky as it feels, as if I am standing in the shower, letting the steam roll into the world beyond me.

"I'm sorry." He slips his hand into my pocket, uncurling my fingers from the knife. "I'm not going to hurt you. I don't want your necklace. I don't want anything that belongs to anyone but me."

Then he leans toward me, as if he's going to kiss me, but he doesn't. Instead, he whispers something, so softly I almost can't hear it.

"What do you want, Jai?"

What do I want? To run away. To grow a vegetable garden, with weeds and flowers taller than my own body.

To run wild in the sunshine. To jump, fly, shout in the air, in front of strangers.

To wander. Travel. Love. Live forever.

To tell my brother I love him, one last time.

To kiss the man who stands in front of me, whether or not he wants me to.

To know. To be sure.

Of him, of me.

Everything.

I say nothing.

I wish I knew.

And even if I did, there's nothing I can say. No words to say it. Only numbers, only the system of our own making, my own father's father.

I can't speak the truth.

I'm not brave enough.

I can only feel it, in the flush that creeps into my cheeks and the way his warm fingers burn against my cold ones.

Then I'm ashamed of myself, of what I'm saying, even if I can't bring myself to say the words at all. I don't think he needs me to say them.

I think he knows.

I draw my hand away from his, out of my own pocket. I clutch the collar of my jacket, holding it close.

His eyes follow me.

"Let's get out of here."

7.2

I have dreams that go like this. I must be dreaming.

We ride on the back of my motorcycle, Jai holding me with small hands. Her hands are warm, even though the night is growing cold. She shivers against me, and I can feel her breathing, her heart pounding. She wears my helmet. It still smells like her, when she hands it back to me.

At least, it will.

That's how it starts, how it always starts. When I dream of One Nine Six Seven, of Jai.

I dream of her almost every night.

Only none of this is a dream. All of this is happening. I shake my head, wondering to myself how one conversation in a lost roadside bar on a faraway continent with Rama could change so much.

But she is real.

I know this, because she clings tightly to me, behind me. And her hands are warm, the way I want to remember them.

The broken streets of *Pinminku* disappear behind us, then widen and open into the vacant stretch of empty highway that will lead us up and into the foothills, circling back on itself until we reach the reservoir.

Everything is ready. It took all day and every penny I had, but I have seen to that.

It has cost me more than the day—probably my job—but I don't question it now. I have other jobs, another job. Not that I will need a job much longer.

I question nothing now.

It's too late for that.

The shade is thick, and the water is fringed with trees. I take her by the hand, leading her to the cliff rock where I have left everything I could find, in a bucket resting on what used to be my bedcover.

In the bucket is everything I know about her. A daisy. A thermos of tea. Rice rolled with meat, how she takes it in the lunchroom. A cluster of grapes that I found off-market, at the cost of my old receiver.

The flask of wine, that was a question. Not something I know; it's there for me.

For courage.

"Do you trust me?" I pour the contents of the flask into a tall plastic glass. She stops me, wine splashing across her hand.

"No." She smiles down at the glass, and I lower the bottle to the tattered blanket on the grass between us.

We are alone now, here at the edge of the reservoir at the far reach of the district. Her ghetto is faraway, her old life even farther.

"I don't drink." That's all she says.

"At all? Ever?"

She shakes her head. "Maybe if you have some water. I sometimes pour a little in. See, like this?"

She fills her glass with water, splashing wine inside. It turns red, not so red as blood, only a faint red, the color of a spilled pomegranate.

"Why?"

"I don't know, I don't like the way it makes me feel. I like to feel—like myself." *I'm scared.* She doesn't say that, but I hear it.

I shake my head. "Not me. I like to feel drunk."

She laughs at me, but her eyes aren't smiling. They're big and dark and staring at me, as if she isn't even thinking or talking about wine at all.

"My brother dropped."

I try to act surprised. It only seems polite.

"When?"

"I don't know. I have his dropletter—I mean, had it. I burned it, most of it. It wasn't dated." She shakes a little, bringing the water to her lips.

I nod. "I'm sorry for your loss." It's what we say. I eye her closely. "Did you . . . know?"

She puts down the glass of red water.

"Yes. No. I'm not surprised. But I miss him. He was everything, all I had left of my family." Her voice catches on the last word.

"I understand."

"Tell me what it's like."

"What?"

"This. To live. To be at the end, like you are. Like Rama."

"The last drop?"

She shakes her head. "Not that." She looks at me more closely. "This."

"Before. You mean, the end of the necklace?"

She nods. "The necklace of raindrops."

"Is that what you call it?"

"In my family. It's what we always did. Even my grandfather."

"It's hard to imagine your grandfather was a poet."

"It was from a story."

I hold up my wrist. On it is a twist of brown string, weathered to the point where it looks like frayed twine. A single clear bead shines from where it is caught in a single loop. I shake my arm in the air between us, rattling it.

"There it is. My whole life, all I have."

"You just wear it like that? Are you crazy? Have you completely lost your mind?"

"Nope."

"What if something happens to it? What about you?"

"If it goes, it goes. If I go, I go." It really is that simple. Each drop of the necklace controls a corresponding nanograin of encapsulated biotoxin, swimming silently in my bloodstream. We get the poison injection when we get the necklace. When a drop's signal dies, whether by command or by being destroyed or lost, the capsule dissolves, and we grow one step closer to the end.

Drop by drop.

One by one by one—until there are none.

When that happens, we die. It's only a matter of time. They're finite and irreplaceable, the drops. They could never be made.

Not by us, anyway,

Only Jai's grandfather and his coworkers—the other gods of the Shenzen Life Calculus—could do that.

Jai knows it. She just doesn't want to hear it.

Her eyes flash dark. "I don't understand you, people like you. Even Rama. Why do you want to leave? Why do you want to go from something to nothing? No matter how bad something is, isn't something enough?"

"You know what your problem is?"

"I have a problem?" She looks irritated.

I nod. "You don't know what everything feels like."

"I don't?"

"You don't know what everything tastes like. The flavor it has, the sound of it. The particular sharpness it brings. The colors." My voice sounds like I am in a dream, and I wonder if I am.

Her breath seems to catch as she looks at me. "What's that? Everything?"

I lean closer, hanging over her upturned face. "It feels like sunlight on the water, shuddering in a breeze that ripples everything, even things it shouldn't."

I slip my arms around her, gently pulling her toward me on the blanket.

"The way it moves the leaves in and out of all colors of green—uncurls the sky in all colors of blue."

She leans against me.

"The way the water can cut through trees and shadows like thick sections of chocolate cake that catch in the back of your throat."

She closes her eyes, settling against my chest. I feel her heart pounding, just over mine.

I don't stop.

I lower my hand to her neck, my mouth to the edge of her jaw. My words become a whisper between us.

"The way a single word, a tiny sound can drift over and around the smallest blade of grass between you and the horizon."

I pull a curl of hair loose from her clipped, black braid.

"The way that glass of wine, right there, can taste like everything you're seeing and nothing at all."

"Water," she says, looking up at me. "It's only—"

Then she says nothing at all, because our lips no longer feel like talking, and there are no more words on our tongues.

It is you, I think.

It was always you.

I could tell her about the deserts I have walked or the mountains I have climbed. I could tell her about the crowded marketplaces and the tents stitched from scarves. I could tell her about beetles that taste like saffron, about creatures that fly when they should swim, swim when they should fly.

The men who ring bells. The bells that bow men.

I tell her nothing, because none of it matters.

I know that now.

It wasn't life.

Not for me.

My pathway, that pathway, led only to her. To an empty cubicle on a crowded street in *Pinminku*. To the worst job of my life, and to her.

Jai.

One Nine Six Seven.

She kisses me. I kiss her.

We are a circle of pathways and arms and eventualities, stitched together with scarves and bells and saffron.

We are more than eight numbers, more than beads in a drawer.

We kiss and I feel my life begin, and the joke is on me, because I suddenly, desperately, want nothing more than to live.

For the first time in my hard-worn life.

I don't tell her that.

I pull her closer, letting her twist in my arms, letting myself twist in hers, until we are swimming in water and wine and kisses and blankets and she tastes like everything and there are no doubts anywhere, for anyone at all.

8. J A I

I become careless. Sloppy. Happy.

I suck in my breath for no reason, gasping at the wonder that is my life.

In the shower, I scream.

When I have nightmares, they are not of death and dropping. They are of my life, before I met Z.

When everything was nothing, sand on my lips.

I forget to buy milk for my tea. I sleep through my first and second alarm.

I wonder if anyone notices.

9. Z

I never understood anything. Now I know that.

I wish it didn't have to end.

I wish I could tell her.

I wish I could ask her brother.

10. J A I & Z

Everything is brighter in the air.

Partly it is the sky, how clear it is, how close they are to the sun. Partly it is the machine, the light shining off the spinning blades above them.

Zhishengji spin quickly, even for choppers.

Partly it is their hearts, pounding themselves into one. A rhythmic arrhythmia, a new beat. Beating itself literally together, and to death.

His lips pressed against her.

His breath in her ears.

The girl, Jai, sits on her scuffed boot heels, staring straight into the sun. The boy, Z, circles his arms around her. To him, she is the sun.

Beneath them, the light glints off the silver rooftops that were the Southlands, that are what remains of the Southlands, spreading like the scattered beads of a necklace that was meant to be broken. Scattered like petals, like leaves in the wind.

Behind them, in the distant blue, is the stripe of ocean that lines the sky. *Haiyang*, as they call it. There are no rooftops there at all. It looks like life, like endless life.

Siwang. The great river.

How Jai imagines it.

Vivid. Dazzling. The ever-present oblivion.

That which is constant.

That which remains.

Love.

Z steadies himself, steadying her. He catches his breath as the chopper twists beneath them.

"Don't be afraid." He kisses her cheek, a soft place he has found next to her ear.

"I'm not." She leans back against him. A touch that is itself a kiss.

"We'll be together."

"You don't know that."

He smiles at her.

"At least we won't be apart."

"Ready?"

The pilot shouts back to them. They only nod. The pilot doesn't care. He gets paid either way.

They clasp hands, ready to jump. Z takes one last look around the chopper. Everything is as it should be. He has been planning this jump for months, since before he knew her. Since the day he met Rama, and they made their plan.

Nothing about this day is a surprise. Nothing except the feeling in his chest. But that's not the question.

Is she ready?

She squeezes his hand, as if in answer.

The chopper lunges in the opposite direction.

"*Goupi!*" the pilot curses. "No offense, kids. If you're gonna jump, you gotta go now."

Z reaches into the pocket of his orange jumpsuit, pulling out an envelope.

"For my parents." He drops it into the box. She smiles, without letting go of his hand.

He knows she has no dropletter. She doesn't need one. She has no one left to tell.

Nothing remains for her but him, but this.

The drop.

"You want a parachute? I know it's kind of pointless, but it makes some people feel better. On the way down."

The pilot turns to look at them, but they aren't there.

They are slipping through the darkness, searching for the beginning of their story, feetfirst and falling.

They're a hundred yards down before the pilot can even turn the chopper around and head back toward the base.

In his haste, he doesn't see the two parachutes missing. He doesn't know about the deleted records, the hacked system that can no longer tell Two Zero One One or One Nine Six Seven when to end their lives.

He doesn't know it is time to begin them.

He doesn't know the biggest secret of all.

That Rama is waiting, that he has always been waiting. That he is every bit his grandfather's grandson.

That he can imagine a new world, and bring it to life, whether or not it is right or wrong. That he can find the man who will bring him his sister for a price, or in the end, for no price at all.

That Rama and his rebel encampment await them in the stretch of oblivion that is the Mojave Desert. In every way, it is the opposite of death.

It is, for the very first time, life.

An uncontrollable storm, more precious than any necklace of raindrops.

The pilot flies on, unaware of the cloud pattern building beneath him.

Instead, the pilot is wondering, as he does every night,

how long it will be until he'll be making that last drop for himself.

The pilot shivers and heads for home. He has a girlfriend and a dog and a love for bread and butter.

It is nearly enough, while he has it.

To keep the drops and his thoughts away.

DOGSBODY

Rachel Caine

WHEN I WAS thirteen, Corporate handed out free tickets to the Cup game to kids on Level K. A lottery win, they said, as they visited each narrow little apartment and listed off kids by name.

By the time they got to Gray, Xavier, I had already heard all about it. Could have ducked it, I guess; my folks were long dead, and at thirteen I was mostly on my own anyway. But I was big, strong, and maybe a little stupid, 'cause I still thought I had a bit of luck, and it had finally paid off.

So I took my ticket, and the Company man crossed my name off on his handheld and told me to have a nice time. He had a tight, empty smile.

Should have known better, about the luck.

See, we *all* knew better, that was the thing; Level K was a hard place, and we didn't get much. Getting a ticket to the Cup was something that happened up on Level A, maybe B . . . not down here in the dark.

But everybody wants to believe in something, and we believed in the Cup game.

So that morning, some two thousand kids arrived painted in crude makeup. They carried makeshift signs to wave and clutched tickets like they were passes to heaven itself. Two thousand shining, excited faces. Mine among them.

The trains pulled in on time—big, shining, sleek things, all lights and glass and gleams. They were so beautiful, so *unreal* they might have been from another planet. Kids watched with rounded eyes, opened mouths as they realized, just as I did, how drab and broken our station looked, with its cracked tiles and rusty metal.

Maybe it was just that I was a bit older than the others, or I was naturally suspicious, but I thought it was strange there were no adults here to see us off. Not one nervous parent, not one idle gawker. *Nobody had come.*

All kids. All alone. Clutching tickets.

Hackles prickled at the back of my neck.

"Zay," a girl's voice said, and a hand caught me on the shoulder. It was Virtue, another orphan; we sometimes scrabbled together; sometimes we fought each other over a particularly good find or job. She was a little younger, maybe twelve, and turning womanly with it. Not in a bad way, though. "Zay, you going?"

"I guess I will," I answered, and shrugged. "Got a ticket. You?"

She held up her ticket for an answer, between thin fingers with broken nails. Then she shook her head, took her ticket and tore it in half, in two jagged pieces, and let it fall to the ground.

"What are you doing?" I blurted; couldn't help the knee-jerk appalled feeling, seeing that coveted ticket go to waste. Could've sold it premium.

Virtue looked tense and very, very serious. "Look around. All these mouths heading up toward the Cup. There'll be prime pickings around here for a while, Zay. Jobs still need doing. We wouldn't have to come to knives over it. You should stay too."

I sent her a long, level look, and said, "You know something wrong about this, V?"

There wasn't much to betray it, a slight widening of her eyes, but I knew I'd hit the mark. She shrugged, just a tiny shiver of muscles, and said, "Nobody here to see us off. Don't you think that's wrong? It's like they weren't allowed."

"You think it's a trap?" I said.

She frowned for a few seconds in silence, then shook her head. "No proof, but I'm playing it safe. You ought to do the same."

Fine, I was thinking, *but what if this is all the luck I ever get? How do I let that go?* "Hard to pass up something like this. A real holiday, and all." I knew she was right, and it made me feel hollow and cheated inside, and stubborn. I was a tough boy. I could take care of myself.

She looked wounded. I knew I'd hurt her; she'd put herself on the line to warn me, and I was throwing it back. "Fine. Go on, get coddled by Corporate. But don't blame me when I grab the good jobs." She started to turn away. I held her arm, just for a second.

"I reckon I'll go," I said. "But if this goes sideways, you take it out on somebody for me, hard. Swear."

Virtue's eyes widened, but she was quick to spit on her hand and hold it out. I spit on mine, and we slapped palms. Deal done.

The trains gave out a heavy, almost human sigh, and the doors opened on every car. Kids shouted and shoved forward, waving their signs and makeshift rag pom-poms. I started to queue up, and Virtue grabbed my arm.

"What?" I asked. "Deal done, right?"

"Sure," she said, and for a second looked outright scared. "Zay, just . . . watch yourself."

Before I could answer, Virtue faded back. I saw her Cup ticket halves blowing in the breeze of the tunnel, and then she was a flicker of movement in the sea of pressing bodies.

Then she was gone.

I joined the flow and was swept into the nearest car, throwing elbows into those who got too close. Most gave me a wide berth; I was a big, strong kid, and had a rep for a temper. Most didn't try to cross me. Nobody did, more than once.

Inside the train, the seats were plush, clean, and a rich shade of red, like fresh blood. I sank down, a little dazed by the metal and the carpets and the softly playing music, as the last of the kids shoved on board and found seats. There was one empty next to me, as others gave me a wide margin of respect. A very small girl, maybe six, was the last one on, clutching her ticket in both hands and looking around in utter terror.

I grabbed her arm and sat her down in the seat beside me. She let out a yelp of surprise and fear and cowered. I scowled. "Name's Zay," I said. "Don't bother me; I won't bother you."

She blinked. She was a tiny thing, skin and bones really, with masses of soft black hair twisting their way into dreadlocks, and eyes like pools of oil. "Pria," she said, and tried for a smile. "Thanks for the seat, Mr. Zay."

"It's just Zay; I'm no Corporate drone," I said, but deep down inside, I was a little pleased. It was the first time in my life anyone had ever called me *Mr.*

Pria's face lit up, and I think she would have talked my damn ear off all the way to the upper levels and the stadium . . . but then the doors hissed open again as a stranger got on board. He was Corporate, there was no doubt of it; he was wearing a black jacket, with the Corporate logo on the pocket, and he had one of those neat, short haircuts and an earpiece, just like you see on the monitor commercials.

Pria's eyes were black, but this man's were *dark*. It wasn't the color. It was what was in them. The kids fell silent, sensing a predator, and I did the same, and squeezed Pria's hand to warn her to be quiet. She didn't really need that, but I needed to do it.

"Welcome to your new life of service," the man said, and took a small, sleek handheld device from his pocket. "I will need ten from this car. Hands up, those who want to volunteer."

Nobody moved. Nobody. I don't even think anybody breathed.

The man sighed and looked put out about it. "All right. It's lottery, then. Seat numbers—" He punched something on his keypad and read off a string of randomly generated digits.

One of them was my seat.

The other kids were reluctantly standing, pale and shaking. Pria looked at me with horrified eyes, her hand still clutched in mine. "Zay," she said. "Don't go!"

The Corporate drone counted heads, frowned, and I saw him identifying seats and finding me. Our gazes locked. "You," he said. "Your number is up."

I stared at him and let my face go blank and stupid. It was something I was really good at; I could look barely functional when I wanted. I'd learned it from Dad, only his hadn't really been faked. He'd gotten his from the gasses in the mines.

"Oh, for the love of— Are you defective?" He shook me. I let some drool wet my chin. "All right, then. You, girl. Get up."

He pointed to Pria, and she sucked in a trembling breath and cowered in her seat. *No*, I wanted to tell her. *Fear doesn't get you anywhere.* But that would make me sound way too smart, so I just stared stupidly at the drone and squeezed Pria's hand once, to let her know I was sorry.

Then I let go.

The drone gestured at her to stand up. She did, shaking like bad machinery, and then her eyes rolled back in her head, and she fell on the clean floor of the train and had a fit.

It was an *outstanding* act. Better than mine. Only I wasn't so sure it was an act at all, because she didn't look good, and then she started vomiting and choking, and I was pretty sure it was for real after all.

I snapped out of it and rolled her over onto her side.

The drone's disgusted stare snapped from Pria to me in an instant, and he pointed at me. "Not so slow after all, are you?" he said, and snapped his fingers. "Up, boy. Over here."

I didn't have much choice. Sure, I could probably take him in a fight—he was Corporate, not much muscle on him, and for sure he hadn't been schooled in dirty fighting—but once I did, what then? I didn't know how to make the train doors open again, and with a lurch, the whole thing began to move anyway.

No real choice. The man was armed; he could burn me down into a grease stain if he wanted. So I stood up, walked to the group of nine he'd already assembled, and stood there like I was part of it.

The Corporate drone nodded, touched something on his handheld, and said, "Don't move, any of you." Some of the kids still seated were crying; some were just staring down at the tickets clutched in their hands. Nobody really thought that we were going to a game anymore. Or if they did, they were slower than I'd pretended to be.

The train ran for about thirty long minutes, smooth and swaying, before it pulled to a stop. The doors didn't open.

The drone cleared his throat and drew all eyes back to him. "You're owed a notice, by law, so this is it. We're over budget. Level K has been exceeding allowable resource levels for five years running. A downsizing order has been given. Your people on the level were notified by drop this morning. You witnessed us choosing random numbers. We try to be fair in any redundancy process."

I heard every kid take in a deep breath, but nobody said anything. Even the kids who'd been crying were silent. *Redundancy*. Somebody was getting the sharp edge of the ax . . . and they'd pulled numbers.

Seat numbers.

They were going to kill us purely to save the cost of feeding and clothing us for the next couple of years until we could earn our bread in the mines or the factories. The bottom line was that the Company had too many human resources.

We were victims of accounting.

"Everyone still seated, please stay in your seats; the train will continue momentarily." I barely heard the drone's voice over the sudden hot rush of blood in my ears. Not that I was scared to die, not at all. . . . Death is pretty much a part of any day on Level K. But I just felt . . . angry. And I was wondering if it would hurt much. Probably not. They needed us gone; torture was just wasted man-hours.

I could hear the murmurs of the kids in the seats, and they were tinged with relief. We weren't a sentimental bunch, we K kids. Everybody had to look out for himself. Couldn't blame them. I'd have been just the same.

The doors opened, and beyond was a tunnel, dimly lit with long strips of glowing glass in a dirty orange. It was clean, but plain. The drone gestured us out, and after a hesitation, I led the way. Better to go first than last, almost all the time. There wasn't anywhere to run. Nothing but a barred gate in the wall, and the trains, and walls.

The drone was the last one out. As I looked down the train, I saw that all the other cars had opened, and drones were leading or hustling out their quotas of ten as well. Ten per train car. Maybe a hundred, total.

There had been worse Company cullings. All of Level H had been made redundant, after food strikes and riots; nobody knew what had happened, exactly, but there hadn't been contact with Level H for four years now, and Corporate had just sealed it off and left it with biohazard warnings on all the entrances. Sometimes on K we told each other gruesome ghost stories and dared each other to break in. Nobody ever had. All ten thousand people on H had just . . . vanished. As if they'd never been.

The Corporate drones in their black jackets and neat haircuts, with their handheld devices, faced the train cars and stood there waiting for something. I saw something flash on our drone's screen, and he nodded and tapped a control.

The doors banged shut on all of the train cars at once, and then . . . then the screaming started. It was a few voices at first, then a panicked wave of sound. A freezing feeling came over me, something that numbed me right down to the core.

I took a step toward the train car. It was stupid, and I wished I hadn't. I wished I'd never looked into that window and met Pria's dark, panicked eyes. Seen her press her small hands against the window and mouth my name.

Because I couldn't help.

It wasn't *us* being made redundant after all. It was those on the train, with their pathetic painted faces and team colors and tattered little banners.

One thousand nine hundred of them, give or take a few orphans.

It was maybe a minute before the last screaming fell away.

I don't remember moving, but suddenly I had my back to the tunnel's rounded wall. Around me, others sank to the floor, crying. One girl screamed and tried to run back for the train car—family in there, maybe, or someone close to it. I grabbed her and wrapped my arms around her as she flailed, until she went limp. I still held her, a warm rag-doll weight, because holding on to someone, *anyone*, felt good just then.

At least it had been quick. Well, they'd stopped screaming quick. Maybe not the same thing.

"Process complete," the drone said, and tapped a

command on his handheld.

The silent, dead train glided on, a smooth and beautiful monster with a stomach full of prey, and the cool breeze blew over us as it picked up speed and pulled away. When the hissing sigh of it was past, the drone turned and looked at us.

"You're all employed at Corporate," he said. "Congratulations. You now hold the job title of dogsbody."

A dogsbody is the lowest form of labor available at Corporate, as opposed to the Operations. The old term for it is servant, or slave, but it's not really either one of those. You're an employee, and you get paid, but you can't ever be more than a third-class dogsbody, unless you make it to the top one percent in your one-year review. If you don't make the top cut, you get culled. Easy as that. Always new, strong dogsbodies being brought in from the levels to replace you.

I was a One Percenter at fourteen, and promoted out of third class. By sixteen, I was second-class dogsbody to Senior Management. I was an appliance. A very reliable machine. And for as long as I worked, they'd keep using me, so I kept myself working, ticking along, growing stronger and faster and deadlier every day.

I could have tried to run; there had been chances, over the years, but running back to the levels was great only if you wanted to die hard, and alone. No, I stayed. I became a good little Corporate drone, and I kept earning promotion credits until one day, just a few days before my seventeenth birthday, my handheld showed me transferred upward to the ultimate top level.

Dogsbody First Class to Tarrant Clark, Global SVP, Corporate Resources. Where I'd set out to be from that very first moment in the tunnel, listening to those screams, because according to everything I'd been able to look up, he was the man who ordered downsizings. *One thousand nine hundred, give or take a few orphans.* I wondered if he remembered anything about it. He was a busy man, after all. He probably ordered hundreds of massacres just like it every year.

I reported for my first day of work to Tarrant Clark's Residence Office—the Res, in dogsbody slang. The man who opened the door to the Res was named Helman, and the insignia under the Corporate logo on his coat pocket meant that he was classified as Junior Administrative Assistant, and he was young and intense and worried.

"You're a big one," Helman said, looking up at me. I presented him with my handheld. "Xavier Gray. Right. You'll be working upstairs, with Pozynski." He pulled out his own handheld, and the two devices talked together silently, then both gave a soft *cheep* as information was exchanged and verified. Deal done. It was more civilized than spitting on palms.

"How's the staff?" That was a question I was allowed to ask of a Junior Admin, and Helman looked pretty casual, in general. "The mood?"

"Tense," he said. "Budget's been running tight this year. Clark's been in strategy meetings for a week. He's due back tomorrow. We're trying to get everything perfect before he arrives, so be prepped for short tempers and long hours."

Nothing new to me.

Helman shut the door with a press of a button, and the lights came up in the entry hall automatically. Clark's home was the size of an entire level where I'd come up; the hall alone was as big as a small factory, tiled in shiny, rare natural stone and with beautiful art on the walls. I'd never seen better, but then, this was my first time inside one of the Res buildings.

"He's had a couple of assassination attempts," Helman admitted. "That's why we're bringing in all new support staff. You came highly reviewed."

I knew I had. I had years in Corporate service, wearing the black jacket, my head wired into the earpiece, taking my orders and doing whatever needed to be done, anywhere, anytime. I'd never had to fry a train full of redundant child-workers, though. Not yet, anyway.

I pointed to the staircase. "Up?"

"And to the right." Helman nodded. "Oh, you'll need to check in with Pozynski, desk at the top of the stairs. She'll give you the credentials."

I nodded and moved on, jogging lightly up the winding staircase toward the second level, and paused in front of a desk on the landing, where a beautiful, willowy blond girl in a well-tailored jacket smiled at me impersonally, our handhelds talked, and she passed me over a plastic bin of things.

Item one, a pistol, with two extra magazines. I took it out

and checked it with professional speed; it was a good weapon, very clean and well machined. It wasn't a Corporate product; I checked the insignia on the side. Different logo. "We're buying weapons from Intaglio?" I asked. Intaglio was a direct competitor in arms and food production. Their headquarters were halfway around the world, which had made it a hell of a lot more difficult to bomb them out of existence. Location, location, location.

"We buy from the vendor with the best price and quality, same as anyone else," Pozynski said. "Sometimes that's one of our divisions internally. Sometimes it isn't. The weapons contract is with Intaglio right now. Problem?"

I loaded the gun. "No problem," I said, and slipped it into my empty shoulder rig, under the jacket. Weapons contracts with out-of-company vendors meant people got downsized. My gun had bodies on it, even before I ever fired it.

Pozynski checked the list and held out a thin metal chain. A collar.

I didn't reach for it immediately, and looked at Pozynski, who raised her pale eyebrows. "Everybody here wears them," she said, and tapped her own with a long, tapered fingernail. "Regulation."

I hated it, but I smiled and said, "I just don't look as good as you in jewelry."

That earned me a more genuine smile. "Oh, you'll look fine." Pozynski stood on tiptoe to put the collar around my neck and snap it in place. It was a thin braid, and she fiddled with it to pull it down a little, make it more like a decorative object. "There," she said, and slipped it under my shirt. Her fingers felt cool and sweet against my skin. "If you don't like the length, just hold it for a few seconds, then pull to drag it lower. If you want it shorter, three taps on the chain to make it contract. It has a safety, you can't strangle yourself with it accidentally. Got it?"

"Got it." I'd worn a collar before, but when I was just starting out. The first year of dogsbody service, everybody wears one. For good behavior. That way, they can end you on a moment's notice, just by pressing a button on a handheld.

I thought I was past all that. Guess not. The chain felt thick and heavy around my neck.

Pozynski pointed up, and up I went. The hallway overlooked the entry hall below—a perfect defensive position, if you were properly armed, because they'd reinforced the wall beneath the banister with ballistic armor. There were gunports, too, though well disguised as ornamental medallions. Position of last resort.

Well, *I* was the last resort, because as Clark's personal first-class dogsbody, I was expected to put myself in front of any danger.

The second door on the right had a palm scanner, which not only read the whorls and loops of fingerprints but also tested for body temperature and pulsebeats. No cutting off some poor bastard's hand to trick your way inside.

I put my hand on the scanner. Light flashed beneath it;

there was a soft, approving beep; and the door clicked open.

I stepped inside, closed it behind me, and immediately registered a change in atmosphere. The carpet was thicker, lusher beneath my polished shoes. The lights were more subdued and elegant. The artwork on the walls was priceless, full of color and swirls and confusion.

There was another desk at the far end of the room, near a dazzling bank of windows overlooking a false, computer-generated sunrise. Behind it sat a woman of about my own age—thin, serious, dressed in a Corporate jacket like everyone else but with a small golden pin on the lapel that denoted her as Senior Administrative staff. She had brown hair, which she'd pulled up into a tidy coil on top of her head, and although she wasn't especially pretty—not on the level of Miss Pozynski—she had a certain gravity to her that drew my steps her way. Again, she was young—younger than I was, this time.

Then she looked up and met my eyes, and I felt a shock of surprise. "Virtue?" I blurted, and immediately stopped myself. My gaze flew to the digital nameplate on her desk. *V. Hardcastle, Senior Administrative Assistant.* Her real name, the one she'd been born with down in the levels. What the *hell* was she doing here? She hadn't been on the train.

"Zay," she said, and gave me a smile that was tense and free of any surprise at all. "Welcome to the Res. Handheld?" I gave it to her, still struggling to accept the sight of a familiar face, here. She matched the handheld to hers, orders digitally transferred and confirmed with the audible ping, and then she relaxed a little as she gave the device back to me. I slipped it into my pocket, and felt my face sliding into a frown.

"*You* got me this job," I said. "Didn't you?"

"I felt I needed someone I could trust," Virtue said. "Like the old days, on the level."

I nodded, still measuring this new Virtue. I didn't know her. A gap of a year in Corporate was more than enough time for someone to shift themselves completely—look at me. I'd gone from a tough, hardscrabble orphan to a tough, hardscrabble orphan with a gun.

And we'd been apart way more than a year.

"Relax," Virtue said, and smiled. I recognized the smile, as I'd recognized the eyes. Warm, guarded, fragile. Her old, familiar smile. "We're not at knives yet."

I raised my eyebrows. "You've done well for yourself."

"Yes," she said. There was a strange flash in her eyes I didn't understand. "I worked hard enough for it."

"Yeah, me too," I said. "Difference is, I didn't apply for the job."

"I know." Virtue swallowed hard, not looking away from my eyes. "I told you not to go, Zay. I told you."

"You knew. You knew all along, didn't you?" I'd spent a lot of time not thinking about the Cup Train, and a lot of time feeling way too much; that's the way of things, when you push them back into dark corners and cage them up. They turn nasty. The surge of rage that swept over me was blinding, and I wanted to grab her by the throat and shake an answer out of her.

I didn't have to. She was already talking over me. "I *didn't* know, I swear! I just guessed something was wrong. If I'd known, I'd have blown the whistle, Zay. You know that. I just had a tingle, and I heeded it."

I believed her. I might not know this present-day Virtue, but *that* Virtue would have screamed the house down if she'd really known what was going to happen. She wouldn't have just saved herself. We were cold, we K kids, but not *that* cold.

"So why did you hire me?" I asked. "Old times' sake?"

"In a sense," she said, and stood up. "Come with me. I have someone I want you to meet."

There was a sliding door concealed in the yellow wall, one that required another access keypad. This one was DNA keyed, from the looks of it, and likely only Virtue was coded to enter directly. She was the gatekeeper.

The door led into a vast warehouse of an office, carpet even plusher underfoot than in the room outside, walls polished dark wood, priceless works of art and sculpture trapped here like flies in amber, for the enjoyment of one person. The entire back wall of the office was windows stretching up twenty feet, pure glass, not monitors. The windows overlooked a real park, green grass, neatly clipped bushes, a riot of colorful flowers. Trees swaying in the wind. A fountain spraying clean water high into the air.

Outside.

I felt it hit me like a punch in the gut, and swayed as I gulped for air. Virtue turned her dark, calm gaze on me. "I know," she said quietly. "It does that. Take a second, then follow me."

She waited while I sucked down a couple of steadying breaths, and at my nod, led me across what seemed like an entire level's worth of carpet, past lush furniture and a library of real, solid books, to a desk that must have destroyed the largest tree that had ever lived. It was real wood, polished and lovingly maintained, and behind it sat a tired-looking middle-aged man with graying hair.

He was wearing a Corporate jacket, but it was a much finer one, and instead of black, it was blue, in the Company color. He had on a tie, faded blue, to match his eyes. A crisp white shirt. He extended his right hand to me as he rose, and I took it automatically. Corporate manners, drilled into me with harsh discipline.

"Is this him?" the man asked Virtue, who nodded. "Mr. Gray. Very nice to meet you. Virtue's said so much about you."

It had happened too fast. He wasn't supposed to be here, not until tomorrow. I had expected to be in control and ready, and instead, I was still struggling to come to grips with the sight of the world outside of those windows behind him, and the tired smile he gave me as we shook hands.

This was the man who'd killed a whole trainload of kids down in the dark, and he looked . . . kind.

"I'm Tarrant Clark," he said. "Global SVP, Corporate Resources."

"Good to meet you, sir," I said.

"Oh, no doubt," he said. "Since I'm sure you've come to kill me."

Virtue took in a breath, then let it slowly out. I said nothing. Clark was still holding my hand in a firm grip.

"Am I wrong, Zay?" he asked, and let go. We faced each other without blinking, and beneath the smile, the kindness, I saw a man who'd survived Corporate life. Someone who didn't flinch. "You're not the first K kid to come here to even the score. Ask Virtue about her first day with me."

I darted a look at her, and saw that he wasn't lying; she'd worked her way here for exactly the same reason I had . . . to get revenge.

Only she hadn't followed through.

I felt the weight of the gun under my armpit, warm and deadly. I was fast. I could draw and fire in a second, and he'd be falling, a bloody memory. I'd certainly be dead about a second later, from any of a variety of automatic countermeasures, but I would have accomplished the one thing that I'd set out to do, all those years ago. What I'd been training to do ever since that day.

"I understand why you feel as you do," Clark was saying. "I won't lie to you; I knew about the planned downsizing. I voted to stop it, but it didn't matter, in the end. It happened."

"Yes," I said. "It happened to *us*."

Clark gazed at me without blinking, still. "Don't kid yourself that it was only you on the level who suffered. A thing like that happens to everybody who touches it, everybody who knows. It's toxic. It changes you."

I was one twitch away from killing him. The powerful impact of the shock of the Outside beyond those windows was wearing off, and so was my first impression of him; the anger was coming back, a red tide that was going to carry me away.

"Yeah," I said softly. "I guess you'd think that." It was sick thinking, to imagine that pushing a button, signing an order would be like *being there*, like *seeing it happen*. Like being one of those dead kids, riding the train to the incinerator. Or like the families who never spoke about it again.

He thought he'd *suffered*? Not by half. Not yet, he hadn't.

She must have seen it in my eyes, because Virtue stepped up and put herself in front of me, between me and Tarrant Clark. "No," she said. "It hasn't come to knives. I told you, Zay. You need to listen to him."

I wasn't going to stop. Not for Virtue, not for anybody.

I made a move to draw, but she was too close, and I was too big to be that nimble. Virtue didn't need a lot of leverage to stop me, she just had to choose the moment. She did, pinning my arm, and hung on with all the wiry strength of her body. "No," she insisted softly, urgently. "Zay, *listen*. Listen to him. Please."

"Let go of me," I said to Virtue. "I don't want to hurt you, but this is going to get done. We swore on it."

"Listen!"

I did, but only because I knew I'd have to kill her first, and

I was weighing whether or not I wanted that debt on my sheet.

"I'm in the middle of a hostile takeover of the Company," Clark said, in the dead silence that followed. "I'm going to take out the CEO. Leo Pannizer is the man who designed and ordered the Cup Train operation; he forced me at gunpoint to sign the papers. It got him the big desk. Now I'm going to downsize him, *tonight*. If you'll hold your anger a little longer, Zay, you can help me do that. You can get revenge on the man who pushed the button."

Corporate. Always *talking*.

I stopped trying to move Virtue gently, and batted her out of the way with more violence than I probably needed. She fell heavily on her side, cracked her head against the wood of the desk, and lay still for a few stunned breaths.

I wasn't looking at her. In the second it had taken her to fall, I had drawn my gun, and aimed it directly between Tarrant Clark's eyes.

He didn't flinch. At all. There was a kind of fatalistic acceptance in his face, a tense knowledge that he'd arrived at this moment under his own power, by making his own choices.

And that made me hesitate, for just a second, that Clark didn't flinch from taking what was coming. I'd never imagined he'd be brave. Never.

Virtue kicked my legs out from under me, screaming out a raw challenge, the language of Level K, not this quiet Corporate haven. I fired as I fell.

The bullet missed Clark, hit the glass behind him, and

simply . . . stopped. The glass didn't break. It held the bullet, perfectly still, in transit. The surface vibrated.

And then I was in the fight of my life.

Virtue hadn't gone soft, not at all, and she was armed with a knife, a little thing, deadly sharp, that flashed and hissed with her quick moves. The skirt she wore left her legs free to move, and she kicked off her severe shoes immediately to give herself better stability. That evened us as much as we could be evened, given the difference in our sizes.

Not that I had ever allowed size to come between us in a fight. Nor had she. Virtue was as dangerous as a rabid weasel when she was committed, and just now, she was fully, fatally committed.

I dodged out of the way of a stab, a feint, another stab that turned halfway and slashed through the arm of my jacket, barely scratching my flesh. The heavy black fabric and the shirt beneath parted with hardly a tug. That was a *very* sharp knife.

I had expected nothing less from her.

I had no knife, but I had a knuckle stunner, which I slipped my hand into in my pocket. I came out with a punch so fast it blurred, and caught Virtue on the chin as she slammed that knife in toward my chest for a crippling blow. The shock jolted my arm, but that was only bleed-through; the vast majority cascaded directly through her body, and I twisted to avoid the knife and caught her on the way down.

I eased Virtue to the carpet, checked to be sure she was

still breathing, and then looked back up at Tarrant Clark.

Who had not moved. The bullet vibrated gently in the glass behind him, giving off a soft humming sound as the field bled off the murderous energy of its passage. He hadn't gone for a weapon. He hadn't run. He hadn't called for backup.

"Is she alive?" he asked.

"Do you care?"

"Yes. I like her. She's a tough little thing."

Oddly, I believed him. I stood up, limping a little from where she'd caught me with her kick, and raised the gun. "I'm not going to miss again," I said.

Clark smiled faintly, and said nothing. He was just as ready now as he had been before, I saw.

I said, "What did you mean about the CEO?"

"I mean that I've been engineering a hostile takeover for a year now," he said. "I've worked hard to load the Board of Directors. Tonight, I call a proxy vote, get authorization, and then my dogsbodies can carry out the redundancy orders. You can head it up, if you want the job." He paused a moment, then said, "I know you don't believe me about the Cup Train. I wouldn't, either. But Virtue will open the records for you. You can see everything you want. Anything you want. I have nothing to hide."

I didn't believe that. Nobody in the entire world had nothing to hide, least of all a Corporate exec. But maybe, just maybe, he was telling the truth about not being behind the Cup Train massacre.

Maybe all my work to get here had just led me to one more step, one more villain, one more link.

Or maybe I could just kill this guy and call it even.

The only thing that stopped me was Virtue, lying insensible at my feet. Virtue hadn't forgotten a single lesson learned down on Level K. She was still fighting. Still fierce.

Still difficult to fool.

So there was a chance, a slim one, that Tarrant wasn't the hard Corporate bastard who'd ordered the deaths of kids, just to save a quarter's results and grab another bonus. There was a chance that if I killed him, I risked the only opportunity for revenge that we had.

I took my finger off the trigger and holstered the gun. "I'll look at the records," I said. "I'll probably still kill you."

"No hurry," Clark said. "I'm here all night."

Virtue was out for almost an hour, which worried me; the stunning, on top of the crack on the head, probably hadn't done her any favors. When she woke up, she was groggy and sick for a while, and finally, shakily, put on her shoes and concealed her knife again and led me out of Clark's office to her own, less distracting work space.

Clark had asked if I required Medical to attend her. I'd refused. I knew Virtue well enough, even at this distance, to know she'd never want to show that kind of weakness, not if she could help it.

It was the sign of a significant injury that the first thing she did, on sitting behind her desk, was open a drawer and take out a dermal hypo, which she pressed against her skin, and dialed for what was probably a combination of headache and nausea meds. They hissed into her system, and she sighed and let her head sag forward for a moment as the drugs went to work. When she looked up at me, she looked almost back to herself.

Only fiercer.

"You really are a hard one," she said, and rubbed at the bruise forming on her jaw. "I thought you'd shoot him for sure."

"I did," I said. "Missed. Doesn't mean I can't try again."

She made no response to that, except to tap her desktop to bring up a built-in keyboard and monitor that rose silently in virtual display from the seemingly smooth surface of the wood. I came around behind her. She smelled . . . Corporate. Clean, sweet, powdered and perfumed. Civilized, unlike the life we'd both come from, where showers were mandatory once a week and perfume was a luxury you saved for to buy your mother—if you still had one—once a year, in a tiny little stoppered bottle.

She'd come a long way. So had I. I was suddenly conscious of how neat I was, too, how *perfect*. Save for the place where her knife had slashed my coat and shirt and dotted the white cloth with little spots of drying blood, I was just like everybody else up here. Owned.

Virtue tapped keys, doing things I only vaguely understood. Dogsbodies weren't cleared for technical training, and it was impossible to get it without authorization, at least at the Corporate rank. Maybe you could sneak a black-market computer class down in the lower levels, but not up here, where every keystroke was tracked.

"There," she said, and rolled her chair back from the desk. "Sit down. You can navigate through anything you like."

I felt a slight flush creeping up my collar, but I sat down, feeling suddenly too large, too awkward. Give me a gun, a knife, a stunner, and I'm as graceful as anyone my size, but keyboards are built for smaller, smarter people. "I don't know how," I said. I hated to admit it, but saw the flash of immediate understanding in Virtue's expression. It wasn't pity. Just acknowledgment.

"I'll do it," she said. "You just tell me what you want to open, I'll open it, you read it. Okay?"

I nodded. She leaned over my shoulder, and immediately the perfume overwhelmed my senses, woke uncomfortable feelings inside me. I could smell *her* under the floral scent, warm and female and very, very close. I couldn't decide whether I wanted her to get away from me, or on me. Something of both. I'd been with a few girls before; it was one of the only cheap pleasures available to dogsbodies.

But Virtue was different. She was from home. And whatever else it was, home was special.

She tapped keys, and a small folder zoomed up and open on the virtual display. It clarified immediately to a resolution that let me read it easily, probably reading my own focus range through receptive sensors.

It was an official memo from Tarrant Clark, sent through official channels, lodging a protest against Operation Overflow—or, as we survivors called it, the Cup Train. He wrote, in passionate terms, about the wrongness of the action, about Corporate responsibility to its workers, core values, all that crap.

He was ignored. Not just once, but over and over. All the evidence was there, including video of the Board meeting where Clark had presented his side and been voted down. Where Pannizer had personally held a gun to his head to make him sign the orders.

Clark had walked out after that. There were more records, detailing a countermeasure team he'd put together via handheld as he sped back to his office. It was a good team, but it arrived ten minutes too late to stop the massacre, which meant that by the time the vote had been carried out, the plan had already been in motion. Tickets delivered, kids loaded on the train.

The votes were a sham. The Board was a sham.

And the man who'd engineered the whole thing was now CEO. *Leo Franklin Pannizer.*

I studied the video of him in close-up. I'd seen photos of him, of course; he was in all the Corporate brochures. But video made him real, not just another set of pixels; he had graceful mannerisms and a nervous, odd laugh, and a bald spot at the top of his head that he hadn't troubled to have fixed. He was married. He had a beautiful wife and three children, all perfect little Corporate specimens, not a single flaw among them.

I had imagined some kind of monster. Some beast with madness in his eyes. And maybe he was. Maybe it just didn't show up on video.

Virtue finally stepped back, rubbing a hand across her forehead. The bruise on her jaw was starting to discolor and looked painful. I wondered if her pain meds were working. "Well?" she asked.

I said nothing. I closed my eyes and thought about it, focusing on all that I'd done to get here, all that I'd learned. All that I hadn't learned.

And then I said, "We'll do it Clark's way. Until I find out he's lying. Then I do it my way."

The role of a dogsbody, at the level I'd reached, was amazingly simple. Stand around. Look tough. If someone attacks, kill them real hard.

It got a little more complicated two hours later, when Clark's messages began to go out, and his takeover plans started rolling. For one thing, Tech Support tried to kill our connections; they sent a single operative, surrounded by three dogsbodies, to the central connection center, where three of Clark's dogsbodies—not me—put all of them down. Next, messages began coming in to Virtue, Miss Pozynski, and

Helman downstairs, warning them that imminent corrective action was scheduled to be taken by Management for breach of contract.

"That's it, we're locked up," Virtue said, and shut down her console. She keyed in a rapid sequence of numbers, and a cabinet opened on the wall of her office. She tapped in another sequence. "Yanna, Aaron, get up here and get armed. We're going to have direct incursion."

The two Junior Admins were there in moments. Miss Pozynski wasn't flirtatious anymore, and Helman wasn't genial. They both had arms training, and it showed in the way that they took and checked their guns.

"You're in charge of the dogsbodies," Virtue told them. "All except Mr. Gray here. He's mine. Last line of defense."

I would be manning the balcony overlooking the entry hall until that last line was required. "Put somebody in the garden," I said. They all looked at me. "I know the glass is ballistic. Just put somebody in the garden."

Because that would be how I would come in. There'd be some flaw there, some hole I could exploit. If it was me, coming for the man I wanted to destroy, then the garden would be my entry point. They all imagined it was secure. It couldn't be that good.

"I need to see the plans," I said. "Every room. Every approach. Every defensive measure. Right now."

Three sets of identical stares, and then Virtue said, "All right," and dismissed her two juniors to their duties. She opened up a cabinet and took out a sheet of smart paper the size of the top of her desk. The paper contained blueprints of the complex and the grounds. I knew how to use these, at least; I'd been trained in reading and analyzing such diagrams. I double-tapped areas where I needed magnification, and the paper obligingly zoomed in for me. "Take this down," I said to Virtue. "You've got a window of opportunity through the service entrance on the third floor."

"I'll close it," she said, and reached for her handheld.

"No, don't. We funnel them through that access, and we control their entry. But we have to make sure that they don't suspect anything. Make sure it's guarded, just not too heavily."

She nodded and tapped the screen, issuing orders. I was probably sending dogbodies like me to their deaths out there, guarding that door. I hadn't meant to, but I'd risen to a management rank within a caste that wasn't even included on the Corporate organization charts. I knew how to make war, and the first tenet is that even if you have disposable people, you don't waste them.

"V," I said, the way I used to when we were kids. "You're the only one with unrestricted access to Tarrant?"

"And you, now."

I wasn't sure that was a bright idea, given the conflicting mixture of emotions inside of me, but this wasn't the time to debate it. "Then I need you out of the fight. You stay in here. This is Secure Level Two. He's Secure Level One."

In other words, Virtue and I would be the last line of defense.

She nodded, perfectly at peace with that.

An hour passed, and nothing. Virtue monitored news and events, as well as private message traffic, on her handheld as she sat perched on the edge of a couch, where I imagine she slept most of the time. There was a blanket folded neatly at the end and a pillow pushed underneath.

"Level K is in revolt," she said. "Somebody started a rumor that the food was being cut off. The stores closed their doors against rioters. Now it's general chaos."

"It's a feint," I said. "They'll stir up as many trouble spots as possible to pull focus away from this place." But I felt sick, because I remembered Level H. So did she. Riots and strikes got put down hard, and permanently. We still had friends down there.

She went back to reading. About five minutes later, she said, in a very soft voice, "A train from Level B has been destroyed. Seven hundred dead. They're talking external competitive attack, but it's a feint. Has to be."

Both of us instantly were transported back to that platform, that slick lovely train, the kids in their Cup game paint and colors. Neither of us spoke. She flicked through messages, faster, faster, and then stopped.

Her mouth opened, but before she could speak, I felt it through the soles of my feet. A kind of harmonic vibration.

Then the building shook violently, rocking side to side, metal bending and screaming all around. Art toppled from the walls. Furniture tipped and slid as the building swayed. I grabbed Virtue and held on as the world shuddered around us.

When it was over, I heard the high-pitched drone of alarms going off. I zoomed the smart paper out to the master view.

Red alerts pulsed in two places: the front entry hall, and on the third floor, at the service entrance.

"I need you to stay in here," I said. "Monitor the garden. If they come that way, get to Clark."

She nodded, face gone tight. I rolled up the paper and stuffed it into my pocket in a wad as I moved for the outer door. I glanced back.

"Watch yourself, Zay," she said.

Same thing she'd said at the Cup Train.

Opening the door of Virtue's office was like opening the door onto a war zone—from soundproofed to shocking in a single burst. I ducked out and to the side, and the door zoomed shut again behind me, the lock flaring red as it cycled down. I was behind the solid ballistic armor of the balcony. I grabbed my handheld and checked camera views.

View one, the door to Virtue's office, where I was crouched.

View two, Miss Pozynski's desk, which had grown a shield around it, and a cannon, which she was firing at will down the stairs. Miss Pozynski looked just as pretty killing people as she did handing them welcome packages.

View three, midway down the stairs. It was a carpet of

bodies. Dogsbodies, of course. Shock troops sent to over-whelm Miss Pozynski, who had been in fact underwhelmed and was still mowing them down with icy precision.

I needed a bigger gun, I decided, and took out my pistol, clicked the Autofit feature, and selected something with better firepower.

Assault rifle. That would do nicely.

There were limits to what an Autofit could accomplish, and so the pistol's basic structure only morphed a little. However, it did give me the ability to fire multiple bursts at blurring speed, although I was likely to run out of ammunition fairly quickly. . . .

"Miss Pozynski," I said into the handheld. "Ammunition?"

"Oh, call me Yanna; we're all friends here. Carl is bringing it to you," she said. "He's on ammunition rounds."

Carl was a kind of stock boy, with a self-driving armored cart. He was a small kid, younger than me, and he pulled up his machine in a hiss of air brakes to toss out a mound of ammunition before speeding off toward Miss Pozynski.

He never made it. A small missile whipped up the stairs in a red rush, avoided Miss Pozynski's armor, and impacted directly with Carl's cart, which exploded in a hail of shrapnel.

Miss Pozynski had a single-use blast shield, I saw, from the red flare that vaporized the shrapnel on contact as it sliced toward her. I had one as well, built into my handheld, and nothing but ash made it through to hit me.

Not much left of Carl, though. Or the ammunition.

I made a run for the armory door. There was an emergency access panel near the bottom, under the theory that if you're in desperate need of ammunition, you probably don't want to stick your head above the bulletproof barrier to gain access. Good theory. I palmed the pad, and the door zoomed open, then quickly shut as I rolled over the threshold.

It was like a candy store full of bullets. I felt positively *warm* inside, but that didn't last long as the whole place shuddered from another artillery hit. I saw plate steel warping at the back.

I consulted the plans. They were targeting the windows in Clark's office, which was what I'd have done.

I loaded up and went back out, opened up a gunport, and fired like there was no tomorrow, because there wouldn't be if this went badly. Dogsbodies in Corporate livery fell and fell and fell on the entry level, and the chic marble floor was a mass of blood, chipped stone, and bullet casings.

Then Miss Pozynski got it, in the form of another smart missile fired from below. It probably would have come for me except that some bright boy had just lit up her metal shield with heat tracers. The missile dived straight for it, sensed the obstacle, dodged, found free space, and detonated *behind* the shield.

Miss Pozynski's personal force field had one use, and this was the second missile. Game over. I got pelted with shrapnel, including something sharp and deep in my side, and didn't look over at whatever might be left of her; it wouldn't be pretty anymore. The fire carried on. Whatever other dogsbodies Clark had around—and I was fairly sure he had a lot—gradually lost to the incoming tide of attackers. The CEO owned a whole army of them, apparently. I checked my handheld. We were down by 50 percent already, and I knew it wasn't close to over.

I heard feet coming up the stairs in a thunder, and without Miss Pozynski there to cut them down, they'd have me in a deadly angle in seconds. As I retreated, I caught a quick glimpse of the man leading the charge. It was Helman, bloody and grinning, and he snapped off shots at me wildly as I opened Virtue's door and slammed it shut.

Virtue, pale and steady behind the desk, clicked keys. "I'm disabling the lock," she said. "It won't stop them long."

"Helman's turned on us," I said. "They must have offered general pardons and transfer and promotion. Could be other defections. You need to change the codes now."

That made her pause, but only for a second before her fingers flew across the keypad. I saw a remarkable variety of emotions flow across her face and out again—anger, fear, sadness, icy determination. "I see that Pozynski is down. What else have we got?"

"Seventeen dogsbodies around the perimeter still register as active and fighting. But they're not going to be enough."

She paused and looked at me, nothing at all showing in her facial expression—but something, some shadow of something, in her eyes. "We're not going to make it," she said. "I never expected them to offer transfer and promotion. That'll kill us, especially if they offer signing bonuses to flip."

"Reinforcements? Alliances?" Because that was the Corporate way to do it; Clark would have strategic alliances, partnerships with other key executives who'd have to offer support. Favors for favors.

"They're *unavailable*," she said with a bitter edge. "In private meetings." They'd been bought off. Tarrant Clark's bid for power had been seen as going nowhere, and accordingly, his allies had bolted en masse. His carefully crafted plans were going to hell, fast.

That left the two of us, effectively. I stared at Virtue. "What do you want to do?" Being a dogsbody, I had no choice. If I tried to surrender, they'd kill me for disloyalty. Virtue, however, was a Corporate employee, a genuine careerist; she could give up Clark and join Helman on the winning side, and nobody would hold it against her, not even on her annual review. She'd probably get a promotion out of it.

"I stay with my boss," she said. "He needs to win, Zay. He *has* to win, or it's all for nothing. Everything you and I have done, been—it's all for *nothing*. You made me promise to make it right. That's why I'm here. If we don't, we might as well have gotten on the train and ridden it straight to hell."

I checked my guns. "Where's Clark's executive escape?"

She shook her head. "There isn't one."

"Bullshit," I said bluntly. "This is a Corporate executive's Res; there's an escape. You tell me where it is now, Virtue."

"Why? So you can run?"

I read bitter disappointment in her eyes, quickly hidden.

"I promise you, I won't be going far. I need you to guard Clark and run some schematics and maps for me."

When I told her what I was going to do, the disappointment disappeared, replaced by a bright, fierce hope. She opened the intercom circuit and got Clark on the line. I could picture him in his still, quiet office, watching the battle rage outside his picture windows.

It was his decision, in the end. I couldn't act on my own, not in this.

"Yes?" he said. Perfectly calm, it sounded like. He had truly excellent soundproofing in there; I couldn't even hear the rattle of gunfire or steady thumping of missiles on his end, although it was plain in Virtue's office.

"Sir, we need you to play for time," Virtue said. "With Leo Pannizer. Call for an official Board meeting. Make a deal."

"He'll never agree. He'll just stonewall me until it's over."

"Yes, sir, I know that. But it's a distraction, and we need a distraction right now. We need him to think you're in a defensive position."

"Aren't I?" I could almost see Clark's eyebrows rise, along with the inflection. "What are you planning?"

"Sir, it's better if you don't know the details. But let's just say that if it works out, you can take credit for the brilliant tactics. We'll need a blanket all-actions-necessary authorization from your handheld."

As an executive, he was more than familiar with that

concept. "All right," he said. "It's posted and on record. I'll try to get Pannizer to talk." If Clark made the call himself, he was more likely to be treated with respect than if Virtue made it on his behalf. Pannizer might even signal a cease-fire until he heard Clark out on a deal. It would demonstrate his fair-mindedness, for the record. I doubted he'd go so far as to call even a virtual Board meeting, but he might. Depended on how much he cared about what the other executives thought about his management style.

Virtue and I pulled maps and schematics, and she downloaded them to my handheld, along with access codes I would need along the way. She shouldn't have had most of them. I wondered, briefly, what Virtue's endgame had been in her own long-term plan; something to do with access, obviously. I wouldn't have been surprised if it had been exactly what I was thinking now.

"Where'd you get the tunneling codes?" I asked her. She shrugged the way she used to, down on K, with just a bare shiver of muscles, and gave me a flash of a smile.

"If it came to it, I was going to go rogue," she said. "Go after Pannizer myself."

"What stopped you?"

"Clark was working on it, so I kept it in the planning stages. But I put in a fail-safe a couple of days ago," she said. "Deadman switch. I wrote together a program that monitors my life signs and launches a nasty little predator e-bomb the moment they fail. If it works the way it should, it'll wipe all base codes and connected backups across the cloud. Bring

down the whole defense grid for at least forty-five minutes
before they can load from off site."

"You mean, the whole *Company's* defense grid?" I was . . .
appalled. And full of admiration. Without defenses, the
Company itself was vulnerable to any kind of armed hostile
takeover . . . just the thing our competitors were waiting for.

Virtue grinned at me, and she was exactly the girl I'd know
back on the level. "We don't have to take out Pannizer directly, if
they get me," she said. "Our competitors come in and do a complete management shakeup. He's downsized automatically."

"I like the way you think," I said. "But since it's a last
resort, let's make sure you don't have to use it, all right?"

"I'd rather win and stay alive," she said. "But if I don't, I'd
rather they don't, either."

We agreed on that much. "Where's the escape?"

"Right over there, in the corner. There's a pad under the
carpet. It's . . . look, you won't like it. It's a fax escape."

My skin crawled, and I felt sickened, but I nodded. A fax
escape meant that I'd be dead on this end, leaving behind a
corpse, as the energy and engrams of my brain patterns and
DNA were ripped away, transmitted, and another body on the
other end was created from vat materials. It'd be a generic
body, no longer my own. Hopefully, there wouldn't be too
much loss of resolution on the mental imprints. Faxing was
definitely the last resort of the desperate.

I stood where she told me to stand, and nodded once to her
to confirm I was ready.

I wasn't.

Faxing hurt like—well, like dying. There was nothing visual; the sensation came from within, like being microwaved, like every cell in your body was burst and flooding out, and you were being burned alive—

And then, I was somewhere else. Some*one* else.

I opened my eyes in a dark, cool, silent tunnel. I sank down on my haunches, my back against the rough stone wall, and gasped for breath as I tried to get used to the new, rubbery flesh around me, the difference in weight, balance, size. Everything was *wrong*, and for a few seconds I teetered on the edge of screaming crazy.

But it passed.

It was icy cold down here, because the fax process had drawn a hell of a lot of energy from all the surrounding area; luckily, they'd included executive clothing on a rack right beside the vat. For the first time, I was wearing full Corporate colors and an executive lapel pin.

There were handhelds racked on the wall; I took one and entered my employee code, and data poured in from Virtue's console, giving me everything I needed to know, including the code for the weapons locker next to me. I loaded up fast.

The bill for this fax would be outright staggering, the price of a year's output of an entire level. The energy-conversion charge was truly enormous. Oh, and the life span of people who were faxed tended to be about twenty years shorter, but then, I didn't expect to see another day anyway. Twenty years of future time was effectively meaningless to me, today.

I calmed myself down with slow, deep breaths, lurched to my feet, and checked position and maps. Virtue had faxed me to a spot right outside of the alarm field, less than fifty feet from where I needed to be. No access panels here, of course; this was serious security, ironclad. You didn't get in if you weren't supposed to get in.

Theoretically.

How Virtue had managed to hack her way into this, the most protected database on the planet, I had no way of knowing. The intricacy of it was staggering. This was her one and only chance to use the information she'd planted. She'd never have another shot.

I strode forward, waiting for the alarms to engage, the kill field to come on and reduce me to bones and ash. Like I said—serious security.

Nothing happened. I walked down the length of the dimly lit tunnel, and it changed gradually to look more finished. The floor started out concrete, then became shiny. Locked, unmarked doors appeared on either side, without handles or access panels. Once again, you had to be meant to enter, or you simply didn't. Nobody in the halls. Nobody guarding it.

And then, up ahead, a dogsbody stepped into my path and said, "Who are you?"

I gave him my handheld. He took it, looked at the orders, checked them against the central computer, and gave the device back to me, granting me the next-level access.

For which I killed him, quickly and efficiently, with a

knife to the heart. It wouldn't bleed much at all. I left him in the hallway, because trying to find a place to hide him was a useless waste of time.

Then I set off at a jog to the next door, which had an access panel. I was cleared for this one. I stepped through it, keyed it shut, and faced the next obstacle.

It went this way for three stops. They cleared me. I killed them. By the time I reached the third stop, some bright spark had found the first guard dead, and the game was up.

Didn't matter. I was already through the last door.

I faced the Senior Administrative Assistant for Leo Pannizer, CEO. According to the nameplate on her desk, she was Naia Wade Lymon. She was good, too; every bit as pretty as Miss Pozynski had been, even better dressed, and a hell of a great shot because she drilled me right in the chest, two taps, before I'd even gotten my own gun trained on her.

Virtue had given me a personal code for the built-in shield on the lapel pin I was wearing; it had been her own, because there was nothing executives guarded more closely than their personal shield codes. The first bullet bounced and put a hole in the expensive wooden paneling nearby. But Virtue's shield, like Miss Pozynski's, was single use.

The second bullet hit, tumbled, and took out part of my lung. I felt it, but I was too busy to hurt, because I was unleashing a precise, murderous stream of fire at Miss Wade Lymon, whose shield was a hell of a lot better than Virtue's, but still not CEO quality. She took five bullets before it failed. Five more after. I ended up with another round in the shoulder, and had to change gun hands. A nuisance, but not critical.

I grabbed Miss Wade Lymon by the collar of her very expensive suit and towed her to the wall, and the access panel, which was virtually identical to the one in Tarrant Clark's outer office. She wasn't dead. Not quite. Which meant that I could enter the code for her, and her DNA would still work the lock, if I moved fast to do it before her pulse failed.

It took Virtue twenty long seconds to send me the final code. We couldn't get it ahead of time; it cycled every three minutes. But I had it, punched it in, and pressed Miss Wade Lymon's shaking, barely living hand to the keypad, then dumped her off to the side as the door slid open.

Leo Pannizer rose from behind his desk. There was a virtual display open in front of him, and I saw Tarrant Clark standing there, looking relaxed and formal and quiet. As if he wasn't under the final act of a death sentence.

Unlike Clark, this man was *not* ready to die. He held up both hands. I could read the shaking terror in his face. "No," he said. "No, please, I'll offer you a place on my own household staff, a generous raise—you can name your own salary. . . ."

I shot Pannizer in the face until the clip was empty, then dropped the gun because it had done no good at all. The CEO's personal shield was better than anyone else's. There were dogsbodies coming, of course, but they'd have to navigate security to make it. I had seconds to live, but those seconds still counted.

I went with the knife. The shield wasn't designed to guard against low-velocity attacks; that was what Miss Wade Lymon had been for, and the dogsbodies, and all the security measures.

Mr. Pannizer surprised me by producing a gun from virtually nowhere, but he never got a chance to shoot. I kicked it out of his hand; slammed him backward to the lush, beautiful carpet; and slid the knife into his chest. I watched his eyes flicker wildly, then start to dilate.

"That's for the kids who died on the Cup Train," I said. I twisted the knife. "That's for the ones who got off."

Then I sat down, knife left in Pannizer's chest, and relaxed, because I'd done my job, and there had never been a way out of this, anyway. It only took about ten seconds for someone to trigger my choke collar. I expected them to throttle me with it, but instead they just choked me gray and left me there, gasping and helpless.

The dogsbodies arrived. So did additional Administrative Assistants. Nobody killed me, probably waiting for orders from the Board, who had to quickly convene to appoint a new CEO. Not to mention deal with the inevitable hostile takeover attempts by competitors, although that really wasn't my problem, or ever would be. Big politics.

No, all I had to do was sit, bleed, and wait for someone to finish me off. And watch the body of Leo Pannizer, the man who'd designed the Cup Train plan, attain room temperature.

That part was kind of a pleasure.

I must have dozed off at some point, because someone

touched my face to wake me up. I blinked. My eyes had trouble focusing.

Virtue. Virtue was kneeling next to me, getting her knees all bloody in the sodden carpet. Her hand felt warm and very good.

"You did well," she said, and her voice was trembling. "Zay. You did it. You made him pay the fare."

I wanted to nod, but instead, I found myself smiling. "You're welcome," I said. I felt distant, somehow. All but gone. I wondered if this was how Miss Naia Wade Lymon had felt as I was using her to get access to Mr. Pannizer. "Did it work?"

She swallowed, and tears bled down her cheeks. "Yes, it worked. Mr. Clark is the new CEO. You just stay still. Medical will be here soon. It's not as bad as that. I'll make sure you get fixed up just fine. He's promised you a promotion, Zay, you won't be a dogsbody anymore. . . ."

There was a commotion across the office, and a wave of people entered—black-coated drones, some higher-level Admins and executives, and in the center, Tarrant Clark, the new CEO. There wasn't a speck of dirt or blood on him.

He stepped right over Pannizer's body and said, to no one in particular, "See that his family is compensated according to the policy, and take care of the cleanup." People scrambled to see who could do his bidding first.

Not Virtue, though. She stayed right where she was, on her knees, looking up at him. Clark nodded to her. She nodded back, smiling a real and lovely smile through her tears.

"We did it, sir," she said. "Zay did it."

"Thank you, Virtue," he said. He still sounded calm and kind. "You've performed amazingly well. You have my sincere admiration for your skill, dedication, and resourcefulness. But you realize that the same qualities that made you so valuable on my way up make you a real liability now that I'm in power. Nothing personal. It's just business."

He nodded, and the dogsbody standing at his elbow pulled out a gun, aimed, and shot her once, in the head. She didn't have a shield on; she'd given me hers, and I'd spent it. The noise blotted out everything for a second, and then Virtue was down, a sprawled weight across my chest. I held on to her, the way I'd wanted to before, and I couldn't wrap my head around it. What had just happened? Virtue—Virtue was *dead*.

For *succeeding*.

"Him too," Clark said, and the dogsbody focused his aim on me now. Oddly enough, Clark still looked kind and sad and a little regretful. "You really gave exceptional service today, Zay," he said. "Thank you. I wish things could be different."

"Why?" My voice sounded thin, but surprisingly normal, all things considered. "Why kill *her*?"

"Because she was brilliant," he said. "And persistent. And sooner or later, she'd have realized that there were flaws in my story. I couldn't leave someone as deadly as Virtue Hardcastle at my back."

"So you lied," I said. I felt distant, only partly there, but some spark kept me going despite all the blood I'd lost, all the punishment. "It was you behind the Cup Train all along.

Should have shot you when I first saw you," I said.

"Yes, you probably should have. But I cultivated Virtue, and you trusted her," he told me. "Not your fault. You've served well, Zay. Both of you have. Thank you. I promise you, I'm going to do a complete ground-up reorganization in this place. You've made it possible for me to make things better."

I started laughing. I couldn't help it. Blood on my lips, Virtue dead in my arms, and I was *laughing*.

"Mr. Clark!" one of the Admins said urgently, and showed him a handheld. "Sir, something's—something's wrong."

Clark waved the handheld away impatiently. "Fix it. That's your job."

"Sir, I *can't*. Some kind of Company-wide blackout. Critical systems are failing, one after another. . . ." The Admin was on the verge of panic. It was real damn *funny*. "Sir, we've just lost missiles. And half the defense grid!"

They forgot about me, even Clark, and for a while there was a lot of suppressed panic, people running, shouting . . . chaos.

Virtue would have been so proud.

Something hit me across the face and startled me awake. I hadn't even realized I'd been resting until the pain came back. The world looked watery and thin, and I knew I didn't have very long now.

Clark was glaring at me. He looked years older now, and no longer sad or resigned. He looked *enraged*. "What the *hell* did you do? The systems are down, all of them are *down*! Tell me what you did!"

"Not me. Virtue. She built a fail-safe. You shot her, and

you triggered the program." I had to pause for breath, and coughed out a mouthful of salty blood. "Was supposed to be her revenge on Pannizer if he killed her to get to you. She never expected *you* to betray her." I watched his face and saw the shock sinking in. "So if you'd let her live, you wouldn't be CEO of a dying Company." I was short of breath now, bubbling blood in my ruined lung, but I laughed anyway and spit up red, right in his face. "For a first executive decision, it sucks."

He shot me, of course. Several times, which should have hurt but really didn't, as if my body had just given up on transmitting the messages. I felt the choke collar engage again, but distantly. And as I slipped off into a comforting, warm darkness, the last thing I heard was him shouting for people to *do something. Fix things.*

But they'd already been fixed, but good.

The last thing I felt was Virtue's body warm in my arms.

The last thought was, *This is the best day I've ever had on the job.*

Retirement came fast, but it came clean.

And that last sound, faint and sweet, was the sound of a CEO, screaming in pain, as the dogsbodies won.

PALE RIDER

Nancy Holder

SHARDS, ASHES, AND a freaking *carton* of batteries. Inside the dusty box, there were dozens of double-A six-packs.

Dana whooped, victorious. Lowering herself to a squat on the balls of her feet, she pushed back her dreads and caressed the treasure with her flashlight beam. Then she set the flashlight on its end so that the light bounced off the ceiling, picked up one of the packs, and wiped off the dust. She turned it over, examining it for an expiration date. The printing was too faded. She grabbed the flashlight and was just about to unscrew the head so she could test a sample battery when she heard the creak of a floorboard. She wasn't alone.

"Shit," she whispered. As quietly as she could, she clicked off her flashlight and stuck it into the pocket of her hoodie.

Then she grabbed the heavy carton and stood, listening. Her heart pounded.

Nothing. Maybe she had imagined it. Or the poor old house was settling some more.

She quietly shuffled out of the room. This was the third time in two weeks that she'd found batteries in places she and her roommates had already searched. She had just *known* to go inside the ramshackle house and step through the filth and the trash to what appeared to be a home office. Even though she and Jordan had been there before and had carted off anything usable. But this time, she could see the floorboards in her mind, and she'd pried them up.

In the disintegrating world, change was not usually your friend, but life had made an exception.

There was another creak, and then a growl, and something charged at her. She screamed and tore out of the room with her carton. Whatever it was, it followed her into the hall, kicking up years of dust and trash while she banged into the walls from side to side with the huge box. She kept yelling, barreling around a fallen door into pitch-black darkness.

My gun is in my other pocket, she thought.

She whirled around and tried to throw the carton at her attacker—where she thought it might be—but the box was too heavy and it just tumbled through the darkness to the floor. Stumbling backward, seeing nothing, she got the gun out of her other pocket and fired. The thing howled. Dog. Coyote. She fired a couple more shots and ran out of the house. The wooden porch gave way and she crashed downward through the rotted boards to her waist.

Bathed in amber moonlight, a mangy dog leaped out of the shadows. Dana was trapped. She let out a bellow as it launched itself at her.

It howled; then its limp body smacked against her right arm and it crumpled in a heap beside her. It didn't move. Panting with fear, she planted her palms on either side of her body, fingertips brushing the dog's dirty, matted fur. She pushed up and out of the hole, propelling herself to freedom as she flopped onto her front then threaded her legs free.

The dog was twitching and panting. *Oh, God, rabies.* Had it bitten her? With a shaking hand, she felt around for her gun, unsure when and where she'd lost it.

No luck.

She tested her footing. Nothing sprained or broken. She stepped back into the house, listening hard, feeling along the floor with the soles of her sneakers for the gun. She still couldn't find it. She could come back for it later, but there was no way she was going to leave the batteries. They were just too precious.

Ear cocked, she groped around for the carton, found it, and picked it up again. She was trembling. She didn't feel any pain. No bites, then. Hopefully.

A creak.

She turned back around to leave. Her knees gave way and she almost slid to the floor.

Silhouetted by moonlight, a man stood in the doorway. Spiky hair, long coat, boots. Her heartbeat went into overdrive.

His dog, she thought, cold and terrified. *He set it on me.*

They faced each other without speaking. She kept it together. You didn't live as long as she had—she was seventeen—by losing your cool. But she was very scared.

"I have a gun," she said.

He raised his hand. "This one?" he said in some kind of accent.

Oh, God. Oh, God, oh, God, she thought. This was what she got. Jordan had told her not to scavenge alone. But she had just *known* they had to get the batteries tonight. Jordan was down with a bug, and no one else had felt like going.

She licked her lips and raised her chin. "I have another gun."

"You can have this one back," he said. The accent was German. He sounded like a movie villain. He looked like one in his long coat. She felt naked in her sweatshirt, sneakers, and board shorts.

"Stay away from me. I'll call my guard dog on you," she said, but her voice cracked and she realized she was losing her grip on the carton. Icy sweat was streaming down her body.

"I mean you no harm, Delaney."

She jerked, even more afraid. That was her given name, and no one at the house knew it.

He raised his hands above his head, and she saw the outline of her gun. She didn't know what to do. Rush him? Run back into the darkness? Where there might be another dog?

Then suddenly, there was no carton in her arms. It was in his. And they were on the sidewalk outside the house.

"What the heck?" she said.

"Schon gut, keine angst."

He was very tall, not as old as she had thought—maybe five years older than her—and in the moonlight, she saw that his hair was blond. His eyes were light and he had a superhero face—flared cheekbones, square chin. Pierced eyebrow. Maybe that was a tat on his thumb. He was muscular, his long black wool coat stretching across big broad shoulders. These days, most people were a little too thin. Like her. She was all crazy black hair, brown eyes, and bones. "I got your name from your aunt. Well, from her things. I haven't actually met her."

"What aunt?" she asked him cautiously. She and her mom had kept to themselves until her mother's death three years ago. She didn't know any of her relatives.

"Aunt Meg." He waited for her reaction. The name meant nothing to her.

"She's white," he added.

Her stomach did a flip. Maybe this Aunt Meg was from her father's side. Dana didn't even know his name. Dana's mom had never told her white ex-boyfriend that she had gotten pregnant.

"What things?" she asked, catching her sneaker toe on a crack in the sidewalk. Their neighborhood looked like a bomb had gone off. Things fell apart all the time. She caught her toe again. Despite the heaviness of the box against his chest, he reached out a hand to steady her. His fingers were very warm and pale against her dark skin.

"Where is she?" she asked. "Aunt Meg?"

"She used to work for my family. In a manner of speaking." He took his hand away. "My distant relatives."

She stopped walking. "It was nice of you to Taser that dog and all, but just, you know, get to the point."

He stopped, too, and faced her. "It's a sad world when someone who knows a family member of yours is greeted with such hostility."

"This world is more than sad. I don't know that you *know* her," she countered. "You're just a name-dropper in a coat." When he kept looking at her as if that didn't compute, she said, "I need more proof."

He nodded. "Fair enough."

She looked to the right, at a boarded-up building, and had a funny feeling. His face came into her mind, and then there was something black and rectangular. She squinted as she walked, trying to make sense of it.

"Hey," said a voice, and she jerked her head up. She and the guy were standing in front of her house, which she shared with Jordan, Lucy, Mike, and Anny. The strays that had become family. Wrapped in his bathrobe and plaid pajama bottoms, Jordan was standing on the porch, shotgun pointed in their direction. "What's up?"

"We have a rule," she told the guy. "No strangers in the house. Ever."

He looked from her to Jordan and back again. "My name is Alex Ritter. There. I'm not a stranger. It's okay to let me in."

Jordan hesitated. "What?" he said fuzzily.

"It's okay," the guy—Alex—said again.

"Cool." Jordan nodded calmly and lowered the shotgun.

Dana was stunned. *"Jordan?"*

"It's really all right, Delaney," the man—Alex—said. "I swear it to you."

"It's not," she insisted. Too late, she remembered that he still had her gun. She bounded onto the porch beside Jordan and reached for the shotgun. "We don't know this guy. And he is *weird.*"

Jordan kept hold of the shotgun and opened the front door. "Come on in."

"Lucy!" Dana shouted. "Anny! Mike!"

Then they were in the house, and her four roommates were oohing and aahing over the carton of batteries, which Alex was doling out to them like Santa Claus with his bag of presents. Dana looked around wildly. She had lost more time. And this creepy man in black was inside her house.

"These things are over fifteen years old," Jordan marveled as he popped a couple of batteries into her flashlight, twisted the head back on, and gave it a flick. Light poured forth. She didn't remember giving it to him. "Awesome."

"They're warm," Lucy said, holding one between her hands. She leaned over and kissed Dana on the cheek. "You're made of fabulous."

"She chased away some dogs, too," Alex offered. Dana

glared at him. Everyone else was taking his sudden appearance in stride. Or maybe she had simply fast-forwarded through the introductions.

She held out a shaking hand. "Give me back my gun."

He did so, willingly, and she stuffed it into her pocket again. Then she turned her back and walked into the kitchen. Out of his line of sight, she slipped through the back door and flew down all the wooden stairs to the cool sand of the beach.

He followed, as she had expected him to, and she pulled out the gun. He looked from it to her face and sighed.

"If you shoot, you shoot," he said.

Then he walked to the water's edge and lifted his chin. "No seaweed," he said. "No seagulls."

But there was something on the beach, next to his boot. She spotted it at the same time that he looked down. He picked it up—tats all over that hand—and his palm blossomed with a pale bluish glow. Her eyes widened as he put the object in his pocket.

"Sea glass," he said, as if that should satisfy her.

He turned his face back to the black water. "I was out here earlier. One good thing about the end of the world: the sunsets are fantastic."

"This is Southern California. Our sunsets are always fantastic." She kept a good grip on the gun. "You'd better tell me what's going on."

"I'm Alex Ritter. From Germany. Berlin."

Despite herself, she was impressed. Eight years ago, people

traveled all over the place. But fuel was getting scarce. Her house didn't even have a car.

"I flew here," he added, as if reading her mind. "I have a plane."

"Holy shit," she blurted. There were still planes in the world. And they cost . . . she didn't even know what they cost. Too much to even think about.

He smiled faintly. His profile was sharply etched against the night. It didn't make any sense that Jordan had let him in, just like that, and everyone had behaved as if it was no big deal. It was a huge deal. He was scary.

"Dana, please, I'm sorry," he said abruptly, turning his face toward her. "There is no good way to have the talk I need to have with you. Let me show you."

Before she could reply, he wiped his face with both his hands and rubbed them together. He moved his head from side to side, as if working out the kinks; then he turned to the sea and opened his arms like an orchestra conductor.

Something hummed against the soles of her feet. A couple of her dreads bobbed in a freshet of wind.

Shimmering blue crackles of energy shot from his fingertips. Then the pulsating sparks traveled to the water and hit it with a sizzle. The waves rippled and flared blue, pink, gold like the aurora borealis, which she'd seen in one of the DVDs she'd found while scavenging.

Dana jumped backward so hard she landed on her butt, and she spastically lifted her sneakers as the water swirled toward her. It took her a moment to realize that he'd clasped her wrist and was pulling her to her feet.

"Don't touch me," she said as she tried to yank her hand away. He was bending over her; there were rings under his eyes and his pupils were dilated. He was jittery and shaky, like he was on something.

She looked from his eyes to the water. The colors were gone. Her mind started spinning rationalizations and denials. She was spooked by the way he cocked his head and gazed at her with an odd, confused expression, like he was trying to remember what to say.

"I don't know how else to tell you this," he said. "But I think it was your Aunt Meg who made all this happen." He waved his hand. "All the chaos. The . . . ending."

"What?" she blurted. "How?" She backed away from him, now holding the gun in both her hands; behind him, the black, colorless surf rolled into the night.

"I don't know how," he said, so softly she barely heard him. "But please, for the love of God, help me fix it."

Then he advanced on her and pushed down her arms. She tried to raise them again but she couldn't. He cupped her face in his hands. Dizziness swept through her and she dropped the gun. He held her still, and she could feel him falling right into her, inside her mind. There was nothing but his blue eyes.

Then warmth raced through her, zinging through her bloodstream, and she began to sweat again. The soles of her sneakers made hissing sounds against the damp sand. Sparks skittered through her veins and arteries.

Then she shot like a comet into the air, into space, among the stars, away from the messed-up world. Suspended above the night, she gazed down and saw Los Angeles in ruins, the way it was, and a huge bloom of red surging toward the shore.

Toward her beach, just below her house.

And then she saw, in that house, two tiny dots of light. She looked at the dot in the kitchen. It was behind the refrigerator, and as it magnified in her mind, she saw Anny's missing house key. She moved on and found Jordan's reading glasses between the couch cushions.

She jerked to consciousness, to find that she was sprawled in the sand. He was on his hands and knees, his face close to hers, and when he saw that her eyes were opening, he leaned back on his heels with a deep sigh of relief.

"What did you do to me?" she shouted, trying to get up. But her muscles were strangely flaccid.

"I think I activated your gift," he replied. She could hear how freaked out he was.

"You *think you what?*" She felt in the sand for the gun.

"What happened?" he asked.

"You know what happened." He just looked at her, and she huffed. "I saw things. First the world, and the mess." She thought of the mass headed for the beach. "Garbage, or something. And lost things."

She told him about the keys and the glasses. He nodded, looking thoughtful. Then she saw a faint glow around him.

She said, "Did you make those things glow so I could find them?"

"No. I can use energy, in some ways," he said. "Like on the dog."

"And on me."

"I'm sorry," he said.

"And you can make people like you."

"Only when they should," he replied.

"*I* don't like you," she said.

And suddenly she was overcome with weariness. She couldn't keep her eyes open. As they drifted shut, she said, "I think you left your wallet in a building on my street."

He was quiet for a moment.

"Thank you," he said finally, into the muzziness of her sleep.

When she woke up just before dawn, she liked him a little more, which was terrifying, because she didn't want to like him at all. He had explained that he'd just found out some unbelievable things—that some kind of supernatural power ran in his family and apparently in hers, too. All his people were missing or dead, but some of them had lived in a castle in the Black Forest. And as soon as he'd gotten inside the castle, he'd turned into Mr. Electric.

Then they were in the house, and he was helping Jordan pull out the refrigerator—a useless appliance except for keeping rats out of boxed food—so Anny could find her house key.

Jordan was overjoyed to find his glasses again. There was no one around to make him new ones.

She put all her own valuables in boxes and Jordan promised to keep an eye on them. Then, with shaking hands, she packed a suitcase. Alex was making her be okay with all this. She could tell. She wanted to make him stop, but she was doing it.

And then she was saying good-bye.

They got his wallet and then he walked her into an alley, where a vehicle sat beneath a protective covering. He pulled it off, revealing a beautiful candy-apple-red Corvette. She hadn't ridden in a car in years. Something loosened in her chest as she slid in on the passenger side. The car smelled of old leather and dust. When they climbed in, he pressed his finger against the ignition, and the engine purred.

"I couldn't find the keys," he said. "Do you see them?"

She narrowed her eyes at him. "Is this some kind of test?"

He shook his head, watching her.

Settling back, she let her lids fall shut. A blur of light passed through her mind's eye; then she felt a stab of sorrow, deep and penetrating. It hurt almost like a physical wound. She opened her eyes and looked at Alex.

"There's something about the keys that's sad," she said.

"The keys are sad?" he repeatedly slowly. As they glided out of the alley, he knit his brows. "In the sense of . . . ?"

"I don't know; I just felt sadness." She crossed her arms

over her chest. "Did you put some kind of double whammy on me?"

"I don't really know what I did to you," he replied.

His jet was bigger than she'd pictured it. It was parked in what had once been a parking lot for the beach. Ready to go, it could cross the Atlantic nonstop. She sat to his right in the cockpit. He took off his coat, revealing lots of muscles and a black T-shirt. His right arm was completely tattooed. Tats on the left went up to his elbow. It didn't make sense that a guy who looked like him would have access to a Corvette and a plane, and that she was flying to Germany with him.

But it didn't make sense that in eight short years, the world had fallen completely apart. First everyone talked about fuel reserves and no TV, no grid, no net, and very few people. It was as if things were melting. Evaporating. As if the world itself was losing time—or running out of it.

They climbed. She looked down at the coastline. The ocean and sky were the same color. Skyscrapers had collapsed. Streets were broken up. There were no birds. Her mother was buried somewhere below her, in a grave not far from their house because, without transportation, they couldn't get her to a graveyard.

Her throat tightening, she brushed tears from her eyes and focused, trying to see her mother's grave in her mind. What she saw was her mother's face, deep black; her lips, so brown, pulled back from white teeth in a smile.

Her throat tightened. She gripped the armrest so hard the beds of her fingernails stung.

"Why did I come with you?" she asked him through tears.

He was quiet for a moment. Then he said, "Why did I come get you?"

Hours later, they began their descent through a sky the color of old copper. The sun was beginning to set. Snow was falling onto skeletons of trees and vast deadfalls. Anticipation skittered through her as his castle came into view. It sat on a hill, as he had said. Half of it had been destroyed; the other half rose into the aged, metallic sky.

They landed and rolled to a stop. Alex had explained that he'd been adopted by a wealthy couple named Aaron and Maria Cohen. They had been on a trip to Greece when the Collapse occurred. That was what he called it. Explosions, earthquakes, riots. Eight years of looking for them. Finally he'd found a key, and then a bank safe-deposit box. There were his adoption papers, saying that he had been born in a town called Ritterburg, in the heart of the Black Forest. He'd lived in the castle for three months before he'd come to get Dana.

"Here we are," he said, sounding nervous.

Alex had brought a little foldable ladder. She didn't really need it. As she climbed down, he retrieved her suitcase and his black duffel. A gritty brown wind brushed over her. Strips of faded blue cloth dangled from flagpoles at the top of the castle, and somewhere a hinge squeaked back and forth in the bitter wind.

Neither one of them spoke as he led the way to the castle. With his long coat and boots, he looked like Neo from *The Matrix*. There were patches of snow on the ground. They were gray and they kind of smelled, but it was the first snow she had ever seen.

Alex put his hand on the small wooden door cut into the larger, older door, to push it open. The rectangle of wood hung in the air for a second, then disintegrated, falling to the snow in a heap of fine ash. He pulled back his hand and stared at the space where the door had been.

"Shit," he said. "Things are getting worse."

"No kidding," she murmured.

He crossed the threshold, and she reluctantly—so very reluctantly—followed him in. There wasn't much left. No roof, piles of stone and rubble, blackened walls stretching up hundreds of feet.

"I've got all the stuff in my room," he said. "Books, research."

Her cheeks warmed. "Do I have a room?"

"*Ja.*" His smile stretched into a grin. "Just across the hall from mine."

"You were pretty sure of yourself when you came to find me," she muttered, crossing her arms over her chest. She didn't like this place. Things were tapping for her attention just beneath her consciousness, whispering just a little too softly for her to hear.

He looked over at her. "I cast a lot of magics to find you, Dana. I didn't know if you would come, but I wanted to make sure you would feel welcome."

"You could just work a spell on me," she said. "The way you did back in LA."

"I'm sorry about that," he said. "I wasn't proud of it."

His manga-man black coat billowed around his legs as he crossed the marble floor. Most of the black-and-white squares had been smashed. He led her down a narrow passage bordered on either side by piles of wood and stone. There was more roof there, blocking out the light. Flicking on a flashlight, he led the way. It was icy, and she wrapped one hand around the other. She became aware that a low-level sadness—no, it was despair tinged with anger—crept up the backs of her legs like a needy, starving dog. Freaked out, she glanced over her shoulder, seeing nothing.

"Something's here," she announced. "I feel it."

"What? What do you feel?" he asked, sounding excited. He painted the walls with the beam from his flashlight.

She told him.

"Maybe it's a ghost?" he said.

"*Maybe?*" she echoed, alarmed. "Damn it, Alex."

He opened a door, pulling back his hand quickly as if he expected it to fall apart the way the front door had. His flashlight passed over a stone floor, swept clean. He moved to a table and lit a trio of candles, except she didn't see a lighter or a match.

He handed a candle to her. In the soft glow, she saw him

open his palm, and a small ball of light appeared.

"I'm not clear what your 'gift' is," she said.

"One of them is light," he replied. "At least, I think it is. I'm on my own figuring all this out."

They moved toward a bed dressed in a thick, furry coverlet and topped with a stack of pillows. Unhappiness rose around her like a mist.

"This place is bad," she said. "Let's get out of here."

"Bad," he said. "How—"

She pushed past him, not willing to stay inside. He joined her in the hall.

"Better?" he asked.

"Not really." She looked left and right. "What happened here?"

"They were attacked, as far as I can tell." He made a face. "There are a lot of bones. And cages." He pointed to an open door. "That's my room."

"*Bones?* I think we should leave," she said. "We'll get the stuff you need from here and go somewhere else."

"Hmm," he answered noncommittally.

There was a sleeping bag on the floor of his room, and a heavy wooden table. Stacks and stacks of leather-bound books and several open boxes littered the surface. Candles, crystals, and herbs were spilling out of the boxes.

"Oh, my God," she said. It would take them days to cart all of it out of the castle.

"*Ja*, you see," he replied.

Then he walked to the table and placed his palm on a black book with scrolled gold writing that she couldn't read.

"I don't know what it says, either," he told her as he flipped it open. There was a loose photograph of a woman with red hair, red eyebrows, and big blue eyes. She was wearing a cat-suit and body armor strapped over that. She had a black helmet on her hip with ZECHERLE in white. He tapped his finger on the lettering. "That's your aunt's last name. Maybe it's your father's, too."

Delaney Zecherle. Her mom's last name was Martin. Her mom's first name had been Tenaya.

He turned the page, edged a small photograph from the crease with his thumbnail, and handed it to her.

She caught her breath at the sight of herself as a little girl in a school picture, grinning away, with no notion of what was to come. She was missing her two front teeth.

"I was six," she said.

She turned over the picture. The handwriting was careful; she read, *Delaney Martin (Dana)*. And the address of their house, the one she was still living in with Jordan and the others. Then, *(your niece!)*.

"Is that your mother's handwriting?" Alex asked her.

She shook her head. "I don't know. We never wrote anything down."

Feelings she couldn't describe swept upward, making her feel out of kilter. She stared at the handwriting, then at the picture. Her heart tugged.

"This was . . . before," she said.

"*Ja*," he said.

They stood shoulder to shoulder, looking down at the Delaney that had been. Stuffed animals and Disneyland—those had been her hopes and dreams. She felt the heat of his skin and wondered what his life had been like with the Cohens. Jets and flying lessons?

"From what I can tell, your aunt was only here for a couple of weeks before everything went crazy," he said.

There were some burned fragments of lined paper. She put down the picture and carefully sorted through them. She looked at a piece of paper.

> things to do
> learn german

On another, she read, I think something's going on downstairs. Something wrong.

She turned another page of the book, to see photographs of other people dressed like Meg Zecherle. They looked like riot police.

"Those were her teammates," Alex said. "They were some kind of security guards. They patrolled along a place called the Pale."

"What's that?" she asked.

"A border. They had to keep something out. I think it got in."

She looked at the massive volumes. "All this, and that's all you've got?"

"Most of this is written in Latin. I think. I think some is very old German." He opened a book at random. "Here or there I found something I could read. Spells." He looked abashed. "Imagine if you came here. Would you know what to do?"

They shared a grim smile. "There's nothing more about . . . us?" she asked, not sure which "us" she meant.

"Maybe you can find something," he said. "There *is* something," he went on, reaching for another book. Bound in maroon leather, it was enormous.

He opened it to the first page. There was a black-and-white woodblock print of a man in a three-cornered hat on a horse, with a small child clasped against his chest. The horse was cantering through the night. Clouds billowed in the background, and in the largest of them, a shadowy face smiled wickedly down at the riders.

Alex pointed to lines of text beneath the picture. It was organized in stanzas like a poem, and he began to read aloud, in German. She listened to his voice.

"It's 'Der Erlkönig,'" he said. "'The Erl King.' Do you know it? 'Who rides so late, through night and wind'?" When she shook her head, he said, "I keep coming back to this picture. I keep reading the poem. I don't know why."

"What is it about?"

"The child is sick. The father is riding with him through

the forest, and the Erl King wants him. The boy can see him. The father can't. He begs his father to save him from the Erl King. But he doesn't."

"Cheery," she said.

The despair tugged at her again, almost like someone pulling on her hand. Anger skittered ratlike up her spine, and she stepped away from the table.

"Delaney?" he asked.

Freaked, she looked around the room. "Is this place haunted?"

"I don't know." His expression told her he had come to a decision. "The town's deserted. We can look for a place—"

A sharp stab of light replaced his face. She saw a circular stone stairway. Saw herself walking down it behind Alex.

She brushed past him and went into the hall. Her thought was to go back out the front door, but instead, she turned in the opposite direction, into the pitch-blackness.

Light flared behind her. She heard the thudding of his boots, and then he was beside her. He had a flashlight. He said something to her in German, gave his head an impatient shake.

"English, English," he said to himself. "What is happening?" he asked her.

"There's something down there," she said, halting before a hole in the floor at the end of the hall. "I saw it. It's a cage."

He was quiet for a moment. Then he said, "There are a lot of cages down there. But you wanted to leave, and I think we should. We can come back."

She nodded. He was right.

But then it happened again: the flash of light. The cage.

And the horrible, horrible despair. Cold, miserable, alone. Dying.

Pleading.

"I think I have to go down there," she said hesitantly.

"Okay, here," he said, turning and aiming the flashlight at a curved stone wall, then downward at a circular flight of stone stairs. "I'll go first."

He started down, taking the flashlight beam with him. She followed for a couple of steps, but then she froze. There was no banister, and she pushed herself against the wall, afraid she'd fall off the edge of the staircase and never stop falling. She was no Alice, and this was no Wonderland. Grief wafted up from the depths below and twisted around her, like people drowning on the *Titanic*. She recoiled and crossed her arms.

She headed back up.

Then suddenly, rage poured right in, crashing over her head.

Just go down and kick him. Kick him hard, and he'll fall down the stairs and break his neck. It was as if someone else inside her was whispering commands. Raging because he was the enemy, and the end of the world was *his* fault.

"Alex," she said, swallowing hard.

Oblivious, he kept going.

She took another step up.

Kill him. They lied. They told us we were doing a great thing. But we were not.

She teetered on the step and went back down. The rage ebbed. Another step down. It faded.

Another.

It was gone.

"Alex, wait," she said. "There's something bad. Really bad."

He was standing at the bottom of the stairs. She got to him, and to her surprise, he put his arm around her protectively.

"There's something that's angry. It told me to . . . ," she began. And then realized that she didn't really know this guy, and she had watched him charm his way into her home.

"To what?" he asked.

What the hell am I doing? she thought. She felt as if she were waking up after a long, strange dream.

"It told me to leave," she lied. "And I think—"

And then she felt the sorrow and the terror. It was longing and keening and fear. She thought she heard a moan and caught her breath. Was someone down here? Someone alive?

"I think we should hurry," she said.

"You're okay, though?" he asked.

"Does it matter?" she snapped, because she was afraid of him. "Why don't you just zap me so I'll do your bidding, master?"

He knit his brows and took his arm away, exhaled, and ran

his hand across his forehead. She saw how tired he was. He'd just flown halfway across the world, for God's sake. But she hadn't asked him to. She hadn't asked for any of this.

He reached out a hand toward her, then lowered it. The flashlight beam glinted off the piercing in his eyebrow. No, not the beam. There was light around him, as if he were glowing from the inside. His eyes were almost luminescent.

"I feel like you're supposed to be here. And *ja*, I pushed to make that happen. If things were different I would *never* have invaded you. . . ." He shrugged. "But they're not."

"Invaded?" she repeated.

He walked on. She walked behind him, staring at the back of his head, at his shoulders. She could almost see tendrils connecting her to him. She didn't feel like she was supposed to be in the castle, but she did feel like she was supposed to be with him. Was that his doing? Was he leading her down there to do something to her?

No, she thought, but how did she know that?

At the bottom of the next landing, a white strip gleamed. Luminous paint. There was a sign in German. EINTRITT VERBO-TEN. She knew *verboten* meant "forbidden."

The sorrow came back. A silver trickle of strange sounds, like wind chimes, breathed against her ear.

"**__*_*_."

Twinkling like starlight.

"**__*_*_."

And she knew it meant "Mama."

"Hello?" she called out.

"Delaney?" Alex said.

"Shh," she ordered. She listened hard.

"**__."

Mama.

"Where are you?" she whispered.

Silence. And . . . weeping, and then a kind of gasping, like strangling. And another voice, higher-pitched:

"__****."

Help.

She ran forward, past Alex, who tried to reach out a hand to her. Then she stood at the beginning of a double row of cubes, or boxes, that stretched far into the darkness. The sounds were all around her now, coming from the boxes. Whispers, cries for help. Help that never came.

She ran to the closest one and stood facing it. There were bars across the front, and what appeared to be shattered glass in a semicircle on the floor. The moan again:

"********."

She felt emotions: Loneliness, misery. Shock. They hadn't expected this to happen to them. Something else was supposed to have happened. Someone else was supposed to be waiting for them. Whatever had been in here had been abandoned, dumped into cells.

"It's evil. So evil," she said.

Then her knees buckled. She felt her eyes roll back in her head. Light blossomed in front of her, reaching to the ceiling in ribbons of color, like the aurora borealis Alex had conjured on the ocean. Shadows appeared, then snapped into sharp silhouettes. Misshapen figures rode huge black horses whose hooves sparked as they galloped six inches above the ground. Tiny, gibbering *things* crouched on the saddles. Dogs, breathing fire, wove in and out between the horses' legs as they cantered along a hill. At the head of the parade, a tall figure wearing a helmet decorated with two enormous antlers turned to look at her.

The deepest fear she had ever felt shot through her soul.

Then everything vanished.

Wordlessly, Alex picked her up and carried her out of the room. Up all the flights of stairs, to the main floor of the castle; and there she felt the rage again. *Kick him. Stab him. Kill him.* He raced across the marble floor and through the rubble and the ash of the doorway. Out to the leveled forest, in the gray, smelly snow.

He set her down on a rock and bent down in front of her. He took both her hands in his. They were cold.

"Are you all right now?" he asked her.

She blinked at him. "What was in there?" she asked him. "And what were the things with the horses?"

"Horses?" He looked bewildered. "What did you see?"

She told him. Then, still not sure it was the right thing to do, she told him about the rage.

"It told you to kill me?" he repeated, the blood draining from his face. "That I was a liar?"

She nodded.

He made a face and muttered in German. Then he said, "I guess it's haunted." His shoulders rounded, and he patted her hand as he got up and plopped down beside her. He gestured to the castle. "I don't think the answer is there." He clicked his teeth and scratched his chin. "I thought you would find it."

She was quiet a moment. Then she said, "You glowed. When I looked at you, I saw light."

"I'm Mr. Electric," he said. He opened his arms. Blue crackles shot from his fingertips. "We can go back to your home. I can make your refrigerator work."

She heard the disappointment in his voice. "But Alex, something *was* going on with your family. They did something bad. And maybe we're here to fix it."

"You can't go back in there," he said.

"I think I have to," she replied, feeling sick to her stomach at the thought.

"But not tonight." He sighed. "I have a car. We can go to the village."

It was a Mercedes; why was she surprised? They didn't even go back for their stuff. They drove into the deserted village. Some shops were still filled with goods; they got toothbrushes and food and changes of clothes. Sheets in packages. They broke into an inn and commandeered two rooms. She wasn't sure which would make her feel better, to sleep in the same room or apart. She wasn't sure of anything. She remembered how great it had felt to find that carton of batteries. It felt like that had happened to someone else. Not here, anyway.

"What did you want out of life, before I came for you?" he asked her, as they shared a bottle of wine—she really wasn't much of a drinker—and ate some canned baba ghanoush. They were sitting on his bed. He was wearing a pair of black drawstring pajama bottoms and a gray T-shirt. She had on an oversized T-shirt and leggings. Not very glamorous, but in a way, that was better.

"Batteries," she said. "Endless quantities of them."

He smiled crookedly. "I'm older than you. I was laying plans for my adult life. We were really rich."

"Did you, um, have a girlfriend?"

"I always had a girlfriend." He waggled his eyebrows and sipped from their bottle. "I was going to follow in my father's footsteps, be rich, then save the rain forest."

"I think you added that last part to make yourself sound more noble." She thought about the voice in the castle telling her that he was a liar. Maybe it had lied.

He handed her the bottle, and she cradled it in her lap. "I wanted my mom not to die. And I wanted to meet my father." Her voice dropped. "And I wanted to be safe."

"I think you need your own bottle of wine," he drawled. "Because you got nothing on the list."

"Are you saying I'm not safe with you?" she asked. She meant to tease him, but her voice shook.

He blew the air out of his cheeks. She wanted to take it back, but she decided to let it hang there, and see how he responded.

"I think," he said, "that we should go to sleep."

But she was too afraid to sleep. She went to her own room and lay down, but she felt too vulnerable that way. She paced, wondering if Alex was awake.

From her window, she could see the castle, and she made a face at it, like a little kid. She never wanted to go in there again. But her purse was in there. Her clothes. She hoped Jordan remembered to take good care of her stuff. She had her mom's jewelry, meager as it was, and some souvenirs from the days before—report cards, birthday cards, a Barbie doll, and her favorite stuffy, Clown Bear.

Sighing, she leaned her head on the glass. Coolness pressed against her cheek and then the sky exploded into colors. Blue, pink, purple, shimmering and flaring; she stared, transfixed, as gray clouds billowed into being. The moon rose and became the face in the book Alex had shown her. Staring at her. Whispering to her, in words she didn't understand. In a rising and falling voice, like someone reciting a poem. She put her hand on the glass and felt such a *pull*.

"Alex!" she shouted.

She heard him spring out of his bed and race across the hall. Within seconds, he was standing beside her.

"I see it!" he cried. "That's the Pale. I know it. I can feel it."

"The face is the Pale?" she asked.

He cocked his head. "What face?"

She pointed. It was staring at them both.

No, it wasn't.

It was staring at Alex.

She looked at him. He was bathed in moonlight, every inch of him. His skin, his hair, his eyes.

She told him, and he held out his arms. "I don't see it," he said. He gazed back through the window. "Delaney, what if *I'm* the lost thing that you were supposed to find?"

And she didn't know why—maybe because he was afraid—but she put her arms around him. His body was very solid. He was staring out the window; now he gave her his attention. She rose on her tiptoes and brushed his lips with hers. Cautiously, he kissed her back. Just the one kiss, chaste, and then she unloosened her arms.

"Just when it couldn't get any weirder," she said, and he chuckled. Then his smile faded.

"I think we should drive toward those lights. Now," he said.

As soon as they got into the car, it began to rain. Wind blew. Alex turned on the windshield wipers as he drove back through the town, to the castle, then past it too, as the lights intensified.

Nothing whispered to her.

"Did I mention that you're very pretty?" he said. "I like your dark skin."

The raindrops painted shadowy tattoos on his face, and

she wondered if he had them in other places, too.

"I like your tats."

"*Danke*," he said.

The rain came down, and she thought about her mom, and as she often did, the faceless man who had been her father.

The lights filled the sky; it seemed that if they drove forward any farther, they would drive into them. Alex stopped the car, and she opened her door.

He came around to her side of the car and laced his fingers through hers. As if on cue, it stopped raining. The earth rumbled beneath her feet. Shadows billowed against the colors, gauzy and diffuse. They started to coalesce and thicken, taking on the shapes she had seen in the castle, by the cages.

"Oh, God," she whispered. He squeezed her hand. She couldn't squeeze back. She was too terrified.

The flares of color vanished, and a figure on a massive horse faced them. It was dressed in ebony chain mail covered with a black chest plate. Its black helmet was smooth, with no eyeholes and topped with curved antlers that flared with smoky flames; fastened at the shoulders, a cloak furled behind like the wake of an obsidian river. In its right chain-mail gauntlet, it held the reins of the horse. Its left arm was raised, and another hand in a gauntlet rested on its fist—that of a rider beside it.

The rider beside it was smaller, dressed much like the other, except that red hair hung over its shoulders. Then it reached up its free hand and pushed back the faceplate of its helmet. It was the woman in the picture. Meg Zecherle.

Her aunt.

She stared at Dana, sweeping her gaze up and down. "Delaney?" she said softly. "Dana? Is that you?"

Alex stepped in front of Dana, placing himself between her and Meg.

"Honey, I have so much to tell you," Meg said, ignoring him. "I was so glad when your mom found me. I was going to come for you. But then . . ." She exhaled. "Then it all happened."

Tears welled in Dana's eyes and she opened her mouth, but Meg held up her hand and turned to the black figure. It inclined its head. Meg seemed to be listening to it. Then she turned her attention back to Dana.

"I'm sorry, but we'll have to save that for later. But we will talk. I promise."

"Just tell me who my father is," Dana said.

"He was a good man," Meg replied. "But, honey, he passed away before you were born."

"Oh." Her voice was tiny. Tears welled, and she knew right then that that was what she had wanted her life to be like, before. She'd wanted to have a dad. That would have been her magic.

"I'm sorry," Alex murmured.

She nodded, a tear spilling down her cheek.

"You're going to have to believe a lot of things that will sound pretty crazy," Meg said.

Dana wiped her cheek. "I think you can skip ahead."

"Okay, but if you need me to slow down, just tell me."

"We will," Alex said.

Meg leaned forward in her saddle. "There was a war. A terrible war, between two magical races. What we might call fairies are known as the fair folk. And the other side are the goblins."

Dana pressed her fingertips over her eyes. She could feel herself tensing, as if bracing herself to hear things she was incapable of handling. She began to shake. Alex put his arm around her waist and pulled her protectively against his side. She did the same. She needed someone to hang on to.

"Hostages were taken on both sides. Infant children, since their code of war demanded that children could never be harmed.

"Finally, it was over. A truce was declared. They agreed to exchange hostages. One baby of the fair folk for one goblin, every Midsummer's Eve, until there were no more. That way, peace would be kept until both sides were made whole.

"For years, my lord faithfully brought a captive goblin baby and laid it in the cradle in the forest," she said, inclining her head in the direction of the tall, black figure. "From the other cradle beside it, he would take the fair child left by his goblin counterpart, and bring it home."

Her lord? Dana thought, with a sudden rush of panic. The stranger who was her aunt called the thing beside her such an archaic name?

"One Midsummer's Night, the local nobleman was riding through the forest. From a hiding place, he saw the exchange. Months later, his wife gave birth to a tiny, sickly girl. The nobleman remembered the swap, and the next Midsummer Night's Eve, he replaced the fair child with his own. What he didn't know was that his baby carried a plague."

"Your . . . lord . . . took the plague back with him to the fairies," Dana ventured, and Meg nodded.

"The humanness of the child went undetected because it was so sick. Nearly all the fair folk died, but the goblin babies in their care seemed to be immune. War threatened to break out again, but the goblins were able to prove that they had had nothing to do with what had happened. But they used the plague as leverage. They demanded the immediate release of all their children. The fair folk couldn't care for them anyway, and asked the goblins to keep their own children safe as well, until the plague was gone."

Dana pictured the cages. "But the humans took the goblin babies instead."

"The noble and his lackeys trapped some of them before the goblins arrived to collect them," Meg said. "In all the confusion, the count was off, and neither side realized it."

"But that happened, when?" Alex said.

"Eight hundred years ago," Meg replied.

Alex's arm tightened around Dana.

"But if they were in those cages all that time," Dana said, "wouldn't they grow up?"

"They only age in their own realm. On this plane, they stayed babies. Miserable. Lonely. Unloved. For centuries."

"*Scheiss*," Alex murmured.

"Alex didn't know," Dana said quickly, and she knew that to be true. She knew he was good. And that she was safe with him. "About any of it."

Meg nodded. "I believe you. I was recruited by the Ritters to guard the place where we're standing. The Pale. The border between magic and nonmagic worlds. They said it was flimsy. Things were getting across that shouldn't."

She looked over at the figure beside her. "What they were worried about was the Erl King. They were afraid that he'd find out about the goblins in the castle dungeon."

"*The Erl King?* Holy shit, Alex," Dana blurted.

"*Ja*," he said, and uttered a string of German.

Meg looked a little confused, but she continued. "The Ritter elders never told anyone the truth. But I found out. I saw the cages. And I busted their lie wide open."

"It was *revenge?*" Alex's voice shook. "The goblins destroyed the whole world because of something my family did hundreds of years ago?"

"It was a rescue mission. Fair folk and goblin. *Your* people fought back," she said to Alex. "During the battle, some of them found out and joined our side. But by then, the Pale had fallen. Magic poured into this world and overwhelmed it."

For a moment no one spoke. Dana found Alex's hand and held it.

Meg's features softened. "Magic made our world sick. The fair folk baby that was stolen was the first domino. The goblins toppled next. What happened would have happened eventually. But not for a long time."

"And the fair folk baby survived," Alex said.

"And had children. And they had children. And that means . . ." Meg's voice trailed off.

"There is still magic in the world." Dana looked at her trembling hands. "As long as we're here."

Alex twined his fingers with hers. "But even if we leave, how many will be left?"

Meg sighed. "We don't know. We don't even know how to find them."

Dana raised her head. The flames on the Erl King's helmet flickered in the night wind. A flake of ash fluttered away, and as she thought about all that he must have lost, too, it began to glow.

She whispered so quietly it seemed as if the wind took her words away, "I find lost things."

CORPSE EATERS

Melissa Marr

HARMONY STOOD OUTSIDE the immense vat of viscous liquid. It looked remarkably like a cross between an aquarium and one of the coffee dispensers at every church dinner she remembered. Inside it, corpses floated. The water was thick with things she didn't want to identify.

"Get out." Chris grabbed her arm and pulled her away from the tank.

She looked past him to where the PBX was attached. The explosives were precious, used only when essential, but this *was* one of the essentials. The body of a girl about her age floated on the other side of the wall where the hole would be.

"*Now*, Harm!" He shoved her toward the door. "You were to be gone by now."

Silently, she apologized to the dead girl for the imminent

explosion—and the damage it would do to her body. On the other hand, it wasn't as if her body would be treated with respect if they didn't do this. She was food now, meat and skin consumed by the creatures that Harmony's group opposed.

The explosions farther into the warehouse began. Hopefully, they'd draw enough attention that she and Chris could escape. Hopefully, only a few of the Nidos would be between them and the door. Hopefully, the monsters wouldn't win today.

"Come on," Chris whispered.

They moved closer to the exit and ducked behind a stack of boxes. His hold on her arm hadn't loosened; she suspected it wouldn't unless he had to fight. It wasn't that she was reckless, not really. It was just that the only time she felt like life mattered was when she was taking something from the Nidos. They'd taken everything from her, from everyone who lived in North America. She liked taking *something* from them.

The sounds of slithering and harsh words echoed through the warehouse. The Nidos were heading toward the explosions. Those explosions were distractions, larger charges causing destruction, but as soon as the vat blew, the Nidos would come.

She felt it as it blew, a smallish explosion in comparison to the others they'd set. The crack in the glass was almost as loud. The fluid began to pour from the hole, and as it did, the crack widened.

They were at the door as the gush of water and human

remains flowed into the warehouse.

"Faster!" she urged Chris. A fight she could enjoy, but being doused with a soup of decaying bodies was the stuff of nightmares.

It was foolishness, but she closed the door behind them.

As if sealing away the sight of it will change anything.

There were two Nidos outside the door, but Chris wasn't willing to waste time on them. He lifted the sawed-off shotgun he had slung across his back and emptied both barrels into the Nido on his side.

"Got you," she said as she threw herself on the back of the second one. The satisfying sensation of slicing his throat wide open wasn't enough, but it helped her feel like all would be right in the world.

He bucked as he died, and she smiled.

When she released him, Chris was frowning at her.

"What?"

"Nothing, Harm." He gestured at the street. "Move before more come."

"I'm gone." She took off in a jog.

When Chris caught up with Harmony, he was exhausted, not from the run or from their work at the warehouse but from the fear that came from watching her take stupid chances. She could've shot the Nido. They both had emergency guns. She didn't even consider drawing hers.

"You're on streetside." He saw her sheepish look, but it only lasted for a blink. Then she shrugged and gestured for him to take the left side, closer to the dark alleyways and shadowed alcoves.

He didn't look at her as they walked, but he couldn't ignore the conversation they needed to have. "Do you try to get injured?"

"Nope."

"You know they have a few openings for transfer to the Midwest." Chris steered her farther from an open trunk on a relatively new sedan.

Harmony circled the car, peering in the windows. "And do what?"

They continued down the street. "You could work in one of the research centers, help with the trainees. It's safer there."

"I'm not qualified. I don't get why . . ."

Chris stopped and held a finger to his lips. She grinned in anticipation of trouble.

He stepped into the mouth of the alley and moved toward the rustling coming from a pile of boxes.

Harmony eased closer.

An old man with rheumy eyes crouched in a nest of cardboard; he remained motionless as they approached.

Chris stepped up to the man, but not within his reach. "It's not safe here."

"Should I go to a nursing home?" The old man rose on his spindly legs and gazed in the general direction of Chris' face. "The caretakers'll send me to the creatures soon as I get sick."

Harmony's voice was soft, neither threatening nor reassuring to anyone who didn't know her, as she said, "No. You should get out of town, preferably at night when they aren't as active."

The old man snorted. "You think? I'm not a fool, but I can't see well enough to drive out, especially in the dark." Bracing himself against the wall, he tottered forward. "But I have a car."

"Really?" Chris examined him more carefully. Cars weren't easy for anyone to keep, especially vagrants.

The old man cackled. "Well, maybe not *have*, but I can start one if you help me drag the fuel out to it." He nudged a piece of cardboard with his foot. It slid to the side, revealing a dirty jug. "Got three jugs saved up. You help me carry the fuel out to one of them cars, and I can wire it."

Chris studied the man and saw no telltale signs of deceit: his clothes were unkempt, his eyes white with cataracts. His health was pretty far gone. The Center had yet to find a case where Nidos sacrificed culinary tastes for strategy.

He glanced at his partner.

"We'll help you," she said.

After a bit of fumbling around, the old man picked up two of his jugs.

Cautiously, Harmony stepped forward and grabbed the third. Chris' already tense muscles stiffened. Their work was always the sort of thing that required all of his attention, but lately, it seemed like every day they were on duty was busier. Being on the front line of the fight was a sure way to see the daily proof that the humans weren't winning this war.

As they moved away from the shadows of the alley, the

man didn't bother to wipe the tears that fell. His voice was low as he said, "I know I'm old, but that isn't any way to die."

"I know," Harmony murmured. "You're not going to die in a vat. Right?"

"Right," Chris promised. They'd get the man to safety, one person saved, and then Chris would go home and get drunk for the two days he had off.

By the time night fell on her second day off, Harmony thought she was going to climb the wall. The down days were to help them recover, rest, and work out. She did all of that—and she still felt like she would go crazy if she didn't *move*. The calm that had come from the last days of work had faded by the end of her first day off. On the second day she'd woken midday, and then she'd watched the sun slowly drop with the same lack of patience she always did at the close of the second rest day.

She paused in front of the mirror. The scratches in the matte black painted surface revealed swaths of the glass. Before things changed, she'd spent hours looking in that mirror. Then, she had prided herself on her healthy appearance. Harmony knew that it wasn't likely that she'd enjoy seeing her full reflection now; better to see only fragments.

When she had first painted over the mirror, she'd dragged her then-manicured fingernails over the still-tacky paint. Tonight she trailed her now-short nails over those scratches in the ritual she enacted every time she went hunting. She couldn't swear that the rote actions had any real impact on her survival, but that first time, not quite two years ago, she'd left angry and untrained—but somehow survived. Now, she was composed and trained. She couldn't do anything more to guarantee her safety, but she took comfort in the small rituals she had. Ritual worked; faith mattered. Everyone on Earth knew that *now*.

"Blasphemer!" her father yelled again.

His fists thudded on the door; the shelf she kept in front of it shuddered. Her mother's porcelain angels, remnants of an old forgotten faith, rattled in time with the pounding as Harmony leaned in close to the mirror and outlined her eyes with smudged kohl, giving herself a sickened look. The shadowed eyes added to her regular pallor and made her whole face look wan and vulnerable.

He threw something in the hall. The tinkle of glass was followed by the bitter stench of alcohol, confirming that he had thrown another bottle. She couldn't see the mess, but she knew what she'd see tomorrow.

As Harmony surveyed her eyes in the exposed stripes on the mirror, she lifted her hand to touch her shaved head. The first night she'd gone hunting, she'd hacked her hair off before shaving it. Now, she could only shave the stubble. It wasn't exactly the same, but it was the closest approximation of the ritual that she could manage.

"They'll find out what you're doing and kill us both. You're as bad as your sister was, and look where that got her," he called through the door. That was almost a ritual too. Sometimes she wondered if she stayed here out of love or because she'd come to associate these pre-hunt rants with survival.

He was sobbing now, drunk and broken, but she'd learned months ago that sobs would shift back to curses if he saw her—and that curses were followed by punches all too quickly.

"Wear your charms," he begged.

A flash of silver was shoved under the door. She paused and stared at it. The chain held a tiny locket, a heart, and a few other trinkets. She had once insisted Chastity wear it, believing it brought her luck, and after her death, Chris had returned it.

"Thank you, Daddy," Harm whispered.

She fastened it around her throat, and then she returned to the mirror. She finished shaving her head, not needing the slivers of mirror for this part of the routine. She closed her eyes and completed the task with the same precision she'd once used for curling her hair. It seemed like such a long time ago that she'd been so foolish, before she understood how dangerous Nidhogg was, before Chastity had died.

Before I knew that gods could be monstrous.

He started pounding on the door again; this time he kicked it too. "I won't die because of you. Are you listening? Harmony!"

She walked over to the door and reached a hand between the shelves barricading it. She laid her palm flat on the door.

"I am," she whispered. "I listen to every word, Daddy."

He couldn't hear her, but their best conversations always

happened when he didn't hear her.

"I'll be home late tonight," she whispered.

She pulled her hand away as he began quoting from the New Scripture. He'd obviously been drinking early if he was already on scripture. Before the New Religion, he didn't drink, but she was grateful that he did now. When he was drunk, he was more likely to stay home where he'd be safe.

Harmony slid a homemade dagger into each boot; then she grabbed her prized blade: a real machine-made serrated eight-inch knife with a good handle that didn't get too slick when it was bloodied. She kissed the side of the steel, as she had the first night, and carefully slid it into the front pocket of her trousers, through the slit in her pocket, under the fabric, and into the sheath on her thigh. Her pants were loose enough now that it didn't show.

"Stay safe, Daddy," she said loudly enough for him to hear. She didn't tell him she loved him anymore. She hadn't said those words to *anyone* since her sister died.

Harmony opened the window and jumped toward the branch nearest the house.

Love is a mistake when we're all going to die any day now.

The familiar burn of her palms connecting with the bark was quickly followed by the thud of her boots hitting the ground. The calluses on her hands dulled the sensations, but it was the reenactment of the steps that mattered, not the sensations themselves.

Chris waited, not nervously but with the ever-present edge that came from the fear that tonight would be the night that she wouldn't show. He'd tried to convince her that sharing quarters was wiser. Most teams did. For reasons he couldn't understand, she refused. Most days, she claimed she couldn't leave her father—but other nights, she insisted that she couldn't step into her dead sister's life.

Although we both know that she already has.

He flicked ash onto the street, realizing as he did so that he'd only taken one drag from the cigarette. He was just about to pinch the cherry off—smokes were far too expensive to waste—when he saw her. She stayed to the shadows, but her movements were deliberate. She looked nothing like prey.

Yet.

Within another hour, that would change. Harmony would adopt the guise of a victim. She'd become the very thing that the devotees of Nidhogg found alluring: weak, sickened, and ready to be delivered to their god.

"You're late."

Harmony shrugged, snagged the cigarette from his hand, and took a drag. It was more ritual than necessity. The first night she'd killed one of them, this was how they met. She clung to those little details, like they would save her. *Maybe she's right.* He didn't try to understand the whole ritual or faith thing. All he knew was that a few drags on a cigarette wouldn't deaden her sense of smell nearly as much as either of them would like. He smoked more often. The childhood warnings about cancer weren't relevant anymore, not to them. If they stayed here, kept fighting, they'd die before there was any time for the carcinogens to have an impact, and the cigarettes helped. Even a slight deadening of scent and taste was a benefit in their line of work. Corpse-feeders stank.

Chris took the cigarette back. "Trouble?"

"Not really. Drunk earlier than usual. Sometimes, I think he hates me." Harmony shrugged and looked away, but not before he saw the flicker of sadness she would deny if he asked about it. For all of her strengths, she still wanted a life that they'd never know again.

When the god awakened, society changed, and short of killing Nidhogg, the odds of finding the sort of society they'd once known were exceedingly slim. Of course, the odds of killing a god were slimmer still. Nidhogg was here, was real, and was staying. To those who questioned, it was pretty obvious that he wasn't as omnipotent as he claimed. If he were all-powerful, they wouldn't be resisting, killing his devoted Nidos, and refusing to obey him.

However, the faith that strengthened him was impossible to negate: he *was* real. Denying his existence was hard to do when he lived, breathed, and consumed them. The more they believed, the stronger he grew. Even those who wanted his death strengthened him with their thoughts of him. It didn't matter whether they loathed or loved him. They thought of him, and that was enough.

How do you deny what is undeniably here?

The answer to that question was one the philosophers in the resistance pondered at length. Chris wasn't a philosopher; even now that a god had come to earth, he wasn't prone to a lot of metaphysical contemplation. His skills were far more practical: he killed monsters.

"Which area did we draw tonight?" Harmony walked close enough to his side that she appeared to be with him. Together they looked like a couple undaunted by the regulations that had spread up most of the eastern part of the country.

"Old Downtown." He draped an arm around her shoulders, reminding himself that they had agreed that it wasn't personal for either of them. *Even though that's a lie.* The illusion required acting like a couple often enough that a good team had to be able to appear completely at ease. They had to look like they were together; teams were a harder target if they were convincing. The challenge, of course, was remembering that it was to be an act.

He and Chastity had allowed themselves to forget, and when she died, he hadn't been sure he wanted to keep living. Of course, loving her was the only thing that had made living matter in the first place. He had no religion, no family, nothing but the fight and his partner. When he lost his first partner, he had tried to lose himself in a drunken haze he'd had absolutely no intention of coming out of.

He lifted bottle after bottle, shook them, and tossed them aside. "Empty. Every damn bottle is empty, Chas."

Saying her name wasn't enough though. He'd kept on talking to her like she was there, but she never answered.

Three more bottles were rejected. The fourth had a good inch of liquid—hopefully gin—in it. Unfortunately, it also had a cigarette butt floating in it. He paused, shrugged, and lifted the bottle to his lips.

"That's disgusting, Chris."

He turned. "Chas?" He lowered the bottle, holding it loosely in his hand. "You're dead."

She didn't say anything, but her head bowed momentarily. After what sounded like a sob, she crossed the room and took the bottle from him. "It's not your fault."

"I was late. If I hadn't been late—"

"You'd be dead too," she interrupted.

"I'd rather be dead."

She slapped him. "You'd rather let them kill you? Let him eat your corpse? What happened to fighting?"

"I can't fight without you." He pulled her to him. He knew now that it was a dream. It had to be a dream because dead girls don't slap people, but he would rather sleep than wake if that meant Chastity was with him. "I need you, Chas. I love you."

She opened her mouth to say something, but he kissed her before she spoke. Her kisses were different, but he couldn't expect a dream to be the same as the real thing.

When he pulled away, he told her all the things he had told her since they'd first fallen into bed. "I love you. I can't do this alone. I need you here. Now."

"You'll fight?" She stepped away. "Promise me, Chris. You'll fight. No giving up. . . . They killed Chastity. You have to fight. Help me fight them."

"I will," he agreed. Something in her words was wrong. He paused, but then she kissed him.

Chastity let him undress her, and they made love.

Later, when he sobered up, he realized that it wasn't a dream at all—nor was it Chastity.

"I need you to train me," Harmony said. "My sister wouldn't want you—or me—to die."

"You're not . . ." He put an arm over his eyes. "I didn't mean . . . Tell me I didn't force—"

"I said yes, Chris. You needed to think I was her, and it's probably for the best. Partners need to be at ease with each other. Now, you . . . you should be at ease with me, right? It'll help."

"Partners?" He moved his arm and stared up at her.

"I'm not interested in replacing her"—she made a vague waving gesture toward the mattress on his floor where she'd just been—"there. I want to be your partner on the streets, though. You trained her. Train me. I'll fight."

"No."

Ten months later, she was every bit as good a fighter as Chastity had been. A year after that, she was more lethal and still looked enough like Chastity that more than a few people mistakenly called her by her dead sister's name, but there was no way he'd ever mistake them for one another now that he'd gotten to know Harmony.

The elder Davis sister had been a good soldier, devoted to the fight; up until the day she died, Chastity had done her job and done it well, too. She killed any of the creatures—human and other—that served Nidhogg. She was still soft though; she wept when she killed humans, not in the moment, but afterward when they were home. Harmony, on the other hand, didn't cry. She also didn't laugh the way Chastity had. Sometimes, when she'd won in a fight where she been outnumbered or overpowered initially, she smiled with the sort of relaxed joy that Chastity often took in little things. But the only things that seemed to make Harmony that happy were victories in the almost-lost fights. Getting close to the edge of death and winning, that was where Harmony found her joy.

Chris stuffed the extinguished cigarette butt into his pocket. The nicotine-stained filters would be recycled again and again until they were so noxious that they were of no use as cigarettes. Some fighters tore little bits of them off to use as nose plugs, but he hadn't yet gotten to that point. If he survived long enough, he would, but counting on surviving was foolish. Maybe if they lived farther north, they'd have better odds, but if they stayed this close to the god's lair, they were just biding time. In the days before the god's arrival, people stayed in dead-end towns, in dead-end jobs, in dead-end relationships rather than take the risk of something new. He'd sworn he would be different, but here he was, staying in a town where dying young was inevitable. *Because Harmony won't leave.* If he could convince her to move, they could try to find a safer place, but she only cared about the fight. *And I only care about her.*

He hadn't meant to fall in love with his dead girlfriend's sister, but he had—not that he'd be foolish enough to tell her: Harmony didn't believe in love. She'd told him early on, "Two of the three people I've loved are dead. The third is a drunk. Love's a bad idea." So Chris kept the words to himself and did his best to keep them both alive.

As usual with Chris, Harmony didn't feel the need to distract either of them with unnecessary chatter. As he did that first night, he kept his arm around her as they walked. Silently, she checked that item off her mental list, too, and he didn't comment on her insistence of replicating so many small details every night they went hunting. All he ever said was that it provided an excuse to keep their voices low as well as presenting a unified front against any watching devotees of the New Faith. Sometimes, in the thoughts she never shared, she thought of her fellow fighters as devotees of a faith, too. They were devoted to a god who hadn't yet appeared, who maybe never would, but she believed he or she had to be out there in the universe. It was a quiet belief, with the sort of small rituals and whispered prayers that wouldn't draw attention—or maybe it was a fantasy as much as Chastity's dreams of a different future. Either way, it was better than the New Faith.

Most of the faithful were zealots, and like all zealots, they focused on some facts to the exclusion of all others. They had proof that their faith was true: their god was here on Earth. They didn't want to discuss the fact that their god required human sacrifice, that he ate corpses, that a great destroyer wasn't doing any favors to the civilization on Earth.

Within months after Nidhogg's devotees revealed the presence of their corpse-eating god, all flights and ships from North America were refused docking or runway access across the globe. Any flights attempting access to foreign nations were summarily shot down; boats were sunk. Humans helped the Nidos—the reptilian creatures that had appeared and served Nidhogg—and the New Faith spread to South America within months. Within two years, most of North and South America was reduced to sporadic internet and telephone access with the outside world.

All of that had happened when she was still a kid. She'd never been outside the country, that she could remember. There were pictures of a trip to Europe when she was in elementary school, but by the time she was nine, everything had changed. There were vague memories of a life before the New Faith, but most of what she'd known was after Nidhogg. At seventeen, she'd lived half of her life under the pall of the New Religion. Sometimes, Harmony thought it was for the best: she didn't want to remember a life that would never be again.

Since Nidos, despite their mostly human appearance, were—like Nidhogg itself—reptilian, they were unable to flourish in the upper reaches of North America. They could also be killed, and that was the chief victory of the resistance so far: they killed monster after monster. No one knew if it had any real impact. Killing the creatures, and the humans who supported them, had led to a few reclaimed towns—and the scant bit of useful intel that they had.

Despite some small victories, the exodus north had continued, but that was as far away from the corpse-eating new god that one could get. Although the access point between Alaska and Asia had not yet been breached by the Nidos, the fear of it was enough that humans weren't allowed to cross into Asia either. People still tried, and stories circulated online of people claiming to have succeeded, but the truth was that anyone who tried to cross that barrier ended up dead for their efforts. The world that Harmony had been born into was long gone, and unless they could kill a god, it wouldn't be returning to the relative safety they'd once known.

Chris finally asked, "Did you hear about Taylor?"

"He was a good guy. At least he got a clean death." Harmony respected Taylor's partner, Jess, a little bit more for putting the bullet in Taylor. Bullets attracted attention, but Jess had risked it to assure that he wasn't thrown into one of the Nidos' vats while still alive. Everyone who knew about the urns filled with decaying corpses was terrified of drowning in one.

When she'd first seen the photographs of the stew of dead bodies that the Nidos lived off of, she'd retched. That image was one of the ones that never stopped haunting her. She still woke from nightmare images of her mother's face in the rot-filled water, from cold sweats in dreams that she was drowning in the decay of people she knew.

"I'd shoot you, you know," Chris assured her; his words filled in the silence that had stretched out while horrors filled her mind. "I'd kill you before I'd let them throw you in one of those things."

"I know." She looked up at him, and he kissed her forehead. For one of those perfect quiet moments, she wondered what life would've been like if she'd been born only a decade earlier. "Is it weird to be comforted by promises to be killed?"

"Not if it's a choice between quick death and something horrible," Chris said.

"I'd kill you, too," she added.

"I know."

They lapsed back into silence then, and Harmony debated asking him about the differences in the world. He was three years older than her; it didn't seem like a big difference now, but he'd known a world she could only try to imagine, been old enough to truly see the change. For as long as she remembered, this was the only world.

Chastity leaned against the wall. Her knees were bent, and she looked shakier than Harmony had ever seen her.

"You're lucky," she whispered. "If we hadn't seen you . . ."

"You did." Harmony listened to the sound of yelling outside their room. Their father had thrown something. Since Mom died, he was drunk more days than not. After what Harmony had seen tonight, she'd thought about stealing one of his bottles of vodka. Bodies floated in various stages of decomposition, arms and legs

tangled together, eyes wide open and staring lifelessly. She'd stood silently looking into the giant cistern of corpses, too disgusted to even scream.

"You can't go back there, Harm," Chastity warned.

"I needed to know. . . . I just wanted . . ."

"Mom's not in there, and anyone that is in there is beyond our help." Chastity reached out, winced, and glanced at her arm. Her sleeve was wet with blood, but she kept her arm outstretched. "Come here."

Instead of accepting the hug her sister offered, Harmony grabbed the first-aid box on Chastity's dresser. Once, they'd both had jewelry boxes sitting there. Harmony's was pink; Chastity had a matching red one. Now, the things that littered the surface of Chastity's dresser included knives, bandages, and bottles of antiseptic.

Their mother had taught both girls to sew, and every time they did this, Harmony thought of her. Of course, she'd intended for them to sew skirts, not skin. Harmony cleaned her sister's wound, and then she threaded the needle with the deep-blue fiber that she would have to snip and tug out later. Not getting the disintegrating thread meant going to the hospital, and hospitals were like grocery stores to the Nidos. It wasn't openly acknowledged, but there had been enough reports of disappearances that anyone who paid attention realized that the claim of "only taking freely offered corpses" was a lie. As the population dwindled, the natural-death rate wasn't high enough to satisfy Nidhogg's appetites.

"Promise me, Harmony." Chastity lifted her gaze from the

needle that Harmony held ready. "I want you to be safe. Once we're able, we're going to get out of here. We'll go north, start over somewhere else. You, me, Christian, and Daddy. It'll be better."

Harmony bit down on her lip, pinched the sides of her sister's knife wound closed, and tried to keep her stitches straight and tight.

"Everything will be different when we get out of here. It'll be better," Chastity promised.

Neither of them commented on their father's drunken ranting on the other side of the barred bedroom door. They were all coping with her mother's death differently. Chastity fought; their father drank; and Harmony tried to ignore the increased number of missing neighbors, the way her sister insisted she stay in after dark, and the stench of her father's almost nightly descents into oblivion.

Things never got better for Chastity or their father, and none of them believed that they were going to improve. Chastity was wrapped in a sheet and set aflame on a bier to prevent the corpse eaters from consuming her. Their father was rarely sober, and Harmony had no expectation of living too many years longer. Chastity's hopes for another life had been a fantasy; this was reality.

Would it be worse to think you had a future and lose it?

Harmony had been eight when the new god arrived. She'd never really known a world where there was any doubt that gods could be real. All she could do was kill the monsters and hope that if *this* god was real, so were other—better—gods.

"Are you going to stay quiet all night?" Chris prodded.

"Sorry." She leaned her head against him briefly. "Dad was weird; we're working downtown; the news about Taylor . . . I guess I'm feeling . . . I don't know."

"Me too," he said.

"We're almost there. Let's go kill something. Maybe if we're lucky, we'll get more than one tonight."

The shift in Harmony's mood as she pondered the inevitable violence in their night was markedly different from Chris' reaction. Every time they cornered a Nido, Chris was filled with fear of losing Harmony. Afterward, he was cheered, but until they were past the fighting, he was apprehensive. Harmony was comforted by the prospect of violence—of revenge—in ways he almost envied.

They entered Old Downtown and started to prowl the clubs. There weren't as many people out this near curfew. Those who were fell into one of four categories: the devoted, the deniers, the deadly, or the dying. Which category a person fell into wasn't always apparent at first sight. There were cues, of course. The people still denying the hell they were living in were the ones most likely to be wearing shoes not suited for running. Admittedly, though, the dying were prone to such folly on occasion. They weren't necessarily rushing to their deaths, but sometimes their "what happens, happens" approach meant that they were as likely to flee from the corpse-feeders as not. The devoted wore shoes fit for running down prey. The deadly were clad in boots, easier to load with weapons and still useful for running.

"My girl's not feeling well," Chris told the doorman as they approached the line outside the Norns. "Can we get inside so none of the N—so no one notices?"

Harmony's posture had shifted as they'd walked. She leaned on him, appearing fragile, and simultaneously tilted her head so that the bruises along her collarbone were visible. "It's okay. I can wait out here," she murmured to him. "I don't mind—"

"I do," he snapped. He pulled her closer, caught her hand in his, and lifted it to his lips to kiss her wrist. In the process, the sleeve of her jacket slid back, exposing the bruised and needle-marked skin of her arm. He wasn't sure what she'd injected into her body. *Drugs? Nothing?* It wasn't disease: he was certain of that. Harmony's pallor, bruises, and demeanor were all lures. She counted on the illusion of sickness, and most nights, it was enough.

Chris caught her gaze. "Harm?"

"I'm fine," she lied. She hadn't been fine in a long time, but that wasn't something he knew how to fix.

The doorman motioned them in. "You shouldn't have her out here when she's sick, man."

The frown Chris gave the man wasn't faked. "If I could keep her somewhere safe, I would."

Harmony winced. "Come dance with me."

Sometimes, he wished they could go out to the clubs for an actual date. Instead, their evenings were spent training, hunting, and killing. It had long since stopped being the life he wanted, but he couldn't leave here without her. He wouldn't. Instead, he kept his arm around her, and together they made their way into the crowd. Time hadn't healed him; no amount of killing seemed to bring him peace. It had helped her, but he had been fighting for a couple of years before she had joined him. Maybe that was the difference: he was tired.

Harmony tensed as she saw her prey: a Nido approached, trying to sniff her out.

Chris wondered how far she'd go to ensnare them. The bruises on her arm were injection marks. As much as he believed that she wouldn't sicken herself too much to fight, he also knew that if she could carry a disease that lured them, she would. Mentally, he made a note to try to get some clothes worn by the recently ill. Doing so was difficult, because the scent of illness faded too soon, but it was a strategy that added a little bit of extra verisimilitude.

"Couple fight now," Harmony whispered as he pulled her toward him.

"Harm—"

"Teammates, Chris. I'm not as vulnerable as I look. You know that." She looked down, so her forehead was resting against his chest while she spoke.

"I still worry," he said. They could only use so many scenarios before they were caught. They rotated sections, rotated clubs within the sections, but even that wasn't enough. Different scenarios made sense.

"It's what we do; it's worth it." Harmony's voice sounded raw. "If we're going to die, it has to be for something, Chris. If we're going to live—"

"I know," he interrupted. *You're my reason, Harm. My religion.* He put his hand on the back of her neck. "I'll be right behind you."

"Not too fast."

"Count five and go." Chris watched the Nido approach with the same trepidation he always felt. He and Harmony had a system, and it worked—but so had the system he and Chastity had used.

"You don't understand." Harmony shoved him and turned away, running into the Nido's arms as if she were unaware that he was there all along.

Now comes the hard part.

Chris stepped up to the bar and ordered a drink. He wasn't going to walk out the moment Harmony left. More than half the time, Nidos in this part of town worked in pairs. It made this section harder to work, but it also meant that hunting here usually meant two kills. Of course, it also meant that their side often took more risks—and more casualties.

In the mirror that hung behind the liquor bottles, Chris watch as the Nido said something to Harmony. In barely three minutes, he had an arm around her, leading her away, taking her outside. The challenge for Chris was in not looking over his shoulder, not racing outside, not scooping her up and insisting they escape north to try to find a safer place to live.

Instead of doing all the things he wanted to, Chris waited, half hoping that the Nido's partner would arrive and half hoping that there was no partner so he could move on to the next step of this strategy: run after his emotional girlfriend.

Harmony nodded and held on to the Nido's arm as he directed her to a side door of the Norns. Her heart was steadier every time she did this, as if there was a calm almost in reach, and she wondered guiltily if the calm was death. She wasn't going to slit her wrists or do anything drastic, but she was well aware that most hunters died. Dying while fighting for a better future seemed like a good way to go, maybe even a way to reach the kind of afterlife where she could be happy, where she could enjoy the sort of existence that people talked about when they talked about *before*.

The crack of metal on metal echoed as the door hit the handrail on the cement ramp into the alley. If she hadn't been going outside to kill him, stepping into the poorly lit alley would be unsettling. As it was, she found the dark comforting.

"Do you have a car or something?" She slid her free hand into her pants pocket to withdraw the knife hidden there, but before she withdrew it, a beam of light flashed on, aimed directly at her and blinding her temporarily.

"You won't need that," the Nido beside her said.

Then another voice drew her attention: "She's my only other child. We'll be even now, right?"

"Daddy?" Harmony stumbled, partly from the inability to

see and partly from the panic that washed over her. "Daddy! What are you doing here?"

She jerked her arm away from the Nido, but he caught her, gripping her biceps with a bruising hand before she could go very far. *Think, Harm. Think.* She couldn't expect Chris to hear her if she screamed; the music inside was too loud. All she could do was buy time until he got there—except every scenario she knew was a blank then. Her father was *it*, the last family she knew she still had. Her sister was dead; her mother was dead.

The light lowered, and she saw another Nido standing beside her father. This one looked like a reasonably attractive woman, and she stood beside Harmony's father like she was his date: a small smile on her lips and a hand resting lightly in the crook of his folded arm.

"She looks a lot like the other one," the female Nido said.

Harmony looked at her father. "Daddy?"

He shook his head. "I tried to save you. I told you what would happen. You didn't listen."

The Nido patted his cheek with her free hand. "We took care of the problem last time, and we'll fix this too."

A cry escaped Harmony's lips. It might have been a word, or it might have been only a sound. She wasn't sure. The Nido restraining her stepped away, and she almost fell. She took several steps toward her father. "How? Why?"

There were two Nidos with her father, and even though she wasn't being held back, she wasn't sure what she wanted to do, much less what she could do.

"Your sister caught their attention. What was I to do?" Her father glared at her through bloodshot eyes. His sallow, fleshy face didn't look anything like the father she remembered.

Harmony shook her head. "And Mom?"

He stepped closer, so he was near enough that she could embrace him. "That wasn't my doing. I didn't know. . . . She was sick, and I only left her at the hospital for the night. I didn't know they—"

"But you knew when you . . . what? Told them where Chas would be?"

"I had to make a choice," he pleaded. "I tried to save you."

Although the two Nidos watched them, they didn't interfere. Harmony looked into her father's face, but she couldn't summon any words for him. Night after night, she'd hoped he would recover from the dual tragedies of her mother's and sister's deaths, but he wouldn't. He was responsible, and now they both knew it.

"You told them where Chastity was . . . and now me too?"

"All I did was add it to the necklace. I warned you, but you wouldn't listen." He pointed at her. "The tracker is on that. I had no choice."

Harm's hand went to the charms around her throat. She yanked the necklace free and threw it at him. "You *had* a choice."

"You don't understand," he insisted. "They would've killed us both. They would've killed all three of us before, when Chastity was blaspheming. I saved you then. What was I to do?"

"Not give either of your daughters to the monsters. If there is another world where we meet after this life, I hope Chastity and Mom are there waiting for us." She slipped her hand into her pocket. "Maybe they'll forgive you, Daddy. Maybe I will too."

She withdrew the knife and shoved the blade hilt-deep into his throat. As the Nidos grabbed her arms, she watched her father clutch his bleeding throat. It wouldn't help. She'd learned where to stab a human; she'd severed his carotid artery.

"If I hated you, I'd have let you go into their foul stew while you were still alive," she told him as he died.

The distant sounds of music, the sizzle of a nearby street-light, and her father's dying were all she heard then. The Nidos gripped her arms, but she kept her hand tight on the hilt of her knife.

I don't want to die.

If she didn't get away, she'd end up drowning in corpses. The images in her mind were almost as vivid as the real thing had been. This time, though, Chastity wouldn't be there to rescue her.

Harmony let her body go suddenly limp, surprising them and dropping to the ground as they lost their grip on her. That was one of the first lessons she'd learned: do the unexpected. Most captives tried to tug away or shove, so her captors were likely to be ready for that.

As she rolled to her feet, she launched herself at one of the Nidos. She knew she couldn't kill them both, but she wasn't going to let them take her away. *Better to die fighting than drown in the dead.* Her shoulder stung from an unavoidable stab wound, and she knew dimly that there were other wounds she wasn't registering yet. None of that mattered though. *I want to live. I want Chris to live.* She knew he should've been there by now, and the thought of reaching him, of keeping him out of their vats, was enough to give her an extra surge of adrenaline.

"Harmony!" Chris yelled.

She wasn't sure when Chris had come outside. All she knew for sure was that she was on the ground, on top of the Nido, and her knife was wet in her hand. A trickle of something dripped down her cheek. She didn't know if it was her tears or her father's blood. The temptation to look at Chris warred with the fear that he'd look at her with disgust.

"Harm," he repeated, softly this time. He had hands on her waist, lifting her up with little effort, as if she really was the rag doll she suddenly felt like. He pulled her away from the dead Nido and her now-dead father.

"You're bleeding," she said foolishly. Bleeding was normal; death was normal.

He took her hand, and uncurled her fingers from the hilt of the knife. "There was one inside, too, or I'd have been here sooner."

"This time . . . I thought . . . I *really* thought I was going to die," she whispered. "I don't *want* to die."

Instead of saying things that would make her fall apart, he suggested the same thing he had not long after Chastity died: "We could go north. Try to get to somewhere safer."

She leaned against his side, not just because of the ritual but because she wanted to feel close to him, and this time, she gave him the answer she never had before, "Yes."

And they walked away from the Norns, away from the father who'd betrayed her, and away from a life that held a too-soon expiration date.

BURN 3

Kami Garcia

THE FACES OF missing children flash across three vid screens above our heads, forming a gargantuan triangle that looms over the street. Children have been disappearing for weeks now. Protectorate officers claim they're runaways, but there's nowhere to go inside the Dome. The truth is no one cares about a bunch of poor kids from Burn 3.

I glance at the screen again and squeeze my little sister's hand tighter, dragging her through the filthy alley.

"Why are we running?" Sky asks.

"We're just walking fast."

I don't like bringing her outside at night, but we're out of purification tablets and she hasn't had any water all day. The dirty streets are bathed in neon light from the signs marking the rows of identical black metal doors that serve as storefronts.

In the distance, towering buildings covered in silver reflective panels rise up around a labyrinth of alleys. Those buildings are all that's left of the city that stood here twenty years ago. Retrofitted and repurposed for the world we live in now. I've never been anywhere near there. It's the wealthy part of Burn 3, no place for poor kids like us.

We reach an exposed stall draped in a black plastic tarp. An old woman swathed in layers of dark fabric huddles underneath. Her face is pebbled on one side, the result of poorly healed burns. Even though the Dome keeps us under a constant shadow, it's dangerous to be outside all day, and I feel sorry for her. But few people can afford the high rent for an indoor shop.

"Two purification tablets, please." I hold out the coins stamped with a crude number three on both sides.

She takes the currency in her gloved hand and gives me two pink tablets. They don't look like much, but they'll turn the black water running through the pipes a safer shade of gray. Before our father died, he told us stories about the world before the Burn. A time when water was clear and you could drink it straight from the faucet, and walk outside to stand in the sun without layers of protective clothing. That was before his mind deteriorated and I couldn't tell if his stories were memories or delusions.

A siren eclipses the sounds around us and an automated voice issues a directive. "Alert: the atmosphere inside the Dome has reached Level 2. Please put on your goggles and return to your domiciles immediately. Alert: the atmosphere inside the Dome—"

"Hurry home," the old woman says, collapsing the tarp around her like a tent.

My sister looks up at me, blue eyes wide. "I'm scared, Phoenix."

"Put on your goggles." I dig in my pocket for mine.

She unfolds the wraparound eyewear that makes everything look bright green, a color you never see inside the Dome.

"Run," I yell, pulling her along behind me.

A man pushes Sky, and she stumbles. He glances at her and starts to turn away without offering help or an apology. Tears run down my sister's face.

I shove him as hard as I can, and grab my sister's hand. She runs behind me until we reach our building, a twenty-story domicile divided into single rooms. The Dome is so crowded that there's nowhere left to build but up, even though it's more dangerous on the higher floors.

Our room is on the eighteenth floor.

I unlock the door and push Sky inside. "Get in the shelter."

She scrambles for the makeshift tent in the center of the room. It's made from Firestall, an engineered material that absorbs heat and UV rays.

The Dome is supposed to protect us from the holes in the ozone layer—holes that turned more than two-thirds of the world to ash twenty years ago. But the sun's invisible hand can still reach into the Dome. The burns people suffer on a daily basis are proof of that. Most of us have been victims at least once, our skin curling like the edges of burning paper.

Some people believe you're more likely to get burned in the buildings without reflective panels like this one. I don't know if it's true, but I can't take chances with my sister. Sky's skin is perfectly smooth. She's never felt the savage itching and heat of a burn, and I'm not going to let her feel it now.

We huddle together in the darkness, and Sky chokes back tears. "I'm scared."

"Don't worry." I pull her closer and listen to the alert repeating over and over until I fall asleep, more worried than ever.

In the morning, I look out the small window and see people wandering through the streets. The alert must be over, though many are still wearing their protective goggles. My father told me this city was called New York before the Burn. The buildings were even taller than the ones beyond the alleys, so tall they seemed to touch the clouds. He said you could see the clouds too—white streaks in a blue sky. A sky filled with beauty instead of destruction.

The Burn happened suddenly, although scientists had predicted it years before. The sky turned red and the temperature rose dangerously. No one could step outside without suffering third-degree burns. Within weeks, the heat was melting steel and plastic. My father said hundreds of thousands died after inhaling the toxic fumes from their disintegrating homes.

For years, people lived in the sewers or underground shelters until scientists developed a compound strong enough to withstand the temperatures in the areas where the atmosphere was still intact.

People traveled hundreds of miles underground until they reached a safe zone—a place without a hole in the sky above it. They built the Dome and named our city Burn 3 because it was the third city in the world to turn to ash.

From where I stand looking down on the black coats rushing through the gray streets, the city still looks like it's made of ash.

I drop the purification tablets into two black cups of water and watch the liquid turn a less lethal shade of charcoal. I choke mine down and leave Sky's on the counter. She's still asleep, blond hair peeking out from beneath the ratty blanket. I can't stand to wake her. The world of her dreams is so much better than the one we live in.

I leave her a note instead.

An hour later, I climb the eighteen flights of stairs with two food packets tucked in my pocket. Noodles with spicy red sauce, Sky's favorite. Orange doors line both sides of the hallways and I can see ours from the landing.

It's wide open.

My pulse quickens, and I bolt up the stairs. Sky would never open the door for anyone. She knows better. "Sky?"

I glance around the room. She's not here, but someone

else was. Blankets are strewn all over the floor, and the shelter is shredded.

"Sky!" I know she won't answer, but I keep calling her name. This can't be happening. Children have been disappearing from the streets, not from the domiciles.

I run for the door and trip over the shredded strips of Firestall. My face hits the cement floor hard, and for a second, the room sways. I push up onto my knees, and something glints under the black strips of material.

A glass bottle the size of my thumb. It has a silver cap with a hole in the top, but the bottle is empty. A white label is peeling off the front. I've never seen anything like it in the stores along the alleyways.

I hit the stairs and notice the open door a floor below me. Clothes and personal items are strewn across the floor. Sky might not be the only kid missing.

I'm back in the streets, running down the alley under the neon signs. "Sky?"

I check the shops she frequents, like the one with hand-sewn dolls that cost more than we spend on a week's worth of food packets. Or the store several blocks away where they sell tea made from roots and the salve that heals burns.

I stop a woman selling bread packets on the street. "Have you seen a little girl with blond hair?" It's Sky's most recognizable feature.

Almost no one has blond hair or blue eyes anymore. My father said they made people more vulnerable to the sun, a vicious sort of natural selection. It's the reason I rarely take Sky outside during the day, and keep every inch of her skin covered when I do.

The woman shakes her head. "Haven't seen no blond hair."

I stand in the middle of the street, the black doors stretching out in front of me, the vid screens above me.

She's not here.

I think about my sister's smile and the way she never complains when we don't have enough to eat. I can see her blue eyes, bright and curious. My mother named her Sky because of her eyes. She said the real sky was just as blue once. I look up at the Dome and the red sky beyond it.

I would trade a real blue sky in a second to find her.

Faces flash across the gigantic vid screens one by one.

Sky's will be up there tomorrow.

I've never been inside the Protectorate. Protectorate officers are dangerous—as quick to draw their guns as the criminals they hunt. And Burn 3 is full of criminals, men with nothing left to lose who will cut your throat over a few coins or a food packet. I try not to imagine Sky in their hands.

The building is made of Firestall, the same material used to construct the Dome. It's only used for government buildings, and the Protectorate is the only government facility in this part of town.

I burst through the doors, and the scanners go off. There's nothing in my pockets except the glass bottle. I don't own anything but the clothes on my back, and I spent all the coins I had this morning.

"Stop right there," an officer shouts. His weapon is pointed at me, the red glow signaling that it's armed. He's prepared to use the heat we all fear to kill me.

"I'm sorry," I stammer. "My sister—she's missing. I think someone took her."

"Scan her." He nods at another officer, with smooth hands a few shades darker than the flesh on his face and neck. Skin always takes on a darker shade after it heals from a burn. Judging by his hands, he was burned badly. Only the expensive salves can smooth the texture of the affected skin.

The officer waves a small electronic device over my body. "She's clean."

The weapon lowers, and I struggle to catch my breath. I notice the cages hanging above us—at least twenty feet from where I'm standing. Arms hang between the bars. There are men inside.

"Someone broke into our room at the domicile, and my little sister is missing. She's only ten."

Please help me.

"How do you know it was a break-in?" the Protectorate officer with the scanner asks.

"The door was wide open, and everything inside was destroyed."

He shakes his head. "Maybe she left in a hurry. Don't you watch the vid screens? You know how many kids run away every day?"

I try to make sense of what he's saying, but I can't. "You think they're running away? Where would they go?"

The one with the weapon leaning against his shoulder shrugs. "The Abyss maybe. Who knows? Lots of kids like it down there. Plenty of stuff on the black market to help them forget about their problems."

"My sister doesn't have problems." I realize how ridiculous it sounds as soon as I say it. "No more than anyone else."

I don't know how to make them believe me. For a second, all I can think about is my father. He died two years ago, slowly poisoned by toxic fumes he and the other evacuators inhaled decades ago when they risked their lives to save others. My father would know what to say to make these men listen.

I shove my hands into my pockets, my fists curled in frustration. The cool glass slides against my skin, and I remember the bottle safely tucked inside. My hand closes around it, but I hesitate. What if they take it? I don't trust these men, and it's the only clue I have.

The officer with the scanner looks bored. "I'm sorry your sister's missing, kid. But we can't chase down every runaway."

I take a deep breath and swallow my anger. If I lose control, I'll end up in one of the cages hanging above us, and I won't be able to look for Sky. "Did you ever think that someone might be taking them?"

They both laugh. "Why would anyone want extra mouths to feed?"

"Maybe they're not feeding them." It's hard to believe

these idiots are responsible for protecting us. But I have to convince them to believe me.

I start to pull the bottle out of my pocket—

"Sounds like a conspiracy theory." He shakes his head. "Did you come up with that on your own, or are you one of those crazy evacuators' kids?"

My whole body stiffens, and I push the bottle back down into my pocket.

The evacuators are the only reason you're alive.

That's what I want to tell him, but the familiar shame eats away at my stomach instead. My father was crazy, a fact I tried to hide when he was alive.

But he taught me to trust my instincts, which is the reason I slide my hand back out of my pocket. Empty.

A cage above us rattles, and something falls, nearly hitting one of the officers. His head jerks up. "Throw something out of there again, and I'll rip your arms off. You hear me? Then I'll send you back down to the Abyss, and we'll see if you can steal without them."

His partner looks at me. "You kids think the Abyss is one big party because there are no rules, but it's full of criminals. If you spend enough time down there, you'll end up in a cage too."

Full of criminals . . .

These men aren't going to help me find Sky. I'm going to have to do it myself.

But at least now I know where to look.

The entrance to the Abyss is a round metal plate in the street. A ladder leads to what's left of the underground city where everyone lived until scientists figured out how to build the Dome. I climb down until the ladder reaches the damp ground, the mouths of stone tunnels surrounding me. Names and arrows are painted on the walls, directions to places I don't recognize.

My father brought me down here once when I was Sky's age. I remember the darkness punctuated by dim strings of tiny bulbs that led to a crowded market of open stalls. He was looking for a friend, one of the guys like him who helped thousands of burned and injured people find their way down here during the Evacuation. He bought me a piece of dried meat from a stall—the first thing I'd ever eaten that didn't come from a sealed silver pouch—and left me to play games with the other children while he spoke to a man with one arm. My father didn't explain the visit, and made me swear never to go down into the underbelly of the city again.

He would understand why I am breaking that promise now.

I don't remember the name of the place my father took me, so I choose a random tunnel and follow the steady stream of water and rats. I can't imagine Sky down here. Everything about her is clean and bright.

I try to imagine my father guiding me, but all I can think about is the last thing he said before he died. When the toxicity levels in his blood rose so high we had to admit him to a clinic. "Be brave, Phoenix. Take care of your sister."

Another broken promise to my father.

My feet are soaked by the time I hear voices and notice a pool of pale light in the distance. The tunnel opens up, and I see the stalls. They're lined up in crooked rows, the ripped awnings forming aisles. Tiny strings of white bulbs dangle above them. I'm not sure if this is the same market I visited as a child.

I scan the crowd, searching for any trace of my sister's blond hair. I move closer to the stalls and watch as customers haggle over the price of burnt books, medicine long past its expiration date, and sweets in clear plastic wrappers instead of pouches. Everything the merchants are selling here is illegal. Things the Protectorate officers would throw you in the cages for possessing aboveground. But here, people are bartering for drinks in dark glass bottles and matches—a controlled substance in Burn 3. The sight of them makes my skin itch as if it's already on fire.

"Whatcha lookin' for, kid? Jerky? Cigarettes?" a man with an eye patch shouts.

I don't know what he's talking about. "Have you seen a girl with blond hair? About this tall?" I hold up my hand to match Sky's height.

His eye narrows, and he glances over his shoulder. "Little girls don't buy cigarettes."

I try again. "Have you seen her? She's wearing a black tunic and outercoat."

He strikes a match in front of me and watches it burn.

"Do you know what this is?" I hold the glass bottle with the printed label in my palm.

His eye grows wide, and he covers my hand with his, closing my fingers around the bottle. "Not here," he hisses under his breath.

"I don't—"

He jerks my arm so hard it feels like he's trying to break it. "Got me those cigarettes back here," he yells loud enough for anyone listening to hear.

I don't know what cigarettes are, but I know I wouldn't buy them—or anything else—from him.

"Come on." He slips between the stalls and gestures for me to follow. The opening to another tunnel waits, but there are no strings of lights hanging across this one. It's completely dark. Even the water trickling from the mouth looks blacker.

I shouldn't follow him. I've heard stories of kids being hacked to pieces in the alleys of Burn 3. Down here, it could be worse. But at sixteen, I'm not a kid anymore—only a year younger than my father was when he saved hundreds of people—and my sister is missing.

"Where are we going?" My voice echoes against the slick walls.

"Shh!" He waves a scarred hand at me. The skin is darker and rough, the mark of a severe burn. I picture a pack of lit matches in his hand and the flame jumping from the matchstick to his clothes.

I blink the image away and listen to his footsteps to be sure they stay ahead of mine. If he stops walking, I want to know. But he doesn't, moving quickly until we reach a dead end.

A lopsided wooden shack leans against the tunnel wall, its windows covered in black tape. Who blacks out their windows when they live underground?

Someone crazy.

The man glances around as if he thinks we've been followed. Satisfied, he sorts through the keys attached to a long chain at his waist, carefully matching them to the rows of locks on the door.

He's just like the evacuators who were exposed to burning plastic and other chemicals. Paranoid. The ones who didn't die immediately went crazy, their minds rotting away from the poison they inhaled to save others. I should know.

I don't want to go in, but what if he knows something about Sky or the bottle I found?

"Get inside." He opens the door and shoves me through.

A cracked bulb buzzes to life, and when I see the room, I realize he is crazy. The walls are plastered with papers, strange numbers and symbols scrawled all the way to the corners. And photos—not digital scans, but actual photos—of children with dirty faces and tired eyes. One stands out.

The boy has blond hair like Sky's. I can't take my eyes off his face.

"Who are all these kids?" I point at the pictures, the edges water-stained and bent.

He takes a long look at the photos and swallows hard. "Mind your own business," he snaps.

I step away from the images and the numbers I don't understand. Boxes of dirty beakers and lab equipment are stacked along the far wall, next to torn and partially burnt books. He must have salvaged the books from somewhere. I doubt he could afford to buy them.

"Know what those are?" He points to the strange symbols and numbers and shakes his head before I have a chance to answer. "'Course you don't. Those are equations. Scientific compounds."

"I'm just trying to find my sister."

He points at my pocket. "Show it to me one more time."

I hand him the bottle, and he holds it up to the light. "Ketamine. Give a kid enough of this stuff and they lose consciousness—or worse."

I clench my fists, imagining someone dragging my sister's limp body out of the domicile.

"Makes it easy to take them to the Skinners."

The word makes my skin crawl, even though I don't know what it means. "What's a Skinner?"

He turns quickly, so he can look at me with his good eye. "Are you messing with me? If you're holding that bottle, you know who they are. Or you will soon."

"Please tell me." I don't know what I can say to convince him to help me. "My father is dead, and my sister is all I have."

"How did he die?" The man's tone is suspicious.

"What?" I don't know why he cares, but he waits for me to

answer. "My father was an evacuator," I say as if that's explanation enough.

He flips his eye patch up, and there's a hollow recess where his eyeball should be. "Then you know what it's like when they take someone from you."

Those are the delusions talking. This guy is too far gone to give me any information, and I've already wasted enough time. I turn to leave. "Thanks for your help."

The man starts pacing in the cramped space, muttering and biting his nails. I remember the way my father paced at night when he thought we were asleep. Sometimes his mind was sound, and others I could see the effects of the poison he inhaled during the Evacuation. Toxins that were slowly killing him.

"Wait here." The man disappears behind a folding screen, and I can hear him rummaging around. He emerges wearing a heavy black coat that makes his thin frame look much bigger.

"I really think I should—"

He slides a rotted panel of wood along the back wall of the shack, revealing the opening to another sewer tunnel. "Do you want to find your sister or not?"

I have no way of knowing if this man has any information—if the symbols on his walls are scientific equations or the delusions of a damaged mind. But something about the photos of the children convinces me he knows something, even if he is insane.

My father had moments of clarity when every word he spoke was the truth. This man reminds me of him, the flashes of sanity grappling for footing on the sliding rocks of madness. If one of those moments can help me find Sky, I have to follow him.

We step into the darkness, and a flame illuminates the void. The man is holding a gold object between his fingers. A small flame rises up from the wick inside it. "Never seen one of these before, have you?"

I shake my head and take a step back. No one produces fire intentionally in Burn 3. The risk of starting a fire is too great when there is so little water to extinguish one.

I picture the flame catching his skin again and wonder if that's how he got the burn on his hand.

"It's called a lighter. You fill this part with oil." He taps on the bottom half of the rectangular object. "Then you turn this dial and it strikes the flint."

I nod as if I understand, and he seems satisfied.

We move deeper into the sewage tunnel, the device he calls a lighter illuminating barely a few feet in front of us. "Kids started disappearing down here first. Bet you didn't know that, did you?"

I remember the photos from his walls. Were they missing children from the Abyss?

"The vid screens don't broadcast news outside of Burn 3."

He shakes his head at my ignorance. "We aren't outside of Burn 3."

"I'm sorry. I didn't mean—"

He waves me off. "Forget it. Children who live aboveground with hair the color of the sun will always be more valuable than ours."

"But the boy in the picture on your wall had blond hair."

His body tenses and I realize I've made a mistake mentioning it. "Don't worry about the kids down here. Your sister's the one you care about."

Heat creeps up my neck, and shame settles in the pit of my empty stomach. The Abyss—the underground sewers I'm walking through—were the only safe place to live for years. Now people don't venture down here unless they want to buy something on the black market. He's right. No one cares if kids in the Abyss go missing.

Yet I expect this stranger to care about my sister. A little blond girl from a world that treats the people in his like rats. "I just meant—"

He cuts me off again. "I know what you meant. Now shut up. We're getting closer."

Closer to what?

The cement cylinder stretches out in front us, murky water splashing under our boots. The stench of mold turns to something more nauseating, one even worse than flesh burning.

I try not to gag. "What is that?"

"The smell of bodies rotting."

"Where is it coming from?" I whisper.

He nods into the darkness. "The old labs where the scientists worked before they built the Dome. The place where they figured out how people could walk in the sun again." His tone is sarcastic. We both know no one can walk in the sun. Everyone in Burn 3 is hiding, above *and* belowground. "The labs are abandoned now. At least, they're supposed to be."

The hair rises on the back of my neck. "Who's in there?"

He stops, the edges of his coat floating in the ankle-deep water. "You really don't know what they're doing down here, do you?" His expression is a twisted mixture of terror and wonder, as if he can't fathom the idea.

I shake my head, afraid to answer.

"They're stealing kids so they can sell them for parts."

I couldn't have heard him right. I want to run and pretend this guy inhaled too much burning plastic—that everything he's told me is the delusion of a rotted mind. Anything to avoid asking the next question I know I have to ask. "What kind of parts?"

He doesn't hesitate. "Why do you think they call them Skinners?"

The ground slides out from under me, and I stagger.

My sister . . .

He reaches out and grabs my elbow to steady me. "If they have your sister and she looks the way you say, we have to hurry."

The words turn over in my mind, but I can't make sense of them. There is only one word caught in the tangled threads of my thoughts.

Skinner.

I push past it, forcing myself to hear what this stranger is saying. "If she looks what way?"

"Light-haired," he says. "It's rare. I haven't seen someone with light hair since—" He stops, his expression defeated. "Rare things are always worth more money to the people doing the selling. And the ones buying."

He is talking about Sky like she is a bottle of clean water or a book—an object to be bought and sold at one of the stalls in the underground market. He doesn't know how kind she is— the way she shares her food packets with the poorer children in the domicile, though she never has enough to eat herself. The way she pretends the life we have now is equal to the one we had when my father was alive to protect us. The way she never doubts me, even when I doubt myself.

I look at the man I'm following blindly. "What's your name?"

Suddenly, I want to know. I am trusting him with my sister's life, which is worth much more to me than my own.

He strikes the flint on the lighter again, and the flame casts a strange glow over his face. "A name is a way to make a claim. No one can claim me."

I watch the familiar paranoia creep into his features. He reminds me of my father again. "A name is also the way you claim your friends."

He turns his back on me and disappears into the darkness. "I don't need any friends."

I follow the echo of his footsteps in silence, hoping with each step that we are getting closer to Sky. I try to ignore the grim reality—that if I find her and this man is telling the truth, she won't be alone.

I need to know more about the Skinners—these monsters kidnapping children to sell their skin. For what? I didn't even know.

"What—" I almost can't ask. "What are they doing with their skin?"

He grabs my arm and pulls me against the wall. There are voices in the distance, but they're too far away to make out anything intelligible. "Shh. The tunnels echo."

My heart bangs against my ribs, and I try not to make a sound while he stares down the black hole.

He pushes his long, greasy hair out of his face. "They sell the good skin for grafts."

"Grafts?" I've never heard the word before.

He rubs his good eye, and I notice how thin his arm is under the long coat. I wonder when he ate last. My father forgot to eat sometimes. He said he lost his sense of taste and smell after the Evacuation, and everything tasted like cardboard—whatever that was.

"You can replace burned skin with new skin. At least a doctor can. They call it a skin graft. Works better than those expensive salves," he says. "And people say it looks almost as good as the skin you were born with."

It sounds barbaric and painful. "Who would do something like that?"

He laughs, the sound laced with bitterness. "Wealthy people who don't want to look like they've been burned like the rest of us."

"They're willing to kill kids to get rid of their burns?" The

Skinners aren't the only monsters.

"Maybe they don't ask questions about where it comes from. Or maybe they do. People are capable of all kinds of evil." He peers down the tunnel again.

"Why doesn't someone stop them?" I realize how accusatory it sounds, but I don't care.

"The Skinners run things down in the Abyss. People that question them end up dead—along with their friends, their families, in some cases whole tunnels full of their neighbors. There's no Protectorate down here. The Skinners are the law. No one can touch them."

I can see the shame hiding in his eyes.

He swallows hard. "Time to go."

We follow the muffled sounds until we reach the mouth of the tunnel. The passage in front of us looks more like a cavern than a sewage tunnel. A gray metal building stands a few yards away, artificial light illuminating the barred windows. This place looks more like a prison than a laboratory.

The man who refuses to tell me his name pulls a gun from the back of his waistband. It's old, and it doesn't resemble the weapons protectorate officers carry.

He notices me staring. "It's a semiautomatic, from the days before the Burn." He slides a cartridge out of the bottom. "This thing doesn't shoot fire. These are hollow-tip rounds. They can kill you in the blink of an eye."

"Do I need one of those?"

"Only have one," he whispers. "Guess that means I'm going first."

He edges his way closer as shadows move in front of the windows. I realize he's risking his life to help me, and I wonder why.

But there's no time. He's already at the door using something to pick the lock. I rush to catch up, my mind racing.

How many Skinners are inside? Do we stand a chance against the kind of people who cut the skin off children?

He grabs my outercoat, his voice low. "When we get in there, we'll only have a few minutes." He nods at the door. "That's the surgical room. Run past and stay to the right. They keep the kids in a box in the back. If they're still here."

A box?

Bile rises in my throat, but I force it back down.

"What if it's locked?" I try not to picture my sister trapped in a box like an animal.

He hands me a thin piece of metal. "Slip this in the lock and jiggle it around until you hear a click. Then get the kids out of here."

"What if they aren't there?"

"If they're still alive, they will be."

"How do you know?"

"I've been here before." It's the last thing he says before he pops the lock.

We step inside and I freeze. Metal tables and trays of crude instruments covered in dry blood dominate the room. A dirty pole with a plastic bag suspended from it looms in the corner. I don't want to think about what they do in here.

Was Sky in here?

My stomach convulses.

"Go," he hisses at me, pointing to the door at the end of the room.

I obey and rush to the dark corridor on the other side. I stay to the right like he told me, working my way to the far side of the building. I hear muffled voices in other rooms, but I can't stop or think about what the Skinners will do to me if they catch me.

Instead I think about Sky. I pretend she's only a few feet away and all I have to do is get there.

The corridor is dimly lit, but I see the rectangular metal container at the end. It looks like a rusted shipping container from a factory. The box.

When I get closer, I see the slats along the sides of the metal. The stench of sweat is everywhere, and it fills me with hope. If the kids were dead, the odor would be different. But it could also be the lingering scent of children who are no longer inside. . . .

I slip the thin piece of metal in the lock and move it around. Nothings happens.

I try again. This time I hear the pop, and I pull the door open, anticipating the worst.

Nothing could've prepared me for what I find inside.

Eight or ten children huddle together in the corner. Most

of them look about Sky's age, but some are older. They're filthy, dressed in torn hospital gowns. But I know if I make it out of this place alive, it's the look in their eyes that will haunt me forever—complete and utter terror.

There's nothing else left.

I run toward them, trying to find my sister in the huddle. "Sky?"

A soft sound pushes its way forward from the back of the group. "Phoenix?"

I try to move the other children out of the way so I can find her. "I'm not going to hurt you," I promise them.

I see a stripe of blond hair.

Sky looks up at me, her face as tormented as the others. Her eyes look less blue somehow. I gather her into my arms. "I'm going to get you out of here. All of you."

Flashes of hope pass across their faces, though some of them seem too weak to react.

"That's a big promise for a girl who's in way over her head."

My neck snaps back to the door.

A huge man stands in the doorway. His face is noticeably lighter than his hands. He's probably used the skin of some helpless child to repair his own. But there are other thin scars—most likely made by knives—running down his neck. His brown outercoat is crusted in dry blood, and he's holding a Protectorate-issue firearm.

I pull Sky to her feet and shove her behind me. "I—I came for my sister."

The man stares over my shoulder at Sky. "She's not going anywhere. We'll get a lot for her skin. Those blue eyes too." I shudder, and he looks me over. "Yours not so much. But if your legs are clean, you'll be worth skinning."

He steps into the small container, so close I can almost reach out and touch him. Another man steps inside behind him, holding an identical weapon. He moves to the corner, covering me from a different angle.

"I'll stay. Just let my sister go."

Both men laugh, and I want to kill them.

"I say you let them all go," a familiar voice calls from the corridor. His expression is fierce, the patch covering his missing eye. He's pointing his gun at the man doing the talking.

"Ransom. I was wondering when you'd come back," the man in the bloodstained outercoat says. "Looking for work?"

"I had no idea what you were doing down here, Erik," Ransom, the man who refused to tell me his name, responds.

Erik laughs. "The lies we tell ourselves."

"You said we were doing experiments to help burn victims."

The corner of Erik's mouth lifts. "Technically, it was true."

Ransom's expression hardens even more. "Today it's going to get you killed if you don't let these kids go."

Erik raises an eyebrow and points his weapon at Ransom. "You shouldn't have come back. I warned you, didn't I? And look what it cost you last time."

Last time.

"I should've killed you then." Ransom winces and his jaw tightens.

"Except you couldn't." Erik glances at the guy in the other corner of the container. "The odds have never been in your favor."

Ransom's grip on the gun tightens. "I'll say it one more time. Let them go."

"No one's going anywhere. Think you can point that relic at me and I'll hand over the kids?" Erik's eyes narrow. "I'm gonna burn the skin off your bones. Then I'll take your other eye and sell it to the lowest bidder."

The man in the corner laughs. "Maybe we should give it away."

Ransom examines the outdated gun in his hand. "This thing is my good luck charm. But I did bring some other *relics* with me."

Ransom opens his outercoat, revealing a black vest covered in bricks of plastic that look like putty. He raises his free hand, holding some kind of switch attached to the vest. "Remember C-4, Erik? It's old, but you used it to blow up plenty of tunnels down here."

I remember when Ransom disappeared behind the screen in his shack. He must have put the vest on then.

The kids start crying.

"Why now, Ransom?" Erik taunts. "You could've come back here a million times. Is your mind finally that far gone?"

Ransom glances in my direction, but he's not looking at me.

He's staring at the wisp of tangled blond hair peeking out from behind me. Just like the blond boy's hair in the photo on his wall.

"I'm doing this for my son. For Alex. You're not taking him again."

I realize he's referring to Sky, and I'm not sure if it's the delusions talking or if he means it symbolically.

Erik's expression changes. He realizes he's not going to be able to scare Ransom. Right now, Ransom is the most terrifying person in the room. And—judging by whatever he has strapped to his chest—the most dangerous.

"You have ten seconds to let them go before I start counting. If you do, I might let you live. But I'm blowing this place either way."

Ransom's lying. He's going to kill them. I can tell by the way he looks almost happy.

Erik nods at the other man. "Turn them loose."

I grab Sky's hand and help up some of the children. They look dazed, as if they aren't really sure what's happening. The ones with bandages on their arms lean against the stronger children as we inch our way between the men locked in a standoff.

I stop in the doorway and look at Ransom—the man who saved my sister and all the other children stumbling down the corridor now.

The man who's half crazy and all hero.

"Thank you."

He nods. "Thanks for reminding me there's always a way to right a wrong. Now get out of here."

We run through the passage and the sadistic surgical room, into the mouth of the tunnel that led me here. We're only a few yards away when the deafening sound of the explosion hits.

The concrete around us rumbles, and I can see the fire consuming the building in the distance.

For a moment, I can't move. I stare at the flames that keep us locked in the shadow of a life only some people remember. Fire has always represented pain and sorrow for me. A sad sort of imprisonment none of us can escape.

Today, it represents something else.

Freedom.

A tiny girl with knotted curls is sobbing. "I don't know how to find my way home."

A boy with dark-brown eyes glances around. "Me either."

Sky squeezes my hand and looks up at me, her eyes the shade of blue I remember. "My sister knows the way."

I study their tear-streaked faces and I think about my father. The way he led so many down here to safety; the way I'm about to lead only a few back up now. I think about the price he paid for it, and what he said to me the last time I saw him.

Be brave, Phoenix.

Today I was braver than I ever believed I could be.

Today I changed things.

Sky is still staring up at me. "You know the way, don't you, Phoenix?"

For the first time, I know I do.

LOVE IS A CHOICE

Beth Revis

I DON'T WANT to kill him, but I will if I have to.

A smooth plastic bottle rests in my right pocket. Inside are three pills. Only three. I have to get more. It's as simple as that. I have to get more. Without the pills, my mind will be contaminated by the drug in the water used to control the populace. Phydus will make me acquiesce to Eldest's rule. It will make me give up.

I grip the knife in my left pocket. It's crudely made from a scrap of metal I found near my hiding place, but it will do what I need it to do. It will get me the pills I need.

I run both hands through my tangled, dirty hair, yanking against the matted knots. I don't want to do this. I don't want to do this. But what choice has Eldest left me? I used to get one pill a day, like clockwork. That pill protected me from the drugged waters that are piped throughout the ship, the chemicals that make nearly everyone else aboard *Godspeed* a mindless minion of Eldest. When I started to question Eldest, though, when I started using this brain of mine that had been sheltered so long by the daily blue-and-white pills . . . that's when Eldest tried to have me killed.

The only reason I escaped is because Doc didn't want to be responsible for killing a kid. I'm not that much of a kid. Practically a man. Nineteen. Doc might have let me go then, to fake my death and try hiding out in a ship that's too small to hide anything forever, but if I don't get more pills, I might as well give myself up to Eldest now.

I take a deep breath. I've been hiding in the walls of the ship for so long that I have almost forgotten the scent of dirt and grass. I had not known before how the stench of metal and dust had woven into my very bones until the clean air purged me. This is the largest level of the ship, the easiest level to hide in. Ten square miles of farmland with a city in the distance, all surrounded by metal walls painted blue to simulate a sky none of us have ever seen. One day *Godspeed* will land on the new planet, and we'll get a real sky.

But until then . . .

I reach into my pocket and clench the knife in my fist.

I keep close to the wall. I can't afford to be seen here. I can't afford to be seen anywhere.

I creep up to the Recorder Hall, a giant brick building that houses all the records of Sol-Earth: literature, history, science, all written before the ship launched, most of it before the authors even thought launching a ship across the universe was possible. The Hall is empty now—no more students, only an ancient old man to wander among the ancient old texts.

The solar lamp is turned off and darkness blankets the ship, keeping me hidden. Everyone should be asleep. Especially the old Recorder.

The Recorder is of the oldest generation, a weak man who acquiesces to any of Eldest's demands, not because he is drugged but because he wants nothing more than to do Eldest's bidding.

Not because he is drugged. He has the pills I need. I just have to take them.

The giant front doors squeak when I push them open. I slip inside and shut them as quietly as I can.

Inside, the entryway of the Hall reminds me of when I was younger, when Eldest favored me. He would bring me here and let me run my hands over the digital membrane screens that decorate the walls, lighting them up with images and vids and music. My fingers ache with a foolish desire to turn on the closest screen. I've filled my time in hiding with my own thoughts—how I can survive, how I can one day take down Eldest, how I can change the ship for the better. I'm sick of my own voice.

"Who's there?"

I freeze. My fingers are hard and numb around the knife in my pocket.

That was not the voice of an old man. That was a woman's voice, clear and strong.

"I know someone's there. Don't make me com Eldest."

Frex.

"Wait!" I say, stepping into the center of the entryway. I let go of the knife, hold up my empty hands.

The lights flick on. I blink, momentarily blinded by the brightness.

"Who are you?" the voice demands again.

"Who are *you*?" I shoot back, rubbing my eyes. "What happened to the Recorder?" I try to think of the old man who used to be the Recorder—he was old, but not so old that he would need a replacement already.

The woman's hand shakes as it hovers over her wireless communicator. She's only a few years older than me, but a childlike fear fills her eyes.

"Don't com Eldest," I plead. "Just—wait."

She steps around the desk. "The old Recorder was my grandfather," she says. "He . . . decided to retire. He let me take his place. We didn't tell Eldest."

The corner of my mouth twitches up. This girl is clever—and so was her grandfather. Much more clever than I would have thought. The grandfather is probably drugged up now, whiling away his later years on one of the farms that produce the food for the ship. By swapping places with this girl, he ensured that she would get his ration of blue-and-white pills, that his granddaughter would be able to think for herself.

And they didn't tell Eldest, who would have put a stop to such independent thinking.

Maybe . . . maybe she'll be on my side. Maybe I don't have to stand up against Eldest by myself.

"What do you want?" she asks, suspicion tainting her voice.

"I—I . . ." I stutter, unsure of what to say.

"I know you," she says.

I duck my head down, hoping my bedraggled hair will hide my features, but it's too late.

"You . . . you're *dead*. Eldest told everyone you *died*."

I glance up, meeting her eyes. "Eldest lied."

She approaches me warily, but I'm not sure if she hesitates because she's afraid of me, or afraid I'll run. I stand very, very still. When she's only inches away from me, she reaches up and touches the side of my face, tucking my hair behind my ear.

She gasps.

I raise a hand to cover the scar on the side of my neck. It's still fresh, puckered and pink, and it hurts to the touch.

She touches the side of her own neck where, just behind her left ear, a wi-com button is embedded. Implanted under our skin at birth, wi-coms provide easy communication with everyone onboard *Godspeed*. But they also provide Eldest with a locator. When I went into hiding, I had to get rid of my wi-com. I rub my fingers together, remembering the way they were slick with my own blood as I gouged the device from my neck.

"Why are you here?" the girl asks, and I know she's talking about more than just why I'm in the Recorder Hall.

"Eldest . . ." I swallow. I've held on to the secrets Eldest tried to kill me for; I'm not ready to give them up to a girl with big, innocent eyes. "I've been in hiding. From Eldest. But I need . . . I'm running out of supplies."

The young woman's face lights up. Even though she's my elder, I feel like an old man next to her vivacity. "Sanctuary!" she says enthusiastically.

"Sanctuary?"

She darts to the other end of the room, to a desk by the wall, and grabs up a heavy book from Sol-Earth. "Just like in this story," she says, running back to me and pushing the book into my hands. *The Hunchback of Notre Dame* by Victor Hugo. "You," she says, "are seeking sanctuary. Back on Sol-Earth, in this place called Pah-rees, if you were in trouble, you'd go to Note-ree Dame, and you could hide there in safety."

I hand the thick book back to her. "You're going to let the Recorder Hall be my sanctuary?"

She nods eagerly. "I'll protect you from Eldest!"

I can't help but smile, even though I'm worried that this young woman has no idea what she's doing, offering sanctuary to me. Against Eldest. Eldest may look like a kind old grandfather, but he rules *Godspeed* more fiercely than any dictator. The few who don't obey him because of the drugged water obey him because of their fear.

Except, maybe, this girl, alone in the Recorder Hall and

ignored by all but the books.

"You can't tell anybod—" I start.

"Of course not!" She cuts me off, looking wounded that I would even suggest that she would reveal my location.

I don't want to trust her. I don't want to trust *anybody*. But the thing is . . . I can't live in hiding in a forgotten part of the ship for the rest of my life.

"My name is Mag," the woman says. She searches my eyes, and I can tell that she wants me to stay.

"I'm—"

"I *know* who you are."

Everyone does. I'm the heir to Eldest's tyranny. I'm the one who was supposed to take over the ship after him.

I was the one he tried to have killed when I disagreed with him.

"I'm not that person anymore," I say. "I can't be."

"You need a new name," Mag says.

I open my mouth but don't speak, my mind racing to come up with a name for her.

"No!" she says, her voice bouncing off the high walls of the Recorder Hall. "We'll find a name for you!"

She turns to the giant digital membrane screens hanging from the walls and starts tapping on one. "Let's name you after a story," she says. "What about Quasimodo? He was in that story I was telling you about earlier. No," she says before I have a chance to speak. "His name's too long and weird. Maybe something from Shakespeare? Like Oberon or Puck?

Or Romeo?" She giggles. Names flash on the screen she's working on: lists of characters in the books preserved in the Recorder Hall, names of authors, charts of the most popular names used on Sol-Earth when the ship launched, a genealogy of the first generations born on *Godspeed*.

"I know," Mag says, stopping her search and whirling around to face me. "I *know*. We'll name you after a constellation. It makes perfect sense."   .

There is something poetic in the idea: name me after the stars we're soaring through.

"Here." A star chart appears on the wall screen, with lines connecting the dots of stars and little name labels beside them.

She steps back, and it's not until she's studiously staring at the star chart that I realize how quiet the Recorder Hall is without her voice.

"What about that one?" she asks, pointing.

"Hercules?" I say.

She nods. "He was a hero in a lot of the really old stories."

"No." I shake my head. I'm no hero.

Mag frowns—not at me, at the chart. This is a puzzle for her to figure out, nothing more.

"That one." I point to a trio of stars lined up. "Orion."

"Orion? I don't know that story. . . ."

I do. "He's a hunter." Much more fitting than a hero.

"Orion," she says to the chart. She speaks slowly, as if tasting the word. Then she turns to me. "Orion," she says, and with that, I am named.

———————

It only takes three months for me to consider life at the Recorder Hall normal. Mag and I share the little room in the back of the third floor of the Hall—I sleep on the floor, she sleeps on the bed. We've slowly started increasing the food rations we take. There has never been a limit to the amount of food given out—with Phydus, people tend to only eat what they need—but we don't want to risk some observant record keeper who isn't on Phydus discovering a sudden spike in food consumption from the Recorder Hall.

Mag's meds are delivered to her daily, one pill at a time, through the automatic dispenser built into her wall. She went to the Hospital with a faked stomach pain, though, and swiped a hundred-count bottle of pills for me. I keep it with me at all times. I have long since learned that if I have the choice between food and meds on this ship, the meds are more precious.

Now I upend the bottle Mag stole for me. Two pills fall into my hand. I put one in my mouth and swallow, then carefully put the remaining pill back in the bottle.

Mag pokes her finger into the dispenser in her wall and withdraws her own pill.

"I need to get more meds," I say.

Mag stares at the blue-and-white pill in her hand. "I'm going to visit my grandfather today," she finally says.

"Why?" I ask.

Her fingers curl over the pill. "I miss him."

I watch her, but she doesn't lift the pill to her mouth.

"He won't be the same," I say eventually.

Her fingers go lax. "I know." She puts the pill on her tongue and swallows.

I don't want her to go. Although it's been months—nearly a year—since Mag and her grandfather switched places, I find it hard to believe that Eldest, who knows everything on this ship, hasn't noticed. Going to her grandfather may draw attention to the fact they swapped roles, and that may bring Eldest here—to her, and to me.

But I can't keep her locked up in the Recorder Hall. I can't ask that of her. Just because I'm trapped doesn't mean I can imprison Mag. Maybe she has escaped Eldest's watchful eye, and she should take advantage of that while she can.

While she goes off to the farms to find her grandfather, I go down to the book rooms. I've been reading up on all the civic and social sciences materials from Sol-Earth. While the civics room is among the smallest of the collections in the Recorder Hall—more than twice the amount of space is reserved for mathematics, and twice that again is reserved for science—there are plenty of books on government to keep me busy.

I find that the volumes I tend to gravitate toward are not the thick, heavy tomes full of history and analysis. Instead, it's the thin books that I spend the most time with. Plato's *Republic*. Thomas Paine's *Common Sense*. Martin Luther's *Ninety-Five Theses*—even though that one's about religion, which I will admit to understanding nothing about, it's also about who has the ability to dictate for others what is right and what is wrong. Sometimes it feels as if the shorter the book is, the harder it is to understand. The Magna Carta is tiny, but there are three books here in the Hall, each more than two inches thick, that try to explain just how important it is.

I push aside the analytical commentaries and look just at the source texts. In one stack I have *The Republic, Common Sense, Ninety-Five Theses,* and now the Magna Carta. I slide over Thoreau's "Civil Disobedience," then add Thomas More's *Utopia.*

On the other side of the table, I have a collection of essays written by samurai on Bushido, Machiavelli's *The Prince,* an Indian book called *Arthashastra,* and *Quotations from Chairman Mao Tse-tung.*

This is the difference. On one side are the books that advocate voting and sharing the government with the people. The other has books that Eldest would agree with: a strong leader using fear or violence to control. This is it, as black-and-white as the pages inside the books.

I draw the stack on the right side closer to me. This is where I should find the key to overthrowing Eldest, making the ship into a world where people can live freely, with the truth and without the hazy acquiescence Phydus provides.

I remember Eldest, when I first learned of the drugs he put in the water.

"Give me that bucket, boy," he said. I was thirteen years old, and felt special that he included me in today's work rather than keeping me cooped up with lessons.

The bucket wasn't big, but the syrupy liquid inside was heavy, and I had to use both arms to carry it. Eldest took it from me one-handed and lifted it to a small spout built into the side of the water pump.

"I thought the vits were already distributed," I say, watching the liquid slide down into the pump.

"These aren't vitamins."

I chew on the inside of my cheek. I don't ask questions: I want to prove to Eldest how smart I am by figuring this puzzle out for myself.

Eldest seems to know I can't, though. He sets the empty bucket down and turns to stare at me.

"What's the biggest danger on this ship, boy?" he growls.

I think for a moment, but Eldest is emanating impatience. "Disease," I say quickly, thinking of the Plague that decimated our population a few gens ago.

Eldest shakes his head. "We can recover from disease. The thing we couldn't recover from?" He waits a moment, but I have no answer. "Mutiny. We're alone out here, boy. Alone. Ain't nothing on the other side of the ship's walls but the vacuum of space. Nowhere to go. If this ship rises up in mutiny, we'll kill ourselves. The mission will be lost. A revolution would be suicide for everyone."

I think about what he says, my eyes drifting to the heavy steel walls that line the room.

"This stuff?" Eldest kicks the bucket. "This stuff prevents mutiny. This saves us all."

I stare at the two stacks of books I've arranged on the metal table.

With a broad sweep of my arm, I topple them into each other, mixing the titles.

It's not as simple as black-and-white, right or wrong.

When I first started questioning Eldest, I was doing just that: asking questions. But I realized soon enough that asking questions was the worst possible thing I could ever do.

I did it anyway.

But even now, I'm still asking questions. Only now, instead of questioning Eldest, I'm starting to question myself. Would a revolution be good? Should I risk everything—even the lives of everyone on board this ship—for what I think is right?

"What are you doing?" Mag's voice cuts through my concentration and makes me jump in surprise.

"I didn't know you'd be back so soon!" I say, masking my worry with a smile.

She doesn't return my grin; her eyes are rimmed with red, her jaw clenched. "I've been gone for two hours."

I bite back a word of surprise. I'd not realized I'd been in the book room so long.

She crosses the small room and sits opposite me. "Are you reading all these?"

"Already read them."

Mag is silent for a long moment. Her eyes stare at the

books, but I don't think she's really seeing them.

"What am I doing, Mag?" I say to the mixed-up books on the table. "I thought . . . I thought it would all be worth it." My fingers go unconsciously to the spiderweb scar behind my left ear, where I removed my wi-com in order to hide from Eldest. "But now I'm just spending my life in hiding, not even fighting." I pause. "Not even sure if I should fight. Maybe Eldest isn't entirely wrong."

"The drugs are wrong." Mag spits out the words, vehemence making her voice rise. "And Eldest is wrong for using them."

I look up at her. I'd noticed her red eyes when she came in, but now I see the sorrow mixed with rage behind them. "Did you see your grandfather?" I ask gently.

Mag growls.

"What happened?" I say.

She looks down at the mess of books on the table, over to the shelves behind me, up at the tiny window high in the wall. She looks everywhere but at me. "He was on Phydus."

She finally meets my eyes. "It's like he was dead inside."

That's what Phydus does. It turns you into a mindless drone, a worker for Eldest to use, and nothing more.

"Weren't you on Phydus before your grandfather gave you his spot here?" I ask.

Mag nods. "Of course. I didn't even know about Phydus. He brought me here and started giving me half doses using his own meds. He'd pop the capsules open and sprinkle the

Inhibitor med onto my breakfast. There was a short time—maybe a week?—when I was starting to come out of the influence of Phydus, and he was starting to fall under it."

"What did it feel like?" I ask. As Eldest's chosen heir, I was always on the meds that prevent Phydus from controlling me.

Mag's eyes lose focus as she remembers. "It was like . . . nothing. It was like living in a state of nothing. Nothing ever really hurt. Nothing bothered me. Everything was so . . . peaceful."

Her answer surprises me. "It sounds nice."

"I think it was nice," she says. "At least, it was nice to be the one on Phydus. But now that I take Inhibitor pills, I see others on Phydus. I see Granddad. And . . . it's not nice to see him like that."

I try to imagine Mag on Phydus. She's so *vibrant*, it's hard to picture her with empty eyes. But then I remember the way Eldest's face hardened when he told me about mutiny. Rage burns within Mag like a smoldering ember.

I don't know if I fear that rage . . . or love it.

I can trace back to that day in the library as the day everything changed. I don't know if it was my words that affected Mag or if it was seeing her grandfather on Phydus, but that smoldering ember grew into a flame. First she read the books I had spread out on the table—all of them. That took her nearly a month, but although she was silent and reserved, I could tell that her passion was only growing.

Then one morning, Eldest makes an announcement.

He coms everyone just as the solar lamp turns on the 132nd day I've been in hiding, ordering them to meet at the statue of the Plague Eldest in the garden behind the Hospital. Mag goes early, but even though so many months have passed and I think I would blend into the crowd, I fear getting too close to Eldest. Instead, I watch from the art gallery's windows in the Recorder Hall.

Eldest takes the grav tube from his level to this one. He doesn't avoid the Keeper Level, but he does make sure that every time he graces the lowest level with his presence, people notice.

He moves quickly from the grav tube entrance down the path, toward the garden. He carries something in his arms, something bundled up and wiggly. I press against the glass to see what he has—and as soon as I do, Eldest pauses and looks up at the Recorder Hall. I draw immediately back into the shadows, afraid he's noticed me, but his attention is quickly diverted back to the thing in his arms.

The sleeves of his elaborately embroidered robe slip, and I dare to lean forward, straining to see. . . .

A baby.

He's carrying a baby.

My replacement.

I watch as Eldest carries the baby to the garden and then raises it up for all the crowd to see. I don't need to hear his words to know what he's saying. He's saying this child is the new heir. He's saying this baby will reign after him now that I am—apparently—gone for good.

I turn away before the crowd starts to disperse and trudge down to the civics book room. The books Mag has been reading are still scattered on the metal table, with tabs and notes sticking out of many pages. She didn't divide the books up by right or wrong, Eldest or not, as I did; instead, she's found something in each title.

I'm just not sure what.

I hear the heavy front doors open—she's back. I rush out of the book room and toward the hall that leads to the main entryway. I'm almost to the front when I hear Mag speak in a loud, ringing voice.

"Just this way, sir!"

I immediately press against the wall, hoping that the shadows of the poorly lit hallway are enough to hide me. *Sir.* That could only mean—

"Thank you," Eldest's voice says, much softer, but the sound is one I'll never forget.

Another sound wafts through the Hall and into the shadows where I lurk: a whimper. Barely audible, soft and gentle. The baby.

"He's a handsome boy," Mag says, but her tone belies her friendly words.

The baby huffs as, I think, Eldest shifts him in his arms. I dare to glance around the doorway—Eldest and Mag are facing the other direction, toward the outer door, and the baby, over Eldest's shoulder, is looking directly at me.

I meet his wide, dark-brown eyes. He can't be more than a few days old. He stares intently at me, as if there is meaning behind his gaze, but there's not. He's just a baby. Already entwined in Eldest's dark plots.

He will be raised just like I was. Passed from family to family until Eldest decides to start training him. Thrust into his role too young, far too young. Eldest will expect him to know everything from the moment he begins training. He'll be punished for silly things, like asking too many questions or walking too fast or stomping too loudly in the Keeper Level. He'll live for the rare moments when Eldest smiles or—even better—lets a compliment fall from his lips. He will spend his whole life questioning whether he's good enough, fearing that he's not. He'll listen to every single word Eldest says, try to uncover meaning in every intonation, and seek with his entire self the hidden secrets he'll need to know to be a good leader after Eldest.

And maybe one day, he'll start to think about the things Eldest doesn't say.

Those big brown eyes blink, and it's only then that I realize I've actually stepped out, past the shadows and into the entryway. If Eldest turned now, he would see me. I suck in a gasp and throw myself back into the dark.

"I wanted to ask you something," Eldest says, his voice snaking across the hall to me.

"Yes?" Mag doesn't let any fear creep into her voice.

"Has anyone been frequenting the Recorder Hall in the past month?"

"No." After a moment, Mag adds, "Sir."

"You've been alone here."

"Yes."

Eldest says something too low for me to hear. Then: "I let you take your grandfather's place, even though neither of you asked permission. I don't want you to get the impression that I didn't know, or that it isn't only because I allowed it that you are in this role."

"Yes, sir." There is fear in her voice now, but still a hint of defiance.

"Someone's been looking at some highly . . . interesting documents on the floppy network. If no one's been in the Hall but you . . ." Eldest lets the accusation hang in the air.

Before Mag can think of an answer, the baby starts to cry. Not the fussy whimpers of before, but an earsplitting wail. Eldest shifts the baby again, but to no avail. The more the baby cries, the angrier Eldest gets; the angrier Eldest gets, the more insistent the cries. In moments, Eldest storms from the Hall.

Mag waits several minutes after the big doors close and the baby's cries fade before she whispers, "Orion?"

I step out of the shadows.

"He knows I've been researching."

"What *have* you been researching?" I ask. I didn't know she'd taken her studies past the books.

"Methods of rebellion. Weapons. Strategy."

"Mag!" Well, of *course* Eldest would have noticed that sort of thing.

She shrugs. "I'm just glad the baby started crying. It'll give me a chance to think of an excuse."

"That baby . . ."

"He's your replacement." Mag's voice is blunt, harsh.

"Still, he's kind of cute. You can't help but like the little guy."

"Yes," she says, very seriously, "you can."

That night, Mag stays in the book rooms so late that I fall asleep without her. I wake up, though, to the sensation of her lips pressed against mine.

I jerk back, surprised, sitting up.

A slow, twisty smile spreads across her face.

"What—?" I ask.

She tucks a strand of my hair—it's getting so long now—behind my left ear. Her fingers linger on the bumpy scar there. Her touch is gentle but unrelinquishing. She pulls me closer.

Her lips touch mine, shy now, but an almost inaudible gasp slips from her mouth into mine, and I'm undone. I grab her and pull her closer, and the kiss deepens, turning swiftly into something else, something more, and we're both lost to each other.

She's gone before I wake up the next morning. I get out of bed slowly, hoping that, perhaps, she'll come back, but no—she's really gone. After I shower and dress, I search the Recorder Hall, but there's no sign of Mag anywhere.

Everything's changed now. How could it not?

I try to think of what the future may hold. I won't hide forever. It's not that I can't—but that I won't.

I think of the baby Eldest will raise as his, to take the place I would have had as leader. That baby holds more possibilities than I can imagine. If I'm patient . . . if I wait . . .

I couldn't start a rebellion on my own. There's no way. Between the controlling power of Phydus and the unremitting strategy of Eldest, any effort to reform the ship now would result in bloodshed . . . a lot of it. There are vids of the one rebellion *Godspeed* suffered, and the ship very nearly died out as a result. I may not agree with Eldest's methods, but I do know that I can't risk the lives of everyone just to take control of the ship for myself.

But maybe with Mag . . .

We could plan. Take it slow. Find a way to filter out the Phydus, bring people to our side one at a time. There is in the history books something called the Glorious Revolution. A bloodless revolt that shifted the power smoothly from one king to another.

It might take a lifetime to engineer, but if we could do it, if we plan just right—

I try to talk myself out of these thoughts, but then I force myself to stop. No. I don't want to talk myself out of these thoughts. I *want* to have my own Glorious Revolution. I want to prove to Eldest that I can rule without the drug, that we can tell the people of *Godspeed* the *real* truth—and then we can all vote, decide in a fair way what to do next. . . .

I go straight to my hidden place, the place where I cowered for so long before daring to go to the Recorder Hall. No one knows where it is, no one but me. Even Eldest, who thinks he knows all, has forgotten about the secrets *Godspeed* still keeps.

In my haste, I don't even think about how I should cover my face outside, how I should make sure no one's following me. I just go, my single thought to begin the plans that will change the ship forever.

When I get to the place, I pause in surprise. While I lived here, it seemed as if the area was small, but almost . . . homey? Now it's claustrophobic.

"This is where you hid before?"

I whirl around—standing in the door, light from the Feeder Level spilling around her, is Mag.

Stupid, stupid, stupid. I should have been more careful. What if it hadn't been Mag who found me?

She steps into the narrow space, closing the door behind her. I flip on the lights.

"It's so cramped here," she says.

But it doesn't feel that way anymore, not with her here, too.

With the both of us here, where I hid alone for so long, I feel the urge to reveal everything to her: the secrets I learned that drove Eldest to get rid of me, the plans I have, the Glorious Revolution I want to stage. I start, though, with Phydus, and how Eldest distributes the drug through the water to ensure that what I want—change—never happens.

Mag drinks it all in, her eyes growing rounder with every new revelation. Even Mag, with her rebellious heart, has not dreamed that *Godspeed* holds this many secrets.

"That's why he uses Phydus," she says softly. "The only way to keep this much secret is by drugging people up so much that they don't care anymore." She turns to me then, eyes wide. "We have to make them care again."

"I've been thinking," I tell her, "about how we can change things. Together."

Her expression lights up. "We *can* change things. *Now.* Take me to the Phydus pump. We'll disable it right now."

I shake my head. "We have to go slowly. We can topple Eldest's control from within."

"That won't be enough," she says, her words so fast that they blend together. "All we need to do is cut the Phydus machine off."

I shake my head. "I can't let you do that."

"You don't have a choice! Now that I know—I'll find that frexing pump myself and blow it up if I have to!"

"Mag . . . *Mag.*" I wait until her eyes are focused on me. "Doing something like that—just cutting off the whole ship's population at one time—that will lead to a huge revolt."

She nods, excited.

"No, you don't understand," I say. My voice is pleading. "Mutiny on this ship would lead to . . . imagine how people will react. When they discover Eldest's lies, they'll want to kill him."

"So?"

"And it's more than that. There are some lies that . . . Eldest has a reason for keeping some things secret."

Mag narrows her gaze. "You *agree* with him. He tried to kill you, Orion! You had to rip your wi-com out of your own flesh and have hidden for months from him! And you *agree* with him?"

"It's not that simple," I say. "I don't think it's right that he's controlling everyone, of course I don't. And I don't like the lies. But Mag—we're on a *ship*. In *space*. It would be so easy—so *easy*—for this to become too much, too quickly. The Feeder Level is a delicate biodome. The ship is not indestructible. We could kill ourselves out."

She waves her hand dismissively, but I won't let the matter drop. I grab a digital membrane screen I'd pocketed earlier and swipe my thumb over the access scanner. For a moment, I'm afraid Eldest has erased my access, but apparently he thought me dead enough to not bother with that. I bring up an old video feed, the same one Eldest showed me when he told me about the dangers of revolution.

I hand the screen to Mag when the vid starts playing. I know the video well: the way the farmers turned their tools into weapons, the way the blood stained the ground red, the way, in the end, nearly everyone was gone, a revolt so deadly we've still not recovered our numbers. While she watches the violent images flash across the screen, I watch her. I watch as the gleam in her eye sparkles, as the corner of her mouth slowly curls up.

In the Recorder Hall, we silently part ways—her to the civics book room, me to the gallery with the window that shows the Feeder Level. Mag still hasn't forgiven me for not letting her switch off the Phydus, and I haven't forgiven her for not realizing that a revolution doesn't have to involve blood.

I stare out at the Feeder Level from my position. The glass is warm, and my face leaves a blurry print. I shut my eyes, letting my full weight rest on the window, then turn and slide down the glass, sitting with my back to the only world I've known.

I touch the scar on my neck.

I cannot forget what Eldest has done. I cannot forget the truths he's covered up with Phydus.

But . . .

I cannot think that everything he's done is wrong. I cannot believe that every truth should be known.

Why did he try to kill me? Because I questioned him. Why are questions wrong? Because questions lead to revolt. Why is revolt wrong? Because revolution would kill us all.

This is what I know is true.

There's only one question left.

If all this is true, why did I push Eldest so hard he tried to kill me?

Because maybe a revolution would be worth it.

I wake up with my face pressed to the window, a slick line of drool dripping down the glass. My neck cracks as I stretch. I glance through the window—there is still mist on the fields; the solar lamp must have just clicked on.

And then I see him: a man, walking up the stairs to the front of the Recorder Hall.

I scramble away from the window, heart pounding. Was I seen?

I should hide. I know I should hide. But instead, I creep down the stairs. Before I reach the hallway, I hear shouting.

"What is going on?"

I know that voice: Doc. Eldest's only real friend, who let me escape death anyway.

"Hello, Doc." Mag's voice is calm, soft.

"He *knows*, you idiot girl, he knows. He's not stupid!"

"I have no idea what you're talking about."

Doc growls in anger. His voice grows louder and quieter, as if he's pacing back and forth. "Information. He keeps track of the network; he knows some very *questionable* documents and vids have been downloaded recently."

Oh, shite. The mutiny vids I showed Mag yesterday.

But . . . what documents?

"And do you really think that he wouldn't notice someone

flipped the Phydus machine off?"

My eyes bulge. She *wouldn't*. Would she? *Would she?* Did she sneak out while I slept and find the Phydus machine? It wouldn't be that hard, not after I showed her my hiding place. Did she just stroll into the pump room and turn the frexing thing off?

"I have no idea what you're talking about," Mag says again, but her tone is a confession enough for me. She did. She *did*. She didn't care about my protests, she didn't care about what I showed her yesterday.

"It's a frexing good thing that *I* caught it first and flipped the thing back on, you stupid girl. If *he* had seen it—"

"I don't care!" Mag screeches. "Let him find out! Let him try to stop us!"

Us.

"Do you have him?" Doc says, panic creeping into his voice. "Are you hiding him? Is he telling you how to cause trouble?"

Doc's footsteps grow closer. He has every right to be scared. If Eldest knew of Doc's betrayal, of the way he let me live, Doc would face the same punishment as I did, and Eldest would watch him die.

"Who?" Mag sounds innocently curious.

Doc starts to say my name, the name I was called before Orion, but he stops himself. He doesn't want to tip his hand to Mag if she really doesn't know.

"He's distracted now by the new baby," Doc says, his voice

calmer. "But he won't be for long. And he knows what you've done so far. It would take weeks, maybe even months, for Phydus to completely wear off the population. Stupid girl. Of course Eldest would know first. You're playing a dangerous game."

"I'm not playing."

And there it is. The threat behind her words.

The room is silent. I want to creep forward and see them, but I don't dare move.

"You've doubled your food rations. I'm missing bottles of Inhibitor meds. And somehow you, a stupid little girl from the Feeder Level, suddenly know about the hidden level of the ship, about Phydus and the water pump. If I can figure it out, you better believe Eldest will. If he hasn't already. And if he finds who I think you're hiding, we'll all be dead."

Mag doesn't answer.

"Do you know what happens when a living body is thrown into the vacuum of space?"

Mag still doesn't answer.

"It will take several seconds for your body to lose oxygen." Doc's voice is cold and calculating. He's trying to scare her. "Your eardrums will explode. Your spit will boil in your mouth. And finally, after all that, your brain will die."

"And Eldest thinks," Mag says slowly, "that doing this to me would stop a revolution if I started one?"

"You fool!" Doc bellows. There's a flurry of motion— I think Doc tries to shake her, and she wrenches out of his grasp.

"You know what I think Phydus really does?" Mag says, a hint of anger in her voice now. "I think it takes away choice. That's all. And I don't care if it does destroy the whole ship—if that's what we choose to do, at least we'll have made the choice."

After a moment, I hear footsteps heading toward the door. Doc leaves without another word.

Mag's determination doesn't change, but after Doc's visit she is, at least, more careful.

I try—once—to ask her to consider slowing down her rebellious plans. Eldest's power extends from more than just the drug. She's risking a lot for a single chance.

We need *plans*. We need contingency plans for the original plans. This is all too important. One wrong move, and the ship descends into chaos. One wrong move, and people die.

But Mag doesn't see it that way.

I was the one who questioned Eldest first. I was the one who was strapped to the table while Doc held a needle full of poison over me. I was the one who hid like a starved, beaten animal, waiting to see if my own exile would finish the job Eldest started.

And Mag is the one who will throw all that away on a haphazard plan to cobble together a revolution as quickly as possible.

"You know I love you?" she asks, both hands wrapped

around the sides of my face. I remember her words about the baby, how easy it was for her not to love him.

I kiss her, the bitter taste of regret mingling on both our tongues.

"It's important," she adds. "Giving people a choice."

I nod slowly. I *do* agree with her. But I worry that we can't carry a whole revolution on just our shoulders.

"But," I say, "you're doing this so people can have a choice. What if they're happier without one? What if they'd rather stay on Phydus? There's that old Sol-Earth saying, 'Ignorance is bliss.' Maybe, when they find out all these truths, they will choose Phydus."

She has no answer for that.

Mag spends more and more time in the book rooms. She pores over blueprints of the ship, schematics of the engine, diagrams of the Phydus pump. She studies how to build explosives and weapons. That's stage two. First, destroy the pump. Then hand out weapons so the people can destroy Eldest. And, I think, the whole ship with him.

When I bring her breakfast, she stares at the little capsule of Inhibitor meds a long moment before she swallows the pill.

"You agree with me, right? You think I'm doing the right thing?" she asks. This is the first time she's ever shown doubt.

"No," I say simply. "I don't."

"But you were the one who first questioned Eldest!"

I nod. "And look where it's gotten me. I was nearly killed; I'm in hiding now."

"Once we start the revolution," she says, "you won't have to hide anymore."

"If there's one thing I learned," I answer, "it's that a real revolution will take much more than a bomb on a water pump to start."

When I come with breakfast a few days later, I find Mag staring vacantly. I wave my hand in front of her face a few times before she blinks back into focus.

"Sorry," she mumbles. "I must be tired."

"Mag, I want to talk to you," I say, pushing the tray of breakfast food toward her. She fiddles with the Inhibitor pill.

"I want you to know," I say, "that I think it really would be better if we wait. There's a lot that Eldest has kept hidden. I think his heir will ask the same questions I did, and when he does, that will be the time to bring him to our side. We can't change anything by ourselves. But if we can crumble the Eldest system from within, we have a chance to really change the ship. We need change, but we don't need a revolution."

I'm thinking now of the things Mag doesn't know, of the secrets that make me question whether or not Phydus really is wrong. I may not agree with Eldest's methods, but at least I understand why he's done what he's done. And I know, I know deep inside of me, with the same conviction that led me to question Eldest in the first place, that a mutiny will fail. It will be crushed just like the first one was.

"No." Mag speaks with more force than I've heard from her in a long time. She swallows her Inhibitor pill dry. "No," she repeats. "I know the only way to do this is with a revolt."

That's fine.

I'm patient.

Haven't I already proven that before?

Another week goes by. Mag's plans crawl, then stop. She goes to the book rooms, but she doesn't read. She just stares.

I place the breakfast tray in front of her. She looks at it, but doesn't think to pick up her fork until I put it in her hand.

"I've been thinking a lot about your grandfather," I say.

"He was the Recorder." Her voice is meek, quiet.

"Yes, he was. And then you were."

"And then I was."

"Mag, remember how he switched places with you?" I ask. She chews on a bit of her breakfast.

"Remember what you said about the baby, Mag?" I ask gently.

"No," she whispers.

"You said you didn't have to love it."

She rests her hands on the table, still holding her fork.

"I realized something then, Mag," I say, still using the gentlest voice I can muster. "I realized then that love can be a choice."

Her big, empty eyes stare at me.

I reach across the table and pick up the Inhibitor pill capsule on her tray. I break it apart between my thumb and forefinger. White dust sprinkles out. "You gave me the idea for this. Or your grandfather did. He opened his own capsules up and sprinkled your food with the meds until they suppressed the Phydus in your system."

I lick my finger and touch the tiny pile of white dust. "I just did the opposite." I press the powder-dusted finger to my lips and taste the salt I used to replace the meds in her pills.

"Mag," I say, forcing my voice into a conversational tone. "I want to thank you. You saved me. You gave me more than sanctuary. You showed me that my mild questioning of Eldest wasn't enough, and that things will have to change."

Her grip slackens, and the fork slides from between her fingers to the table.

I set it back on the tray. "But I can't risk your carelessness. I've faced Eldest and nearly died for it. This is too big, too important, for you to throw everything away with reckless plans. It doesn't matter if I like you or not."

"Like? Love?" she whispers, the words struggling to escape from her Phydus-fogged mind.

"I can choose to love you," I say. "Or I can choose not to."

I help her stand. She follows meekly beside me as I lead her to the door of the Recorder Hall. "Go back to your grandfather. Go back to your other home. I will be the Recorder now."

She doesn't look back as she descends the stairs. I knew she wouldn't. That's what Phydus does. It makes you easy to control.

I stand in the shadow of the Recorder Hall, watching her go. I will stay here. I will be the Recorder. The Hall is rarely used, and I can stay in the shadows. As long as there's no more trouble, Eldest won't bother to come down here again. He hates to be reminded of the world outside his empire of steel.

And meanwhile, I will learn every single last secret that Eldest has.

When the time is ready, I will make my move.

It might be years. A decade or more. But while I wait, I will construct a plan so foolproof that, even if I die, the revolution—the freedom—Mag wants will still be ensured.

If I loved Mag the way she thought I did, I would have stood beside her and died a ridiculous, noble death.

But love is a choice.

And I can choose not to love her.

MIASMA

Carrie Ryan

THERE WAS A time when men had cures for things like the disease that swept through Portlay that summer. That was before the cities grew sick and crumbled into themselves, before the waters rose and the swamps swallowed what was left of civilization.

For a while divers took to the waters trying to salvage scraps of the old world, but they always came to the surface sickened and weak. The mortality rate became alarmingly high, and eventually people stopped pining after what came before.

What they didn't expect was that generations of toxic soup would eventually belch up diseases that wafted through the air like a stench with no way for a body to defend against it. And without medicine, civilization turned to darker ways of handling outbreaks of the fever: doctors with beaks like birds and their plague-eating beasts.

Once the beaked doctors were invited in to quash sickness in a town, their rule became absolute and their decisions unquestionable. They bred monsters who lived off disease, and then they starved them, sending them into the streets to sniff out their next meal.

If you had any money, you could pay off the doctors to pass by, or, if you were wealthy, you could pay for a private room at the hospital and a chance at recovery. Unless your tears ran red; by then it was too late. That meant the walls that held the inside bits of your body separate from one another had already begun to crumble and disintegrate. Your lungs had begun melting into your heart, and your stomach into your intestines, until you became nothing more than a jumbled mass of deteriorated cells barely held together by yellow-tinged flesh.

The moment you cried red, they took your body to the hidden tunnels underground and left you to the plague eaters.

Someone started a rumor that the plague hadn't come to Portlay until the beaked doctors arrived—that they were the ones to unleash the fever in order to feed their monsters—but Frankie knew that wasn't the case. She saw them come riding into town. She'd been hiding in the cemetery during the darkest hours of the night on a dare from her friends Cecily and Bardost. They'd told her that in the silences between the midnight chimes, you could hear the dead shift in their coffins, but Frankie didn't believe them and aimed to prove them wrong.

Except that when the bells tolled the middle night, she did hear something. At first she was afraid it might be the dead, and her heart stormed against her rib cage. Then the noise resolved into the pattern of hooves and carriage wheels, and that was when she caught a glimpse of the first doctor.

Growing up, she'd been told stories about them—every kid in Portlay had heard: *If you don't eat your vegetables, your skin will grow green, and we'll have to send you to the beaked doctors.* Frankie had always imagined them as bent crones with long, sharp fingers, but that was not what she saw on the horse at all.

The first doctor was tall and straight, broad-shouldered with large hands cloaked in thick gloves. He wore black from head to foot, every possible hint of skin covered and covered again. But the face . . . that was exactly what Frankie had pictured: a bone-white mask with a long curved beak stretching an arm's length beyond where his nose and mouth would be. Two holes were drilled in the tip of it, and a thin trail of gray smoke wafted from the holes to mix with the midnight mist.

It should have been impossible for the doctor to see anything through the thick black lenses of his goggles, but he turned his head as he passed the cemetery, and Frankie could feel his eyes on her. She should have ducked behind a headstone or raced back to the shadows of the trees, but she just stood there, bare toes curling against the fecund dirt of the dead.

Stacked neatly in the cart trailing behind the horse were groupings of cages draped in black cloth. Frankie thought the sight of the doctors would be enough to send her heart tripping hard for hours, but it was the cages that truly sent the fire of fear through her.

She'd never seen a plague eater before, and most people got quiet if the topic was ever mentioned. Some things were too terrifying for even whispers. A few years ago a kid down the block had found the skeleton of a ferret and tried to trick up the bones to look like the doctors' pets, but it hadn't fooled anyone for long, and he'd regretted it after the beating he'd gotten from his father.

Frankie found herself staring after the cages as the cart rolled toward the hospital in the center of town. She wondered if reality could ever be as horrid as her own imagination. There was a tiny part of her that wanted to sneak after the cart and lift one of those blankets and peek inside the cage. She just wanted to *know* what they were up against, something visible to aim her hate at.

But Frankie was smarter than that. Instead she faded back toward her home along the edge of the swamp, enjoying her last night of freedom out in the midnight air. If the beaked doctors were here, everything in Portlay was about to change.

A few hours later, the beaked doctors knocked on their door, and her mother let them in. As one of them entered their tiny shack of a house, he didn't utter a word, just loosened the leash attached to his beast and let it approach each of them in turn: Frankie, Cathy, and their mother. The beast was smaller than Frankie had imagined, with a long, thin, ferret-like body covered in mangy patches of fur.

Its nose was narrow and pointed, barely concealing sharp teeth. Its forked tongue slithered out, raking against Frankie's flesh before moving on to her sister. It let out hisses and growls—until it reached her mother. Then, it grew agitated and began to screech.

Frankie tried not to be mesmerized by the thing, this nightmare made flesh, but she couldn't help it. Here was the threat that had always hovered unspoken over Portlay. They'd known that eventually the swamp would drain, and the miasma would run thick. They'd known the fevers would come, and with them the beaked doctors and plague eaters.

They should have been prepared. They weren't. Frankie didn't even realize her mother was sick and should have said she'd seen the beaked doctors riding into town, but she hadn't wanted to get in trouble for sneaking out. And now the doctors were here, in her house, with their plague eaters howling.

Her mother tried to swat at the creature, but the gesture was useless. The beast had talon-like claws that it used to climb her body, ripping her skirt and tearing into the skin of her legs.

Cathy started wailing, and Frankie reached for a log from the pile by the fire, brandishing it like a weapon. The doctor swung to face her, long white beak breathing smoke, eyes empty disks of glass. He towered over her, larger than any human being had a right to be. With one swipe of his arm he could knock her unconscious. He raised his walking stick in a warning.

Her mother pulled out a ragged purse and dug through it for money—offering out everything they had. It wasn't even a full day's wages, as earlier they'd been to the market to buy food for the week. The doctor gazed down at her mother's trembling palm, and Frankie held her breath, waiting.

"It isn't enough," the doctor pronounced. "Next time have more."

Frankie froze. More doctors came in and bound her mother. "Take care of your sister," she shouted as she was dragged away. Even though Frankie was the younger sister, she knew her mother was speaking to her. Cathy's brain didn't always work the way it should for a girl her age, and Frankie had learned early on how to be the older sister in responsibility if not in years.

The next statement came out muffled as one of the doctors shoved a rag into their mother's mouth. "Remember I love you!"

And then she was gone.

The quarantine was instantaneous. Not that it took much work to shut down the little town. Portlay was squashed between the swamp and the sea—the only way in was either by ship or the rickety bridge leading out past rotting water and wilted trees. What was left of the mainland civilization was miles and miles away.

Most people knew it was suicide to try going through the swamp this time of year anyway—the miasma hung thick as fog, just waiting to lay waste to whatever crossed its path. Of course that didn't bother the doctors. Their long, thin beaks were stuffed with incense and herbs; their clothing was doused with scented oils to keep the bad air at bay.

Once the doctors made it into town, they didn't bother with gates or guards to seal off the entrance to Portlay. Instead they sent out the diggers to pull up the foundation for the first section of bridge. The men did as they were told, shirts off in the heat and backs glistening with sweat, as they stacked the old brick on a slice of dry land.

Three days later most of those men were crying red tears and being taken into the bowels of the hospital so that the people of Portlay wouldn't realize just how many were dying on a daily basis. It was one thing for people to abstractly gauge the scope and breadth of the disease, but another for it to be so blatantly visible in the form of dead bodies piled outside for family members to claim. The numbers would incite a riot, and that would disrupt the order of things. How would the Oglethorpes' gardens be maintained, and the Tybees' tea be served, and the Musgroves' linens be changed if the masses took to the street in protest?

For those who lived behind pruned hedges with proper-ties wrapped in sweet-smelling gardens, the fever was nothing but a nuisance. Their houses stood tall on the tops of hills, well above the weight of miasma, so that the scant wind of summer could stir the air through rooms, dispelling any sour odor that might lead to illness.

Those families had ample stores of sweet-scented oils and incense and candles with smoke that smelled like irises and clouds. Their water ran through layers of filtration before being pumped into basins and sinks.

Frankie knew well the lengths the wealthiest in town went to avoid contact with illness and how vexed they became at any interruption to routine. And so the night after her mother was taken, she bent over the last of their candles fighting with needle and thread as she cut her mother's Oglethorpe uniform to a size that would fit her own much smaller frame.

On the other side of the bed Cathy whimpered in her sleep, and Frankie noticed the sheen of sweat along the back of her neck and a flush to her face. For a long while she watched her sister sleep through eyes thick with tears.

She should have fought harder for their mother. She should have been better prepared. She'd failed their tiny family—what was left of it—and she refused to let that happen again. From now on there would be a tub of water always standing ready, and at the first hint of a beaked-doctor raid she'd shove her sister into it and coat her with rose powder to fend off the scent of sickness that seemed to be spawning inside her.

Frankie slipped from the bed and prodded at the fire, hoping the smoke could keep the bad air from the swamps at bay, if only for a little while.

Frankie had only been working at the Oglethorpe house for a few days when she sneaked off to the courtyard garden and plucked free a fresh bloom.

"I saw that." The voice was male and much too close.

Frankie's back stiffened. She felt the weight of rose petals in her pocket, and her hand itched to clasp tightly around them. But instead she kept still and silent, letting her chin dip forward in deference.

The owner of the voice drew near, polished leather boots crunching along the cracked oystershell path. In the distance a cannon blew, the enforcers of Portlay trying to clear miasma from the air.

Frankie expected the voice to demand an explanation and perhaps dismiss her on the spot, so she was surprised when long fingers wrapped softly around her wrist to draw her hand forward.

Everything inside her wanted to look up, to search out the expression on the man's face, but she knew that the slightest hint of defiance, even a flash in her eyes, could get her dismissed. She couldn't afford that.

She clutched the stem of the rose she'd just clipped and felt thorns break into her skin. Frankie refused to wince.

Gently, the man pried her fingers back until he could pluck the flower from her grasp. "My mother would be incensed if she found out," the voice said.

So now Frankie's fears were confirmed. He was part of the family, an Oglethorpe. Her lips began to tremble, and she bit at them furiously. She was in even more trouble than she could have thought.

Excuses ran through her mind. Not for the man standing in front of her—trying to beg her way out of this situation would be useless—but for her sister for when Frankie came home early with only final wages in her pocket.

"I beg your pardon, sir," Frankie murmured, trying to keep her voice even and subdued.

A silence stretched between them. The man still held his fingers around her wrist, and she became far too aware of the feel of his touch. His skin was so much softer than she'd ever imagined possible. Not like the thick calluses of her mother and sister or the blisters that peppered Frankie's own palms.

"Why?"

At his question Frankie lifted her head, remembering too late to keep demure. She'd expected someone much older than the young man standing in front of her. By the ornamentation on his boots and the sharpness of the crease in his pants, Frankie had thought he must be a brother to the Mistress or perhaps a far-flung cousin. But this boy was hardly much older than she was.

His hair was oiled smooth and his skin scrubbed fresh. She could see where sandalwood powder dusted along the edges of his collar, giving him a crisp, heady smell that mingled with the roses surrounding them.

"Are you going to let me go if I answer?" Frankie asked.

He glanced down at where he gripped her, and his hand released her arm immediately, as if he was stunned to still be holding her.

"I meant, are you going to dismiss me?" she clarified, and just in case he misinterpreted that term as well, she added, "Fire me?"

He considered for a moment and then said, "If you lie."

Already he wore the mantle of the Oglethorpe name easily along his shoulders, and Frankie wondered what it was about growing up in these houses that could make someone so sure of themselves so young. It was the exact opposite of how Frankie felt every moment of every day. She was always questioning, always wondering, as though her life were a hand-me-down pair of shoes that had previously conformed to someone else's stride and never fit her own.

For a fleeting moment Frankie considered giving him the truth: her sister was ill, and she needed the rose petals to keep the stench of bad air at bay. But she couldn't tell him that. If he knew where she went home to and where she came from every morning, he would tell his mother, and she'd call out the plague eaters, and before Frankie could make it home her sister would be gone.

And so she told him a part of a truth instead. "My mother was a maid here, and once, when I was little, she brought me to work." Frankie's eyes widened in panic as she realized how she'd misspoken, and she rushed to clarify. "I know she wasn't supposed to, but my father had just . . ." She struggled for the right words.

"It's okay," the Oglethorpe boy said.

After a hesitation Frankie heaved a shaking breath and continued. "It was washday and I was supposed to stay quiet in the kitchens, but I followed one of the servants to deliver tea, and when she walked through the gardens I . . ." She struggled again for how to express the feeling of that morning and was stunned to feel tears burning at the corners of her eyes.

She dipped her chin back into her chest. "I'd never seen anything like that before. The pure beauty of roses speckled with dew waiting to be taken by the sun. That kind of thing doesn't exist for people like me. And I guess I just wanted to remember what it was like to stand in the garden that morning, longing to cast off my clothes and roll across the lawn."

Her cheeks blazed pink as she realized that perhaps she'd spoken too much, and when she risked a glance up at the Oglethorpe boy she noticed his face was a bit flushed as well.

She waited for him to say something, to demand a deeper truth, but he was silent as he seemed to consider her story.

One by one he plucked the petals from the rose he'd taken from her and placed them in the cupped palm of her hand. When he was done, he cast the thorny stem back into the thicket and curled her fingers closed.

"Don't let my mother find out," he told her. His touch lingered longer than necessary, his eyes darting around her face. Then he cleared his throat and strode away, his shiny boots crunching along the path.

Every day Frankie showed up to work at the Oglethorpe house, it was the same ritual: rough hands stripped her bare and pushed her toward a room with a large, overflowing tub. She was given five minutes on a good day but more like three when things got busy.

Frankie was never the first to arrive for work and so by the time it was her turn to wash, the water would have taken on a bit of murk and sheen. While the rooms upstairs were stocked with soft soaps subtly perfumed, the help were given a cup of gritty detergent that smelled of pine straw and licorice.

From the first day, Frankie learned to be quick and thorough scrubbing herself. If the house manager caught a whiff of unpleasant odor wafting from any employee, they'd be reprimanded and, on subsequent infractions, dismissed. The Mistress of Oglethorpe refused to allow a hint of miasma into her home, and since most of the servants lived in the neighborhoods along the swamp, she was diligent about every one of them going through a deep cleaning before being given entrance to the house.

Frankie found that if she washed quickly she could spend the last stolen seconds with her head dipped below water. It was this moment of the day she loved best: when her head slipped under the surface for as many heartbeats as she could bear, and the world fell silent and numb.

Underwater there were no beaked doctors or plague eaters, and she could forget about the night they came for her mother and the fever flush on her sister's face in the evenings. She didn't have to worry about the rumors that the doctors were taking healthy people from her neighborhood, somehow causing their monsters to alert on them even though they weren't ill.

It was in those stolen moments that Frankie allowed herself to imagine a life different from the one she lived. Instead of dirt floors there would be carpets of woolen flowers; instead of plywood walls there would be rows of gilt frames boasting centuries of oil-captured ancestors. Instead of the sickly stench from the swamp there would be the gardens.

And in the gardens there would be the voice. There would be the touch of the boy who cupped his hand around hers, and he would pluck rose petals as he did before, but instead of dropping them into her palm he would brush them over her lips and eyelids and down along the ridge of her throat.

In her imaginings his touch would dip lower, but by this time Frankie's lungs would be burning and no matter how hard she willed herself to stay below the surface, to keep the daydreams fresh and alive, her body would betray her and force her up for air.

Nothing was ever as acrid as that first lungful just as her lips broke free and the oil-slicked water sloshed around her chin and shoulders.

Even though she'd scrub her skin almost raw with rags, she could always remember the stench of the swamp that clung to everything in her neighborhood: decaying leaves piled upon dead animals and forgotten civilizations buried deep in dirt that had been damp for centuries, slowly churned over by worms and scavengers and steeped by rain that dripped from tree limbs casting everything in perpetual shade that never dried.

It was that smell that brought the fever, the minuscule bits of toxic rot floating in the air, drifting on currents and inhaled through nostrils and mouths to settle in lungs and leach into the bloodstream, touching death to what was left of life.

During her days at the Oglethorpe house, Frankie might smell pure and sweet, but it never lasted. At night the miasma of the swamp would seep into her pores and burrow under her hair as if to claim her and remind her that she was not, nor would she ever be, like the boy she had met in the garden of the Oglethorpe house.

Frankie was never supposed to step foot into the Mistress of Oglethorpe's personal chambers, but one of the other maids was flushed and didn't want to risk the chance of being seen and dismissed for the possibility of being sick. As a favor, Frankie offered to fill the rose water carafes and change out the incense burners in the family's private suites.

She'd understood that the Mistress was out at tea most

afternoons, and so Frankie chose that time to sneak up the back stairs and slip through the rooms, her goal to get through the task as quickly and efficiently as possible.

But when she made it to the Mistress' bedchamber, she let out a soft gasp and could go no farther. The room was teeming with plants, their green leaves crisp and polished and unfurled against the sun streaming through triple sets of double windows. Tendrils and vines crawled up the posters on the bed and gripped the molding along the ceiling.

It was like living in a garden, down under the canopy where light turned green and raw. Frankie felt her lungs relaxing, even her skin delighting in the coolness of the room and the freshness of the air.

Tiny pinpricks of flowers dotted the foliage, and the scent of gardenias and tea olives was overwhelming, almost making Frankie drowsy with their headiness. She wanted to collapse on the bed with its thick down comforters and freshly pressed sheets and just spend the rest of eternity inhaling deeply.

But in the distance a cannon boomed, clearing the air along the lanes of the districts between the hills and the swamps, and the sound of it snapped Frankie out of her reverie. Reluctantly, she returned to her task, dribbling the fresh rose water as slowly as possible to prolong her exposure to the room.

If I could bring Cathy here, she thought to herself. The clean air would keep the sickness at bay and might even cure it. Frankie closed her eyes and allowed the thought to unfold in her mind. The sheer absurdity of it was enough to make Frankie's heart pound thicker—which made her remember how, before the plague, she'd sneak out of the house and take wild dares like spending all night in the cemetery.

There had been a time when Frankie had been brave. But now she barely found the courage to linger in the Mistress' bedchamber and dream.

Over the next few days Frankie invented a thousand excuses to go back to the family suites, but none of them came to fruition. She offered to take other maids' duties on top of her own, to swap out chores—anything—but no matter how hard she tried, she couldn't finagle a way upstairs.

She'd been relegated to the washhouses and kitchens, which meant she spent the day bathed in heat and sweat. And once one had enough sweat, that person wasn't allowed inside the main house for fear of the stench.

Frankie felt she might go insane if she didn't see that room again. The memory of those few moments breathing in the freshest air she'd ever imagined and being surrounded by the bright green of plants had become almost an obsession for her. A craving for it had burrowed deep under her skin.

The next morning she arrived early for duty, so early that the sky was still black and the water for the servant baths retained a bit of warmth. After she'd scrubbed the smell of the swamp from her skin, she grabbed a stack of fresh linens and shuffled them up the back stairs.

The only light came from the scented oil sconces along the walls, their flames turned dim, and Frankie kept herself to the shadows as she crept toward the Mistress' chambers. The Mistress would be asleep still—Frankie knew this—but she just needed to peek into the room and inhale the freshness of flowers.

As she drew closer, the sound of the Mistress' snoring filtered through the air. Frankie bit her lips, cursing the loudness of each inhalation she took. The door stood ajar, and for a long time Frankie stared at it, willing the courage to poke her head inside.

Just for a moment. Just to take one deep breath.

But then behind her she heard the rattle of feet pounding on stairs—not in the back passages but from the main rooms downstairs, which were reserved only for family and guests. There was nowhere in the long stretch of hallway for Frankie to hide, no alcove or shadow deep enough to conceal her.

She hadn't expected anyone to be awake, and even if they were, it never occurred to her to realize that servants were always moving about and she wouldn't be noticed as out of place. But *she* knew she was where she shouldn't be, and that was the only thought that flashed through her mind.

If she was caught, she was fired. If she was fired, they lost the small amount of wages that she'd been using to pay off the beaked doctors who came to the door relentlessly every evening for Cathy.

Frankie panicked and she couldn't think. The steps on the

stairs were gaining ground too quickly—they were like thunder in Frankie's ears—and she reacted, needing to escape.

She slipped through the cracked door, straight into the Mistress' chamber. It was a stupid decision, she realized, but it was done, and she held her breath as she waited to hear if the Mistress' snoring changed pace or rhythm.

The steps slowed as they ate up the ground along the hallway, and then they were passing the door, and from the bed behind her Frankie heard a pause and then a snort and a snuffle.

Frankie squeezed her eyes shut. If she was found now she wouldn't just be let go, they'd likely call the enforcers on her and have her locked up for her ingratitude. Drops of sweat gathered at the small of her back and began to trickle down.

Frankie knew that terror sweat smelled the worst. She'd spent nights with it as her sister tossed and turned on the bed next to her.

"Is that you, Charles?" a muffled voice called out from the bed.

The footsteps moved closer to the door, a shadow passing in front of the gap.

He's going to push the door open, and there's nowhere for me to go, thought Frankie. She knew that the floor was crisscrossed with vines, and if she stepped wrong she could accidentally pull a pot from one of the shelves. Blood careened through her veins as sweat beaded across her forehead and along the seams of her uniform.

"It is, Mother. I'm home." The figure shifted, and Frankie saw Charles for the first time. She tasted blood from biting her lip so tightly to keep back the gasp of recognition—it was the boy from the garden, the one who had dropped rose petals in her hands.

She had to remind herself that he'd never traced the contours of her face with them or dipped his lips to her own. Those thoughts had been just in her dreams, but seeing him standing there, the darkness making the edges of him hazy, they seemed almost real.

Charles started toward the door and Frankie shook her head, as if by that gesture alone she could stop him from coming. He paused and tilted his head, and for a terrifying moment Frankie was convinced she was caught.

"You're later than usual," the Mistress said, her voice still sleep scratched.

Frankie could swear Charles was staring straight at her. She thought of the night the beaked doctors rode into town and how one of them had turned to look at her, though it must have been too dark and the goggles over his eyes too thick for him to see her.

The light from one of the oil sconces on the wall flickered over Charles' face, making his cheekbones look sharp and his chin pointed. He was dressed all in black so that his head with its closely cropped hair seemed to float in the air. It was clear he'd been gone for quite a while, and Frankie wondered where he'd been all night and with whom.

She had no idea how people like him lived.

"Something smells off," the Mistress' voice took on a hard edge. Frankie dared a sniff. She reeked, her nervous body pouring sweat. If the Mistress could smell Frankie from the other side of a room washed in the sweetness of gardenias, then there was no way Charles couldn't smell her as well.

Frankie kept her eyes pinned on his face, waiting for his features to shift to anger and for him to call her out.

"Did you wash afterward?" the Mistress asked.

A flash of disgust rolled over Charles' face, and he moved away from the doorway. "As always, Mother," he responded as his steps pounded down the hallway.

The Mistress shifted in her bed, and Frankie feared she'd light a candle or call for her maid. But instead the Mistress huffed a sigh and settled back into snoring, giving Frankie the opportunity to flee. She ducked her head and slipped out of the room, her movements no longer demure as she raced toward the servants' stairs and made her way down to the kitchens.

For the rest of the day Frankie kept herself enveloped in the steam of the laundry, not caring that her hands became a raw red from the boiling water or that sweat drenched her uniform. She needed to get the stink of fear from her pores.

It was late afternoon headed toward dusk by the time Frankie finally made it home that day. Her mouth felt dry, and the blisters on her hands were cracked and weeping. Cathy had already drawn the bath for the evening, and she urged Frankie to go first. Usually Frankie would protest, but tonight her limbs felt weak from the strain of the morning, and she let her sister pull her free of the Oglethorpe uniform and settle her in the tub.

Even though the night was overwhelmingly hot and still, they set a small fire burning in the hope that the smoke would drive away the bad air. Periodically they'd hear their neighbors discharging rifles or setting off crudely made fireworks, the tart brightness of gunpowder a poor substitute for the power of the cannon's roar farther from the swamps.

The knock on the door that night came earlier than it ever had in the past, and Frankie cursed as she splashed her way from the tub. Cathy's fingers fumbled with her skirt as she tried to quickly undress so they could switch places. It was always more difficult for the plague eaters to sense the fever on someone immersed in water, and it's what had kept the creatures at bay for the past several nights as Frankie tried to pull together more money to pay the beaked doctors off.

"Go," Frankie hissed at her sister, and finally she just shoved Cathy, fully clothed, into the water, not caring as waves sloshed over the edges of the tub and sent rivulets toward the fire that set the embers to hissing.

There was another knock, and Frankie didn't have time to dress, so she grabbed a dingy sheet from the bed and wrapped it around her body twice before opening the door.

"Oh." It was the only word she could say.

She'd been expecting the towering black-draped doctors,

their masks gleaming in the darkness as sweet-smelling smoke drifted from the tips of their beaks. Instead she found Charles Oglethorpe standing on the threshold.

It took a moment of her staring before her brain kicked in. "You shouldn't be here." She pressed her hand against his chest and pushed. He deftly sidestepped her and twisted so that he came behind her and entered the tiny shack.

Cathy sat in the tub, shoulders hunched and knees tucked up under her chin. The edges of her clothes drifted along the surface of the water in swirling patterns.

Frankie recovered herself and followed him inside, closing the door behind her. The man living next door—too close—set off a series of shots, but Charles didn't even wince or seem to notice, he was so intently examining their little hovel before ultimately turning his eyes on Frankie.

The sheet draped around Frankie was thin, and already the dampness of her body had seeped through, making it almost transparent. She began to blush, every inch of her skin heating.

She suddenly saw her life through Charles' eyes, then, and this made it all worse. He was used to heavy silver cutlery, thickly piled rugs, and painted plaster walls bordered by heavy trim. Here there was a dirt floor going to mud where the bathwater sloshed out and a hole in the roof to let smoke filter into the sky. Embarrassed tears pricked Frankie's eyes, which made her mad. Making her even angrier was the sight of her sister huddled in the water, her only clean set of clothes now drenched and unwearable.

Frankie raised her chin—something she'd never be allowed to do anywhere on Oglethorpe property—but this was *her* house and her domain. "Why are you here?"

Charles' eyes skimmed around the room again, and he walked toward the bed shoved into the far corner; not even a scrap of cloth hung from the ceiling to afford any privacy. This made Frankie stiffen because it was such an intimate part of her life. This was where she lay down at night, where she dreamed (often of him), and where she was most vulnerable.

For a fleeting moment she remembered him this morning and how he'd come home so late and his mother had asked if he'd washed. She wondered if this was something he did every evening—follow a girl home, stare at her bed, and maybe spend the night with her before returning to his proper life.

Bile churned in her stomach. This wasn't what she wanted to think of him. He'd been kind to her, once, and maybe even twice if he'd known she was hiding in his mother's room this morning.

Maybe he thought it was time for her to repay that kindness. Her eyes flicked toward Cathy. She would do anything to keep her sister safe and alive. *Anything* to keep the plague eaters from crawling over her skin and braying that the illness nestled inside her.

Cathy had been sick for two weeks now, almost three. No one had ever survived the plague that long, and this alone gave Frankie hope. If she could keep piling fresh flowers around her and keep the miasma from the swamps from creeping into the house, Cathy stood a chance.

"What do you want?" Frankie asked Charles again, trying to keep her voice icy sharp.

Charles leaned over and rested his hand on the blanket draped across the bed. Frankie swallowed, wondering where she could send Cathy to be safe while whatever Charles wanted to happen here tonight took place.

And then Charles was on one knee reaching toward the floor. When he straightened, he held a wilted rose petal between his thumb and the knuckle of his forefinger.

"From the Oglethorpe garden?" he asked.

Frankie's stomach tensed. She'd been surreptitiously taking more flowers from the property, always making sure she wasn't seen. She wanted to explain, to say that she had no choice when her sister's health was at stake, but she bit the insides of her cheeks instead.

He walked around the room toward Frankie, whose skin was pricked with goose bumps as the bathwater dried along her arms. Cathy shifted in her tub, sending little ripples to shush over the rim, but other than that she made no noise. Even though Cathy was her older sister, Frankie had been the one to step into her mother's shoes after she was carried off. It didn't take much for Cathy to defer to her.

As Charles drew closer, Frankie saw, now, that he'd collected an entire handful of shriveled flowers from the floor. He didn't stop at a respectable distance but instead came nearer than necessary before letting the petals drift from his fingers. Several of them clung to the damp patches of Frankie's sheet, one pressing against the edge of her right breast. She inhaled sharply as her eyes were drawn to the bright splotch of color, and then she spun around abruptly once she realized that Charles' gaze was focused there as well.

Cathy started to stand from the tub, but Frankie cut her eyes to her, telling her to stay put. The beaked doctors could still come at any minute.

"What do you want?" It was the only thing Frankie could bring herself to say.

But Charles said nothing, and when she glanced over her shoulder, she saw him staring at her sister. Cathy's eyes grew wide, and Frankie rushed to stand between them.

"She's sick," Charles stated.

Frankie made no move to confirm it but she knew she couldn't deny it. Why else would her sister be sitting fully clothed in the bath? "It's none of your business," she ultimately answered.

"My mother would disagree," he replied.

"I'm not sick, and I'm the one who works there." Frankie crossed her arms over her chest, trying to hide the rose petal and the thinness of the sheet covering her. "That's all that matters. The health of my sister is irrelevant."

He raised an eyebrow, and Frankie chewed harder on the inside of her cheek.

"It's why you needed the roses." Charles' words came out

as a statement rather than a question. His eyes flicked past Frankie's shoulder to where a chipped cup contained a struggling gardenia cutting, and another sprouted one bud from a tea olive. Barely enough to sweeten the air.

"Why are you here?" This time Frankie's voice finally cracked. All she could see in her future was getting fired from the Oglethorpe house and losing her wages, which meant that when beaked doctors knocked on her door she couldn't pay them off, and they'd let their plague eaters scurry across the floor with sharp muddy paws that would pierce her sister's skin as they climbed up her flesh and howled about her sickness.

Charles reached out and took Frankie's elbow and tugged her toward him. Now all she could picture was what would happen next. How he would use this knowledge about her—this weakness—to have his way with her. She hated that she'd once believed the best of him when he so clearly only deserved the worst.

"Don't make her watch," she begged him in a whisper. "Please." Her voice was desperate.

He hesitated, his eyes searching her. She couldn't help it when she glanced at the bed and then back at him.

Realization dawned on him, and he dropped her arm as though it were on fire. He took a large step away from her and then another. "What do you think of me?"

Frankie could come up with no answer that wouldn't offend him and get her fired, so she kept her mouth pressed tightly shut. Charles glanced again at Cathy, whose chin trembled against the surface of the water, sending out patterns of tiny ripples.

He reached for Frankie again and pulled her to the door and out onto the street. Already she could smell the hint of incense that led the procession of the beaked doctors. She heard the howl of a plague eater and then wailing as a family was wrenched apart.

How long until they took Cathy?

"I'll do anything to keep this job . . . Charles." She forced herself to say his name, to make this personal, but it felt wrong the way it fell from her mouth. If she were on his property, he would be Master Oglethorpe, but never Charles. Just as his mother was Mistress and never Camellia.

"If she's sick, they're going to take her eventually," he said when the door closed shut behind them.

"I know." It was all Frankie could muster.

"How you've kept her hidden this long I don't know."

He already had so many of her secrets to lord over her, another didn't matter. "Most of them accept bribes. Even small ones."

His head shook. "They won't for much longer. Their sweeps are becoming more aggressive, taking more people. Things have gotten worse; even the families from the hills are looking for a way out."

This revelation shocked Frankie. It had never occurred to her that the wealthy families with their gardens and filtered water and soft breezes would be so worried about the plague that they'd abandon their property. It would take only hours for those left along the edges of the swamp to fight their way in and take the estates over in the families' absence.

"But I haven't seen anything . . . packing or preparations," Frankie said. "There hasn't even been a rumor."

"They're afraid that if the servants know, then their plans will go wrong. If the help sees us leaving, what's to stop full-bore panic? And if there's panic, the enforcers will lock down the harbor even tighter than it is now, and then no one will escape. As it is, they think only one more ship will be able to rush the blockade to freedom."

Frankie leaned her head back against the side of her shack, trying to find the stars through the hazy mist drifting from the swamp. "Why are you here? Why are you telling me this?" she finally asked.

Next door her neighbor set off another round of fireworks, and the air filled with spent gunpowder. How this type of smell didn't cause sickness while the one from the swamp did, Frankie never understood.

Charles took a long time to answer. "I was there that morning when you came to Oglethorpe with your mom and you sneaked into the garden."

Frankie twisted her head toward him. She didn't remember him at all.

"My tutor sent me out to draw something in nature, but I couldn't find anything interesting. I'd spent hours staring around, looking for something exciting, but nothing caught my attention. And then you came sneaking down the path, and you had this look on your face like you'd suddenly found a kind of heaven. I could tell, everything was a wonder to you. You took none of it for granted, even the flowers that had wilted and aged."

Frankie sank back into her memories, trying to remember him, but she could recall nothing.

"I drew you," Charles said simply. He reached into his pocket and pulled out a sheet of paper folded several times over. With careful movements, he began to unfold it. "I couldn't bear to show it to my tutor. It felt too personal."

He handed the page to Frankie, and she swallowed twice before taking it. She noticed how her hand trembled as she shifted for better light. Sketched in pencil across the page was her, hands on her knees as she bent so close to a daffodil bud that the fringy edges of it caused her nose to crinkle.

This moment she remembered. The brightness of the yellow, the crispness of the scent. She'd even picked that flower, and the sap from the stem had pulled into long saliva-like strands that draped over her fingers.

Charles kept talking. "I'd never thought to find something so simple as a flower quite as mesmerizing as you seemed to. You took delight in things I'd always dismissed."

Her cheeks were hot under his scrutiny, and she remembered again about the thinness of the sheet draped across her body and how she wore nothing underneath.

"I never knew who you were," he continued. "I waited in the garden for you to come back so I could talk to you. I thought you had to be a daughter of one of my mother's friends, but I never saw you again. I was so young, but I think . . ." He hesitated. "I think I fancied myself in love with you."

Frankie's heart soared until Charles let out a kind of laugh as if the very notion of him caring for her was ridiculous. The blood that only a heartbeat before had sung through her veins froze, and she struggled to keep her shoulders from sagging.

She pushed the sketch back toward him. The creases crossing it were frayed, the pencil faded along the well-worn lines. "I'm sorry." Frankie had no idea why she said those words. She'd done nothing wrong, and yet still she felt somehow inadequate.

She despised being embarrassed about where she lived and the life she'd been born into—one she had no control over. She wanted to shout at him that she was a hard worker and a smart girl and none of her surroundings were her fault. She was trying—damn it—as hard as she could to hold her life together, and she didn't need his scorn.

"You know who I am now." She kept her voice stiff. "Not the wealthy heiress to some fortune with a house on the hill and a cottage out along a stretch of sand somewhere down the coast." She hated how her lip trembled. "I'm a servant in your mother's house, as my mother was before me and her mother before her. And the only garden I own can be contained in two broken teacups."

Charles said nothing. A cannon roared in the distance as she stared at him and let him stare back. The scent of incense had grown stronger. Soon doctors would knock on her door, and she only had two days' wages to offer them to pass without stepping inside.

She waited for Charles to say something, to tell her it didn't matter where she came from, but those were words reserved for dreams, not reality. She could see the beaked doctors down the street, and she was sure, now, that they never traversed the neighborhoods on the hill but rather spent their time in the communities along the swamp.

First in the procession came a thin boy shuffling slowly with a silver censer that he waved back and forth in intricate patterns, filling the air around them with smoky blue incense to ward off the miasma.

Behind him came the doctors in their sweeping black cloaks, their long white masks piercing the night in front of them. Their goggles made them appear as though they had no eyes and therefore no souls. In their gloved hands they wound leather leashes that barely restrained plague eaters scrabbling toward the hovels they passed.

The creatures were hideous, a perversion of nature, with their long mangy bodies and their forked tongues licking the air, tasting for fever. They grunted as they walked, the talons of their many toes digging into the cracked dirt of the road.

Frankie needed to be inside preparing Cathy. By this time the water in the tub would be cold, and Frankie had to dump rose powder over her head and dunk her under to mask the scent of illness.

This was her life, here with the swamp and the bad air and the sickness. Charles belonged on the hill with its freshly scented breezes. She was stupid to have ever dreamed about them. She'd given him enough time to respond to what she'd said to him—to deny the truth of it—and still he was silent, and it hurt because she hated to lose the idea of him to reality.

He was just a boy in a big house with a lovely winding garden. Nothing more.

"Go." The word she spoke was simple and effective. He paused, only a moment, and then nodded before striding off. She was surprised, at first, to see him heading toward the procession of beaked doctors, but then she remembered that he had nothing to fear from them.

Frankie turned back to the door and took a deep breath before plastering a smile on her face for her sister. She would not fail her family again.

Once Cathy had been dunked under several times and coated liberally with sweet-smelling powder, the two sisters sat and waited for the doctors to knock on the door as Cathy's bathwater grew cold. Frankie perched on a stool by the tub, holding her sister's damp hand in her own. Neither of them spoke as they heard and smelled the procession grow closer.

But the knock didn't come that night, and Frankie let out a long breath of relief. Tomorrow when they came, she'd have three days' worth of wages for them. She hoped it would be enough.

The next day Frankie paid more attention to the goings-on around her as she performed her duties at the Oglethorpe house. Now that Charles had told her of the family's plan to escape Portlay, she could sense the nervous thread of energy vibrating through the rooms, the harshness of the Mistress' voice as she made demands for certain linens to be folded more carefully or her favorite dresses to be pressed.

There was a quietness to the servants as well; the maids moved about with tense lines of worry around their mouths, and Frankie couldn't determine whether they were caused by fear of the fever or fear of when they would all be forced to find employment elsewhere.

And that's when Frankie realized the enormity of the situation. If the Oglethorpes left, there would be no need for her, and she'd be fired without any kind of notice. She'd been walking through the garden when the understanding overwhelmed her, and her feet fell still as she struggled to breathe.

For the first time she ignored the beauty surrounding her and the crisp sweetness of the air because all she could think of was Cathy. A sense of panic began to claw its way through Frankie, and her mind scrambled for a solution. She could sneak in after the family left and dig up the roses and plant them in the dirt of her home. That would keep the illness from advancing through her sister, but it wouldn't keep the beaked doctors from knocking on the door and demanding their bribe.

Frankie's legs felt weak, and she allowed herself to sit on a nearby bench. On any other day such action would lead to a severe reprimand, but what did that matter if Charles was telling the truth? And he had been—she could see it in the small details of the house, the tiny preparations for the family to flee.

A flicker of movement caught her eye, and Frankie raised her face, scanning the rows of blank windows surrounding the courtyard garden. Most days the curtains were drawn to keep the sun from heating the rooms during the long summer mornings, but today one was open along a third-story corridor.

Charles stood, watching her, his hand cupped around the sill. Frankie thought she saw one of his fingers twitch, and she couldn't tell if it was a greeting or merely a muscle spasm. It didn't matter. She was sitting when she should be working, raising her chin toward family when she should be bowing.

She stumbled to her feet quickly, the stack of linens she'd set in her lap fluttering to the ground. Instantly she dropped to her knees, pulling the fabric into a pile and gathering it in her arms before scurrying toward the kitchen. She was happy to have an excuse to hide her face from him.

That night when the knock on the door came, Frankie felt confident that Cathy was scrubbed bright and clean and that the three days' worth of wages she'd scrounged would be enough to keep the beaked doctors at bay.

Her heart still pounded as she cracked open the door, but the flood of terror that accompanied this ritual most evenings was set to simmer rather than boil. Still, the sight of the doctor looming outside, the long, slender beak of his mask protruding from a cloud of thick incense smoke, caused her breath to hitch.

The plague eater strained at the leash by the doctor's side, a low hissing growl causing its body to vibrate.

Frankie clutched the wages in her hand and held them out, but the doctor only glanced at her offering for a moment before pushing her aside.

"Wait." Her voice sounded high-pitched and afraid. The doctor's robes swept around him as he strode toward the center of their tiny shack. As on every other night, Cathy sat in her bath, knees drawn up to her chin and eyes wide. The tips of her hair floated around her, shielding her nakedness from view.

Frankie moved between the doctor and her sister and held out her hand again, but the beaked man ignored her. Instead he focused on her sister while the beast by his side lunged and struggled against its harness.

"She's not sick," Frankie insisted. "Neither of us is." She watched in horror as the doctor gave slack to the plague eater's leash and the creature ran once around her, merely hissing, before moving toward the tub. It rose on its hind legs, stretching its long body tall, but still it couldn't reach over the lip of the basin.

"No," Frankie cried out, attempting to grab the leash, but the doctor held out a thick walking stick, pressing her against the wall. This couldn't be happening. Outside other beaked doctors milled. The boy with the censer swung it in ever larger arcs, filling the air with such acrid smoke that Frankie felt she couldn't draw a proper breath.

She became frantic, tears blurring her eyes as the doctor pointed toward Cathy and ordered, "Out," in a muffled voice. Frankie tried to stop him again, but he was stronger and kept her at bay.

He had the courtesy of turning his head away when Cathy rose from the water and shuffled toward her clothes, not even taking the time to dry herself before pulling them on. She looked so frail bent over herself as she dragged on her skirt.

Frankie wondered why the doctor bothered to show any courtesy at all before sending her to her death.

"Please," Frankie whispered, but she wasn't sure if the doctor could hear her through the layers of cloth and leather protecting him from the stench of the swamps.

Once Cathy was dressed, the doctor let loose the plague eater again, and the creature lunged hungrily forward. Frankie moaned, but Cathy was silent as the beast licked its tongue along the flesh of her leg, leaving a trail of saliva that glistened in the low light of the fire.

The thing's nose twitched, and it pawed at Cathy's foot,

causing her to wince as sharp talons scratched her skin. It still hadn't howled, and for a moment Frankie let her held breath seep from her lungs. Perhaps her sister was clean enough for the plague eater not to alert on her. Maybe the scent of the rose water would throw the beast off, and the beaked doctor would leave their house, and her older sister would be safe.

But before the dream could fully crystallize, the creature began to whuff, sucking and snorting, and then its lips pulled back from razor-sharp teeth, and it began to howl and growl. Before it could take a bite, the doctor yanked hard at the leash, causing the beast to twist and grapple as it toppled through the air. It landed with a hiss, its ears pinned back and body held low to the ground, growling.

Frankie's eyes darted around the room, looking for a weapon. She was still desperately searching for a way out when the doctor reached for Cathy.

"*No!*" Frankie screamed, and she lunged. Her fingers were like claws when she attacked the man, but her efforts were useless. His body was too well protected for her to do any damage, and he didn't even bother to fight back.

Another doctor swept through the door just then, pulling her away from his companion. The first doctor raised his walking stick, preparing to bring it across her back, but the new doctor raised a gloved hand, holding him off.

His other hand clamped around her bare arm, and she felt something off about the touch. When he pulled away, she looked down to find a trail of slickness smeared over her shoulder and oozing toward her elbow. Then the plague eater, which had been huddling on the ground, leaped to attention and struck toward her.

Frankie backed frantically into the corner. "I'm not sick!" she cried out. But the beast was more agile than she was. Already its talons bit into her as it climbed her body, tongue darting toward the slick on her arm.

She'd heard about the rumors—of doctors starting to take the healthy as well as the infected—but she hadn't been willing to believe them. Now she had no choice. This new doctor had done something to her—wiped something that caused the plague eater to alert. Even more doctors streamed into the house, the lot of them indistinguishable in their midnight robes and beaked masks.

"You can't!" Frankie shouted. "You can't!"

Her brain wasn't fast enough to come up with something else to say, something that would stop the men binding her wrists and stuffing a gag into her mouth. They tied a rope between the sisters and dragged them from their home.

Frankie was horrified and angry, so enraged she couldn't think or react. She saw tears in her sister's eyes, saw the way her body shook, and she wanted to tell Cathy that she was sorry, but her mouth was stuffed with cloth.

Out in the streets there were others bound and gagged, and most of them stood with blank stares, some of them with faint red trails down their cheeks, evidence that the fever had raged too close to death for recovery.

Frankie didn't understand why they weren't fighting. Why her neighbors were hiding behind curtains and doors and weren't trying to stop the doctors from taking them away. But of course last night and the night before that for weeks, Frankie and Cathy had been the ones hiding, not taking the risk to defend the people who'd once been friends.

The boy with the censer led them through the streets, and the ranks of the bound sick grew, and Frankie still couldn't figure out a way to escape. Beaked doctors surrounded them, their hidden eyes watching for any attempt to break free of the ranks. Soon they'd finish their rounds and they'd start the long walk to the hospital. That would be the end for Frankie and her sister.

They certainly didn't have money to purchase a private or even a public room for treatment. They'd be shunted toward the basement where, rumor had it, fever victims were piled in old tunnels and left as food for the plague eaters.

Frankie worked one hand free enough to find her sister's fingers and grip them tight. She didn't want to think about what came next.

All too soon the doctors began to shuffle them toward the road along the coast that led to the hospital. They moved slowly, some of the sick unable to walk quickly, and everyone else unwilling to hasten their fate.

Frankie pulled her sister to the back of the group, hoping to find a chance to slip through, but they were too closely guarded. And then something that felt like a stick slapped against her shin, tripping her. Her arms were bound, and she couldn't control her fall. Because Cathy was tied to her, she stumbled as well, and they collapsed together in a pile.

When Frankie looked up, one of the doctors hovered over her, the tip of his smoking beak mere inches from her face. She wanted to slap at him, but could only glare, which was small comfort.

The man reached for her, his grip painfully tight as he jerked her to standing. His treatment of Cathy was a little more gentle, for which Frankie was grateful, but not enough that she didn't fight the moment he turned from her. Frankie felt her toe connect with something that felt weapon-like, and she saw the doctor's walking stick rolling across the ground.

She knelt, pretending to be dizzy after the fall, and reached for the staff. The rest of the group had already traveled a distance away, leaving Frankie, Cathy, and the doctor to catch up.

When Frankie rose, she was already swinging, and the beaked doctor couldn't have seen it coming because he did nothing to defend himself. The stick cracked loud against his head, causing him to stagger.

But he didn't fall. Cathy and Frankie barely made it far before they heard the scrabble of talons chasing after them, and the horrible huffing and hissing of the plague eater as it closed in. The doctor had dropped the leash, either in the confusion of the scuffle or from being hit or just to track them down.

The creature was faster than either of the girls, and it caught them easily. Frankie still gripped the walking stick, and she beat at the thing, but it seemed immune to her efforts, coming after them again and again.

Then the doctor was there. A thin crack ran across his goggles, and the long, slender beak was broken open. Smoke poured out, wreathing his head in a cloud of incense that caused Frankie's eyes to water and lungs to constrict.

He stepped on the plague eater's leash, then jerked the creature back under control before reaching for the rope tied between Frankie and Cathy. Tears trailed down her sister's face, and Frankie could tell from the curve of her shoulders that she was close to giving up.

She wanted to pull Cathy into a hug and whisper into her ear. She was used to being the strong one, but sometimes it was overwhelming to carry everything for the family.

And she'd failed too many times already. Oh so many times.

It took Frankie longer than it should have to realize that the doctor wasn't dragging them after the departing flock toward the hospital but rather toward narrow alleys weaving along the edge of the docks.

Ever since the quarantine had been enacted, most of the buildings around the port had become abandoned, the warehouses slowly emptying of goods and no ships allowed in to replenish them.

Frankie wondered if the man was taking them somewhere to punish them for acting out and striking him. Horrid images of the doctor tying her to a post in an empty room and just letting the plague eater have its desired meal flickered through her thoughts. She tried not to imagine what the teeth would feel like as the beast gnawed on her skin. She knew the doctors kept them hungry so they'd alert on the ill. How hungry would this creature be? Enough to kill her and her sister quickly?

The doctor stopped them next to a full water barrel in the darkest bowels of a narrow street. The few windows along the building towering over them were dark, several of them broken, and Frankie knew that even if she weren't gagged, she could scream all she'd want and no one would come to their rescue.

At their feet the plague eater hissed and lunged, and Frankie could tell that the doctor kept it restrained with effort. Slowly he pulled the leash tighter and tighter until the beast was forced to climb up his thick black robes. Once it was within reach, the doctor grabbed it and slammed it into the barrel's murky depths.

Water sloshed over the edges, splashing against Frankie's legs. Even as he held the plague eater under, the doctor didn't shift his attention from the two sisters, his body tensed and ready as if to chase after them if they tried to escape.

Frankie was mesmerized by the sight of the drowning animal. The beast thrashed, and the doctor grunted with effort. Every now and again bits of the creature would break the surface, the long pink tail whipping against the doctor's arm as it fought for life.

It took a long time. Frankie never realized just how hard something would fight for life. But eventually the water grew still. The doctor continued to keep his hand buried underwater just to make sure. The smoke from his beak began to disperse, and for a moment Frankie thought she could see the edge of his chin. She realized his mouth was open as he panted from the recent struggle.

She'd been easing Cathy along the wall, putting distance between them as she tried to figure out a way to escape. As if he could read her mind, the doctor stepped closer. He reached for her hands. Frankie punched at him, but he deflected the blow. She kept struggling, and the doctor pushed his body against hers, pinning her to the wall so she couldn't fight him.

When the rush of sensation began stinging her fingers, she realized what he was doing: setting her free. And then he moved and unwound the rope from her sister as well.

Frankie ripped the gag from her mouth and then pulled her sister into her arms, feeling Cathy sob against her. Her relief was short-lived when the doctor put a hand on her shoulder as if to usher them farther down the alley toward the wharf.

Frankie pulled away, keeping her sister tucked safely behind her. She couldn't see past his goggles, and so she couldn't meet his eyes. He held his arms by his side, gloved fingers splayed open to show he meant no harm. It didn't matter. Frankie began to step back from him, putting more distance between them.

"Wait," the doctor said, his voice muffled by the mask and the billow of smoke that accompanied every exhalation.

Frankie continued to draw away. The doctor fumbled with his robes, finding a slit and then reaching into the pocket of his black pants. When he pulled his hand free, Frankie could only say, "Oh," as the doctor held out a palm full of rose petals.

Nestled among the damp, wilted petals sat two large, gleaming coins, more money than Frankie's family had likely ever seen since arriving in Portlay generations ago.

"The last ship leaves soon," the doctor said as he gestured toward the wharf. "It's docked out in the harbor." Frankie glanced over her shoulder, but she saw nothing except water reflecting back the thin gleam of stars.

"She's running black sails," the doctor added, and now that she knew what to look for, Frankie saw a spot of sea with no reflections, as though something great and hulking were sucking in all the light. A small boat slipped between it and the shore.

When she turned back to the doctor, he was by her side, and she watched him as he talked, seeking out the familiarity now. "These"—he pressed the coins into Frankie's hand—"are for the last two spots on board."

"Charles?" His name felt just as strange on Frankie's lips tonight as it had the evening before. But she recognized his voice now, and the way he held his shoulders straight and the shape of his mouth and chin.

She couldn't believe how well she knew these tiny details of him.

"You're one of them?" She had no claim on him, yet she felt betrayed all the same. That he was someone rounding people up and sending them to their deaths or taking bribes for them to have just one more day with their families disgusted her.

His silence was his answer as he stood wearing the beaked mask and black robes.

"How?" she asked. She didn't know if she meant how did he become a doctor or how could he stand himself.

"Sometimes you have to do things you don't like in order to make a change in the world," he said. "Becoming one of them was the only way I could find to help you." He curled her fingers around the coins. "The ship will take you past the quarantine, somewhere safe."

This didn't make sense to Frankie. "What about *your* coin? Your spot?"

Charles cupped his hand over hers and she felt the warmth of him through the soft leather gloves. "You have it."

She didn't realize that he'd been pushing her and Cathy forward until she heard the gentle lap of the sea against the pier, smelled the tangy freshness of salt water. "But you're coming, right?"

"That boat"—he pointed to the narrow craft halfway between the larger ship and shore—"will only wait one minute when it reaches the dock. If you're not there, it will leave you."

Frankie noticed other people hovering in the darkness, tucked into the shadows cast by the empty warehouses. A few were already sneaking toward the pier, dark shawls wrapped tightly over their heads and faces. Cathy watched it all with wide eyes, but Frankie's attention was focused on Charles.

"Why? Why would you ever give up your chance to escape? Why let us go instead?"

More and more people swelled from the darkness, beginning to race for the tiny boat. She heard a few of them whispering to one another, but one voice began to rise above the rest.

"Charles?" It came out as a hiss, and Frankie recognized Mistress Oglethorpe standing regally thin with her sharp nose. Her eyes scanned the crowd, searching. "Charles?" she called again, a sound laced with the beginnings of panic.

Frankie's stomach grew heavy. She wanted to leave so desperately, and her sister needed to be somewhere with softer, sweeter air, but she wasn't sure she could actually take Charles' place on the ship.

She began to shake her head, her throat tightening as she forced herself to decline his offer. "I can't. It's not right." The panic surrounding the wharf made her heart beat faster, the blood scour through her veins.

Charles gripped her shoulders with both hands. "Your sister's ill," he told her. "You can keep her alive if you leave. But she'll never make it here. The plague's getting worse—more people are falling sick, and the city's going to start cracking down hard on anyone who shows the slightest symptoms. This is the only chance she'll have."

The boat slid against the dock with a thud that vibrated through the damp wood. Around them the air filled with the tension of so many hopes pulling tight and frayed. People began leaping aboard, all trace of order abandoned with the fear that any moment they'd be caught.

"Charles!" Mistress Oglethorpe wasn't even bothering to keep her voice quiet as she called for her son. Someone tried to herd her toward the boat, but she broke free. "My son's supposed to be here," she said. "He's not here. Charles!"

Her hysteria over her missing son was so clear that it physically hurt Frankie. She knew what it was to love something beyond yourself like that, to risk anything for their safety. "You take Cathy, and I'll stay," she said, pushing her sister toward Charles.

The boat was growing full, only a few stragglers left. One of them had to physically force Mistress Oglethorpe to board, his hand cupped over her mouth to keep her from screaming and giving away their position. In the distance a cannon roared, and Frankie heard shouting.

Suddenly a bright light swept across the wharf, eliciting a few muffled cries of alarm from the boat. Two men dipped oars into the water, ready to push back for the ship waiting farther out in the bay. Not too far away whistles began to blow, a siren amping up to roar.

Any minute the wharf would teem with enforcers and beaked doctors and anyone else tasked with maintaining the quarantine.

"Go," Frankie urged Charles, but he pushed her and her sister closer to the boat.

"If the enforcers catch either of you here, you'll go straight to the bowels of the hospital. Trust me," he said. Charles pried Frankie's fingers open until he'd pulled free one of the two coins. He thrust it at Cathy and shoved her hard enough that she teetered on the edge of the dock before tumbling toward the boat. Her arms pinwheeled, and she would have hit the water if one of the oarsmen hadn't risen to catch her and eased her on board.

"Then what about you?" Frankie asked. "You'll get in just as much trouble."

"I'm only a beaked doctor trying to keep the peace." He grabbed her shoulders. "I was attacked trying to keep you from escaping. There's nothing they can do to me."

Frankie's throat was tight, her eyes raw. Charles tugged off one of his gloves and held his soft hand to cup her cheek. Frankie reached up, tentatively, and began to pull the mask from his face.

At first she felt him stiffen, resist, but then he allowed her to free him and trail her fingers along the raw bruises where the straps had bitten into his skin.

Lights began to blaze in the warehouses, and the oarsmen started to pull the boat away from the pier. But Mistress Oglethorpe must have seen that it was her son standing there because she cried out for him and lunged toward the dock, holding the boat in place.

Men tried to break her grip, but she kicked them away. "Charles!" she cried out. "Jump! Come on, Charles!"

Frankie felt his hands tense on her shoulders and knew that in one heartbeat or two he would shove her toward the boat just as he did with Cathy. "What will happen to you?" Her voice was a broken little noise in the dark night.

He touched his lips to hers, just barely grazing her mouth. "The plague will pass, and you'll come back and you'll walk up to the house on the hill, and I'll be in the garden waiting for you." He pressed the kiss deeper, as though he could breathe hope into her, and then broke free. She tried to hold on to him as he pushed, but he was too strong.

"I promise," he added as she fell backward toward her sister's waiting arms.

Men wrestled Mistress Oglethorpe toward the center of the boat as she screamed for her son. Oars lit against the water, no longer caring about stealth or not creating a wake. All along the sides of the craft, people dug their arms against the surface, adding any momentum they could to escape the rush of enforcers crowding their way onto the wharf.

The ship with black sails was already under way when the little boat with the last of her cargo caught up at the mouth of the harbor. The escapees climbed rope ladders and huddled on the deck, where they stared into the dark unknown, some of their faces gleaming with tears at all they were leaving behind.

Frankie stood with her sister at the back of the ship, the wake from the rudder dissipating back toward the fading lights of Portlay. The night air felt fresh and full, and Frankie inhaled it deeply, letting it seep into her lungs and clear out any lingering miasma from the swamp.

She could hear that Cathy's breathing came easier as well, her cheeks flushed not with fever but with the crispness of clean air. She didn't know if the sickness would ever fully leave Cathy, but for now they were safe.

Frankie looked down at where she clutched the rose petals Charles had tucked in her palm as a promise. Already the color was fading, the scent only a lingering memory. She imagined Charles going back into the town with the ranks of the beaked doctors and saving those few people he could, either by finding a way to smuggle them free or giving them another day with their families before being dragged away. She wondered if he'd spend his afternoons surrounded by the flowers, thinking of her.

She closed her eyes and pictured the gardens covered in snow, ice clinging to the bare vines and dripping in frozen daggers from trees. Her feet would leave a trail as she made her way up the hill to the Oglethorpe house, everything around her silent and still. The house would be empty—any servants who survived the plague would be allowed home to care for the families that remained.

Frankie would push open the trellis gate and maybe it would creak on its hinges from disuse. And there he'd be, sitting on the bench, waiting for her. She'd bring him a fresh hothouse flower from wherever Cathy and she settled after escaping, and she'd let him trail it over her lips and down along her neck.

He'd plant her a garden in her room and another in Cathy's room, and from then on they'd live out their lives surrounded by blooms and beauty.

As the last glow of Portlay faded on the horizon, Frankie breathed in the fresh smell of the sea and clutched the rose petals tight in her hand. Her sister was safe, they were both free, and for a moment Frankie allowed herself to believe in dreams once more.

ABOUT THE AUTHORS

KELLEY ARMSTRONG ("Branded") has been telling stories since before she could write. Her earliest written efforts were disastrous. If asked for a story about girls and dolls, hers would invariably feature undead girls and evil dolls, much to her teachers' dismay. Today, she continues to spin tales of ghosts and demons and werewolves, while safely locked away in her basement writing dungeon. She's the author of the #1 *New York Times* bestselling Darkest Powers/Darkness Rising young adult series as well as the Otherworld and Nadia Stafford adult series. Kelley lives in Ontario, Canada, with her family. You can visit her online at www.kelleyarmstrong.com.

RACHEL CAINE ("Dogsbody") is the *New York Times, USA Today,* and internationally bestselling author of the Morganville Vampires young adult series as well as the Weather Warden series, the Outcast Season series, and the new Revivalist series in urban fantasy. She has published more than thirty novels and has been translated into more than twenty languages around the world. You can visit her online at www.rachelcaine.com and on Facebook and Twitter @rachelcaine.

KAMI GARCIA ("Burn 3") is the *New York Times* and internationally bestselling coauthor (with Margaret Stohl) of the Beautiful Creatures novels. *Beautiful Creatures*, published in forty-four countries and translated in thirty-three languages, is currently in preproduction as a motion picture with Alcon Entertainment. She is also the author of *Unbreakable*, the first book in her solo series, The Legion (Little, Brown 2013), which is currently being developed as a major motion picture by producer Mark Morgan (of the Twilight Saga) and Black Forest Film Group. When she is not writing, Kami can usually be found watching disaster movies or drinking Diet Coke. She lives in Los Angeles with her family and their dogs, Spike and Oz (named after characters in *Buffy the Vampire Slayer*). You can visit her online at www.kamigarcia.com.

NANCY HOLDER ("Pale Rider") is the *New York Times* bestselling and multiple award–winning author of the Wicked, Crusade, and Wolf Springs Chronicles series. She's written tie-in projects for "universes" including *Teen Wolf, Buffy the Vampire Slayer, Angel, Hellboy*, and *Saving Grace. Hot Blooded* and *Vanquished* are her newest young adult novels. She also writes comic books and teaches in the Stonecoast MFA program at the University of Southern Maine. She and her daughter, Belle, are published coauthors, and they spend every dime they make together at Disneyland. You can visit Nancy online at www.nancyholder.com and on Facebook and Twitter @nancyholder.

MELISSA MARR ("Corpse Eaters") is the author of the *New York Times* bestselling Wicked Lovely series, *Graveminder*, and *Carnival of Souls* as well as a manga series (Wicked Lovely: Desert Tales) and various short stories. She is also the coauthor, with Kelley Armstrong, of the upcoming children's series the Blackwell Pages and is coeditor of the *Enthralled* anthology (also with Kelley) and the upcoming *Rags & Bones* anthology (with Tim Pratt). When not writing, editing, or traveling, Melissa is buried under a plethora of books, dogs, and children in Virginia or online at www.melissa-marr.com.

BETH REVIS ("Love Is a Choice") is the *New York Times* bestselling author of the young adult science fiction novel *Across the Universe* and its sequel, *A Million Suns*, as well as several other short stories set on the spaceship *Godspeed*. A former high school English teacher, Beth drew inspiration for her novels from her students and their lives—although she took the claustrophobic feeling of being trapped in a small town and enclosed her characters on a spaceship instead. Beth currently lives in rural North Carolina with her husband and dogs, and she believes space is nowhere near the final frontier. You can find out more about her online at www.bethrevis.com.

VERONICA ROTH ("Hearken") is the #1 *New York Times* best-selling author of the dystopian thriller *Divergent* and its sequel, *Insurgent*, the first two books in the Divergent trilogy. Her books are inspired in equal parts by her Chicagoland upbringing and her twisted imagination. She currently lives in Chicago with her husband and can be found online at www.veronicarothbooks.com and on Facebook and Twitter @VeronicaRoth.

CARRIE RYAN ("Miasma") is the *New York Times* bestselling author of the critically acclaimed Forest of Hands and Teeth series, which has been translated into more than eighteen languages and is in development as a major motion picture. She is the editor of the anthology *Foretold: 14 Tales of Prophecy and Prediction* as well as a contributing author to the Infinity Ring series. A former litigator, Carrie now writes full-time and lives with her husband, two fat cats, and one large dog in Charlotte, North Carolina. You can visit her online at www.carrieryan.com.

MARGARET STOHL ("Necklace of Raindrops") is the author of the forthcoming futuristic thriller *Icons* and is the *New York Times* and internationally bestselling coauthor (with Kami Garcia) of the Beautiful Creatures novels, which have sold more than a million copies in more than forty countries. *Beautiful Creatures*, named Amazon's Top Teen Title of 2009, is currently in development at Warner Bros. Studios. Studying

American literature while living on Emily Dickinson's street in Amherst and earning an MA at Stanford University, Margaret came to her love of the South much as she comes to her love of everything—through books. Margaret spends most of her free time traveling to faraway places with her husband and three daughters, who are internationally ranked fencers. She can be found online at www.margaret-stohl.com.

WANT MORE FANTASTIC SHORT STORIES FROM FABULOUS AUTHORS? PREPARE TO BE

EDITED BY MELISSA MARR AND KELLEY ARMSTRONG, *Enthralled* IS A COLLECTION OF ENTICING STORIES FROM AUTHORS CLAUDIA GRAY, KAMI GARCIA, MARGARET STOHL, AND MORE!

HARPER
An Imprint of HarperCollinsPublishers

www.epicreads.com